West of the Sound

A Novel

B. ALEXANDER OWEN

Dedication

VIII • XI • MMXIX

This Book Is Dedicated With Love To Fred

On This Milestone Day

My Brother from Another Mother.

Thanks to Larry David, Jerry Seinfeld, and Mike Judge for brilliant motivating humor. You guys can get away with it, I cannot.

Also, thanks to Paul and Ringo, George and John. I've spent my life listening and loving your words and music.

Thanks to Nick and Nate Diaz for your inspirational warrior spirit.

Thanks to all of you for sharing this space in time.

Special thanks to my wife for everything. How did I get so lucky...

Rock on!

B. A. O.

Contents

West of the Sound

B. ALEXANDER OWEN

Chapter 1

The Appointment

5:31 A.M. Tuesday, July 4th, 2017

STEVEN HUFFAM BAKER was known to his friends, family, the police, ATF, and FBI as Stiv Huffam Baker. As a concealed weapons permit holder his nickname was both public and federal record. When he was a baby, his older brother's three-year-old mouth pronounced Steve as *Stiv*. The name stuck. He liked the name so much, he considered having it legally changed, but never got around to it. Like a Navaho Hogan, his fourth-floor condominium had an unobstructed eastern exposure, the rising sun acting like an alarm clock when his bedroom shades were open. Slipping out of bed, he went to his bathroom, washed hands and face, went back to bed, and immediately fell back to a deep morning slumber, chasing the sexy dream he'd been having. Instead of the blonde nymph, he dreamed a bizarre scene so alive he could smell the night air in the distant galaxies of his mind.

The old Black man stood in the middle of a tree-lined highway on a cloudless starry night. He wore faded overalls shirtless, his wrinkled chest bare and caved. His eyes red-rimmed and tired from a lifetime of thankless labor. A thin Black boy stood in front of him. The old man's long-fingered

9

hands held the child close for protection. The boy was dressed the same as the old man but looking cold and hungry. Wind blew past like a lonely ghost, flashing stars dotting the cobalt sky like a trillion fireflies. Stiv stood on the road across from them leaning slightly forward wearing jeans and a T-shirt, feet bare.

"I'm on my way to the dentist." Stiv's voice echoed off distant mountains, returning loud.

"Can you take my boy to the dentist? He's my grandson and never went to no dentist," the old man said, his voice deep, smooth, and soothing like Morpheus, god of sleep and dreams.

"The dentist might pull the boy's teeth, might hurt him," Stiv said.

"That's okay, son. Life is about pain, he needs to learn, and his teeth need pulling because they ain't nothing more than poor White folks living their lives in pain and darkness."

Stiv woke, struggled to understand the dream's meaning. But knowing dreams could be deceitful, he promptly forgot about it, feeling no need to get up except for his doctor's appointment later that morning. Stiv loved his doctor. The man stayed open on a national holiday.

Three weeks before, Stiv was fired from his lucrative job at the massive pawnshop he helped build and co-manage. A long-expected argument started with a fellow manager becoming aggressive, then morphed into a shoving match before escalating into a fistfight. Security cameras showed Stiv as the aggressor. It did not help that the video clearly showed him attacking with one of his favorite moves, learned thirty years before in his dojo in Japan. A fast jab, right cross to the face, roundhouse kick to the side of his co-worker's head, pushing him back against the wall, then grabbing his shirt and headbutting the man to unconsciousness. Because Stiv still practiced karate two or three times a week, the move was fast and accurate. It did not matter that the co-worker was a so-called tough guy—you cannot work in the pawn business otherwise—the co-worker had no chance against the move. Stiv always thought the guy a coward anyway, but that did not matter. He stood over the unconscious man with other co-workers holding him back. Blood flowed from his victim's nose and lips, a purple bruise growing on his forehead.

Stiv was fired for violence in the workplace and damn lucky the police weren't called. The security video was a smoking gun for an assault-with-intent charge, a no-questions-asked arrest. Humiliation and betrayal were complete in Stiv's drugged-out mind, refusing to let him believe he was in the wrong.

He was used to losing jobs, well not exactly used to it, but he had some practice over the years. It was the loss of a regular paycheck that bothered him most. On that day, he understood why a disgruntled, terminated employee might go back in with a firearm and light a place up. Not that he condoned the response, regardless of circumstance. But he could understand the anger, and pain.

His termination was keyed as *Cause, not eligible for re-hire*, so he could not collect unemployment. This was a problem. He'd lost six jobs in twenty-six years, an embarrassing circumstance. In the end, he didn't care so long as he had his wife, his drugs, and what he considered his good health. Humiliation notwithstanding. It was times like these he was glad they were intentionally childless. A conscious physical effort.

They had savings; a 401k plus his wife's income from her graphic design job and proceeds from her surrealistic oil paintings she occasionally sold. Her artwork was blended abstract visions from her brilliant mind, in Stiv's opinion. Another negative: the loss of their medical insurance. His wife's company offered insurance, of course, but they opted out, taking Stiv's company's coverage. He refused to pay the ridiculous price of COBRA, nor wanted anything to do with the Affordable Care Act. As far as medical coverage was concerned, they were screwed.

At 8 a.m., Stiv lay staring at the bedroom ceiling wondering what the 4th of July 2017 would offer. He also wondered where his wife slept. She should have been next to him.

He grabbed his cell phone charging on the bedside table and punched up daily news. He began to read headlines. A guy broke his annual hotdog eating record, consuming seventy-two dogs and buns in ten minutes at Nathan's Famous on Coney Island. That was pretty cool, although nauseating. A sleepy truck driver in Australia crashed, releasing 7,500 crazed chickens on some major highway. That wasn't bad either although also nauseating. North Korea rattled its saber a bit with another rocket launch and the American and Russian presidents were planning a sit-down in the near future. Such boring news could put him back to sleep, so he punched up Facebook to see if anyone had something relevant to say. But as expected he was greeted with holiday salutations, political attacks, and the same old song and dance. He thought about Ari on that July 4th back in 1976, forty-one years earlier. Now that was a reason for a time machine. Since time travel wasn't an immediate option, he let that memory float away like a leaf on a slow-moving stream. He closed his phone and continued to stare at the ceiling.

After his doctor's appointment, he planned to apply for jobs, send out a few resumes. Fortunately, beating the pavement was a bygone method of searching. Looking for a new job was torturous and embarrassing at his age. He sincerely wished he never had to work again.

He also planned to get stoned and make a few music CDs. He called the collections Vicomixes, after Vicodin. He'd be high on narcotics when making music mixes. Stiv selected compositions from his vast Cd collection and a music-sharing app, snagging music from private hard drives from all over the world. He was amazed at the obscure music he found, not to mention the readily available porn. These were a couple of his many hobbies, another benefit of no kids and few responsibilities. At 8:20 a.m., he was up making coffee, and listening to Zero 7's bluesy song, Destiny.

Stiv looked out at the sunny day through 180-degree bay windows. This was an expensive view he soon would not be able to afford. He watched small waves breaking on the beach four floors below, several hundred yards away. A murder of crows and neighborhood seagulls floated in the morning breeze like slow motion riders, adding colors to the day. Sitting at the kitchen table, he reached for his vitamin container waiting like a well-trained pet next to the antique silver napkin holder. Seven little marked compartments contained a mega multi-vitamin, 500 mg of B complex, 1000 mg of vitamin C, 500 mg of magnesium, an 800-mg horse-pill-sized ibuprofen, and most important, the tiny blue pill with M stamped on one side, 15 on the other. This was the only pill he cared about, and the only pill that mattered. Oxycodone, 15 mg.

He couldn't explain why he took the other pills except the cocktail turned his piss green. This gave him the false illusion his body received all the vitamins and minerals it needed. Palming the small gathering, he popped the pills in his mouth chasing them with the last of his coffee, which he took black and bitter. In his heavy drinking days, he took a blood pressure medication and an anti-gout pill, but since he quit two years before he stopped taking both.

Sitting at his desk next to the living room windows, he looked out at the wonderful view of the Sound's blue waters. He kept his little drugstore in a half-century-old, weather-worn Dutch Master cigar box he removed from a desk drawer. Stiv was most interested in how many Oxycodone pills he had left. He also considered his large supply of Valium, thinking one of these days he would count the stash. He figured there were close to four hundred 10-mg blue bombers and about two hundred 5-mg yellows in another plastic bottle. He had been illegally hoarding Mother's Little Helper for years.

Currently, the contents of the cigar box with The Syndics of the Drapers' Guild on the cover, held an inventory of fifty 1-mg Xanax bars, sixty 2-mg Klonopin pills, forty-two 30-mg hits of Adderall, and eighteen 10-mg hits of Ritalin. A Ziplock baggie held at least an ounce of sticky, grayish-green marijuana buds. Not a bad personal pharmacy except for the lack of Oxycodone.

Chapter 2

Drugs, Death, Denial

8:35 A.M. Tuesday, July 4th, 2017

He used to hide the stash box in his bathroom behind and under the bottom drawer of the vanity. The box and its contents fit perfectly, an excellent hiding place. Stiv had been lying to his wife about his drug use for years, even though he'd been using long before they met. She forgave his drinking as a legal vice, sort of, but narcotics were a very different story. He knew she suspected him often searching for what her inner voice whispered. She searched his closet, safe, desk, and bathroom, much like his parents did when he was a teenager. Her exasperation was a pleasure to watch knowing she would never find the box. For the most part, Stiv was a happy functioning drunk—depending on one's definition of functioning. She hated his drinking but tolerated his binges because she loved him.

Or so he thought.

When he finally cold turkey, abstinence put a new dimension of happiness in their marriage. He wasn't exactly sober, but more like white-lie temperate. But sobriety confused him. Was it worth the emotional and physical pain? Life offers few true loves. Stiv firmly believed giving up a love during his short existence showed a shocking lack of moral fiber, also a flat contradiction to his being. He knew only too well, life is short and soon the guiding moonlight would be gone. Everybody got one quick crack at the mortal farce. He loved alcohol, but he loved her too.

She loves me, she loves me not, she loves me, she loves me lots.

Effeuiller la marguerite.

Stiv's wife had strong beliefs in universal underlying energies. Unseen powers propelled their lives to new insights. Powerful guidance from the universe, and the angels she secretly conversed with. She'd been gathering transcendental ideas for years, even before they met. Stiv suspected the benevolent charms of hummingbirds informed on him, ratted him out, taking her side. He knew she communicated with the tiny, high-energy Aves. Gemini girls have that power. Stiv could not prove his theory but lived by it. His wife was a textbook Gemini: the twins, gentle, affectionate, adaptable, but ruthless and sadistically violent.

Late one summer afternoon a few years before, she found a tiny 10-mg white pill on the floor of their condo. Recklessness often shadows the addict. She asked Stiv about the medication even though she already knew its pharmacological properties.

Oxycodone.

He lied and denied everything. That's right, Stiv was a member of the big bitch club. Habitual User. And so, he did what came naturally to self-preservation types; he washed the evidence down the blackhole drain of the kitchen sink, sending the pill to a watery grave. This was antagonistic and weak. The wife immediately said so and he would pay the price going forward.

From that moment she became the silent, inspired, tireless detective searching out the truth, determined to expose the drugs she knew he hid, abused, and lied about. Her top-notch detective work paid off on the worst day of Stiv's fifty-plus years on planet Earth. The day his Pops passed into the Afterworld.

News came by text message from the Wolfpup, his youngest brother and closest sibling to their unpleasant stepmother. He sent the text because he could not speak for sorrow. Stiv understood. The text was just three lonely words: Pops Is Gone.

Stiv was off that day. He sat in their living room watching an old movie. His wife was out shopping for art supplies when the agonizing news came through the airwaves. An evil messenger from beyond. Even though family and friends knew the end was near, the news floored him like a rogue wave, knocking him to the far side of despair.

Pops years of hard drinking, smoking, and carrying on finally caught up with him. It took death eighty-five years to catch up to his lifestyle. Even though Pops was a tough old goat, the cancer was aggressive. Pops was too weak to fight on. The news stung like a cloud of hornets because Stiv thought Pops would live forever.

Wrong again.

After the initial shockwaves the three words radiated, *Pops Is Gone*, Stiv sobbed while death-marching to his bathroom head down, shoulders slumped in search of numbing pharmaceuticals. Oxycodone and/or Valium would calm the storm in his heart. The prescribed medication now had a real job to do.

On his knees, bathroom door closed and locked, overhead fan buzzing loud, he quietly pulled the secret hiding place open. Even though the wife wasn't home, he still followed protocol. Reaching into the dark, cool plot, his hand desperately searched, reaching, feeling each inch of the empty space. His fingers and heart slowed to a stop, time passed, breath held, blind fingertips exploring the now meaningless, hollow space. His heart began to beat again like a deep-toned single kick on a twenty-six-inch bass drum.

Boom! Boom! Boom! Boom!

His treasured Dutch Master cigar box was gone. Gone like the wind, gone like the tide of time. Gone like his Pops. His brain screamed in alarm. In place of his beat-up discolored cigar box was a scented sheet of flowery stationery. Peaceful pastel pinks, blues, unicorn, and mint colors decorated the paper with one noun neatly written in gleaming blood-red ink:

LIAR!

The declaration burned him slowly, charring his heart. Stiv was on his knees holding the note in both hands reading the solitary word over and over. He could not believe what he found and lost. He tried desperately to make the meaning of the solitary word change. But no matter how hard he tried, praying to whatever god of vocabulary and literature might be listening, it would not change. Was it too much to ask? Just one lousy word, the dictionary was full of them.

Synonyms danced wildly in his mind like kernels of corn popping out of the super-heated pan of his brain. Synonyms ricocheted everywhere.

Cheat! Charlatan! Fake! Chiseler! Rogue! Crook! Hooligan! Phony! Fibber! Falsifier! All rained down like acid, burning his conscience. Finally, reality slapped his brain. His devastation and mourning should be for his dead Pops, not lost drugs. He was losing his mind slowly in the murky waters of guilt and despair. He needed help. Fast.

Where was his wife? Where were his drugs? Where was his Pops? Where was he?

He rolled over onto the tiled floor curled into a fetal position, weeping, the obnoxious synonyms giving him no respite, his sobriety an amplifier of turpitude.

An hour later he sat on their bed thinking about his own personal exit from the light, joining his Pops. The Model 38 a willing collaborator.

Pops was dead.

His wife had busted him cold.

She had confiscated his desperately needed anti-withdrawal narcotics.

He was going to pay for his lies for a long time to come, his wife a slow methodical torturer when he wronged her. His life flashed before his eyes, mind racing through space. It was not a smooth ride. Had he really let drugs and alcohol guide him to where he sat? Since he had no drugs to relieve the pressure, he decided to cash out, he did not want to go on.

While contemplating which handgun would be best for the job, he heard the front door bang open. He cringed. With a Gemini woman you never knew which twin you were going to get, Glinda, the sexy Good Witch of the

19

South, or Elphaba, the violent, apathetic, sadistic, Wicked Witch of the West.

Stiv shuddered at the thought of her coming home an hour or two later, finding his last messy artistic decision splashed on the bedroom wall like a drugged-out Jackson Pollock painting. But she was home now, his liberating angel, and he would never conduct his final exit with her home. He continued crying softly, relieved to still be cognizant and among the living.

Soon, his lovely muliebrity sat next to him on their bed looking at his downward profile. Stiv had not heard her come into the bedroom. He could not look at her or bear to see her accusing eyes. The traitorous vanity drawer sat on the bathroom floor visible from where they sat like a bloody kitchen knife at a murder scene. He did not slide the plasterboard collaborator back into place. Why bother.

The hiding place had served him so well for so long, a perfect clandestine vault though ultimately, like any trusted scheme, betrayed him in the end. The tangled web of deceit had ensnared him like a weasel with one paw in the sharp teeth of a trap. Better to gnaw its own paw off than be taken and skinned. Stiv had no escape.

She was crying. Women often lose their good looks in the slow-motion contorting, grimacing, and misshaping their faces undergo when they weep. Halloween masks from the five and dime store. Not her though, she was fine as hell in mourning. Stiv was happy, but this would be his only happy thought, and fleeting like the back-stabbing hummingbirds.

Each of her soft gentle sobs drove another spike through his heart. But her sorrow excited and turned him on, he felt his blood rise. She respected her father-in-law and owned the experience the pain and final loss caused her. Unfortunately, Stiv's betrayal hurt her more and she told him so after putting her hand on his leg. He flinched at the touch he always longed for. Her fingers felt alien and sharp.

Stiv was terrified on so many levels. A new chapter in his life was beginning without his advisor, protector, and friend. His Pops. A new chapter without his wife, too, and worse, a new chapter without his drugs.

"I'm sorry about Pops, Stiv. I know this is an inconvenient time, but we need to talk about what I found. I knew you were lying all this time. You're a liar. What else have you been lying about?" she asked in her pretty voice.

"Can I please have my cigar box back?" he sobbed, not wanting to say drugs.

"I can't do that; I won't do that. Not until I am certain you aren't doing anything illegal. I live here too. I was going to throw that nasty old box off the balcony but didn't because I know how important it is to you. Why, I don't know, but whatever."

"I'm not doing anything illegal," he lied. "I have a prescription for everything," he lied again. "You know what that box means to me. I've had it since I was a kid."

"Yes, I know that. That's also why I didn't destroy it, Stiv. I have respect for your things even if it's not deserved."

"I could really use something to calm me. I'm having terrible thoughts, please?" He mumbled.

"No. Not until I speak to your doctor's office which I cannot do until Monday. I am sorry, the answer is no and if you don't understand my reasons, that's your problem. But you really should understand."

"I'm sorry I lied to you, please forgive me," Stiv said weakly. "I need the pain medication for my back and the Valium for stress and anxiety. Please, at least give me the Valium. It's in a prescription bottle with my name on it, so of course it's legal. If you don't, I don't know what I'll do," he moaned gazing into her brown teary eyes.

"The answer is no. I'm sorry I caught you lying on this of all days. I've been searching ever since I found that little white pill on the floor. I looked in your bathroom drawer many times since then. Today, I pulled the whole drawer out. I didn't even know the drawer came out. The strangest part, I walked straight into your bathroom, pulled the drawer out, and there in the back of the space was your cigar box filled with all your drugs. Like I knew exactly where to look even though I had no idea, like I was guided there, Stiv. I pulled the drawer out, saw your cigar box like I was seeing it through someone else's eyes. The whole experience was unnerving. You know I've always been suspicious, I found your drugs today, as if— well, I don't know why. I wasn't even looking, Stiv. How can you explain why I found your secret hiding place this morning? I've been waiting to catch you for years because I knew you are a deceitful drug addict," she said slowly and with scorn. Her pretty voice had morphed into a shout in the silent room of mourning, finally unable to contain her wrath.

"How can you say that to me?" Stiv moaned, thinking about the sneaky spying hummingbirds. "Please, if you're going to be this nasty on the day my Pops died, I'll go into my safe and just end it all. Fuck this," he stated with bloodthirsty psycho seriousness.

"Well, I didn't know Pops was going to die today Stiv, and I am sorry," she said, wiping her eyes on a sleeve. "I loved him even though he didn't like me very much. I don't know what made me look behind that horrible drawer."

Stiv stared silently at the carpeted floor. He began counting carpet fibers.

"Your Pops was a wise man, Stiv. I'm going to miss him.

Just so you know, I took all your guns and hid them too. I did this for you, Stiv...for us. Everything happens for a reason, can't you see how clear it all is?" she said, staring at him.

"I only see a long dark tunnel of sadness. I can't believe this is happening to me, to us. It's the worst nightmare I could imagine. What are the chances? What's going to happen next?"

"Well, Pops loved you in life, now he loves you in death. And make no mistake Stiv, there are no coincidences. We're guided to our own destinies but walk there alone. As for ending it all, I really wish you'd stop talking like that. It really hurts me. You know I hate guns, making death threats only gives me more reason to throw them in the Sound. Threatening me with your suicide is foolish and mean," she stated, looking under his face so their eyes met. "I guess you could jump off the balcony if you're determined, but you'll probably just break your legs, and trust me, I'll leave you there. But until I know you are not breaking any laws, I'm keeping the drugs and your guns. Sorry. You can have that moldy cigar box back, but it's empty. I still might throw your guns in the Sound. What do you need them for anyway? You are not a police officer, I really don't get it."

She stood up and leaned over him.

He looked up into her eyes hoping for magic compassion. His were red-rimmed and sore, he was about to say something, anything, but she beat him to it.

"And please Stiv, we can comfort each other, get through this together like we always do, but please don't use the f-word around me. You know I hate when you do."

She let this demand descend, her lips now touching his forehead moist and warm. Her breathing tickled his flesh. She turned and walked out of the bedroom.

He fell to the cold comfort of their beloved bed, screaming emotional agony into his tear-dampened pillow. Fortunately, their bed was magically comfortable, reassuring like a private sanctuary. A euphoric garden for intimacy, love, and rejuvenation. He knew she was right, they would get through their painful loss together. It was always them, together against the world.

He was thankfully off that ghastly day, an overcast autumn offering from the god Notos, bringer of wind and storms. The god Notos stated clearly and authoritatively, in a raspy Bronx accent in Stiv's head,

"Sorry, kid, this is the day we take your Pops, sorry it ain't sunny, he liked sunny."

"Yes, he did," Stiv answered aloud. "Camping, fishing, hunting, and boating. Why don't you leave him with me another day, one more sunny day so we can talk. I want to thank him one last time. A little more time won't matter, right? Just one more lazy sunny day, who's gonna care? Can you do that for me please?"

"No. We take him today, kid."

Remaining supine for hours, then curled up and guilt-ridden, filled with festering regrets, he needed some conclusion. None came until around 9 p.m. His wife returned sympathetic with a glass of water and two 10-mg Valium tablets.

"I see you have a prescription for this medication, so you can have some. I hope it helps, but we are going to have a long talk later when you are feeling better. You hurt me and now you are paying. What is it you like saying so much? 'If you wanna dance, you gotta pay the man.' Well, you're paying the man for what you did to me, to us. Sorry the price is so high."

She handed him the glass of water and the two blue

tablets. Stiv sat up, accepted both. He tossed the drugs into his mouth and drank the cool water. It was like the Great Flood chasing the pills down to the pit of his empty stomach. Before he fell back to his pillows, she held him tight, hugged him and whispered promises of love and dedication, calming his shaking body. Later that night she gave him back his cigar box full of drugs. Everything was there. She kept the handguns hidden for a few days before telling him where the mini arsenal was, neither saying anything more about it.

———

That was two years before. Stiv did not hide his drug stash anymore, his wife never asked about his little pharmacy. Stiv proved his drugs were legal, well, sort of. Perhaps she stopped caring— a bitter pill to swallow.

———

He had prescriptions for the Oxycodone and the Valium. All the other pills he received illegally, a federal crime actually.

Jemena, a twenty-five-year-old female co-worker liked him and gave him drugs. She explained the surplus was prescribed to some or all of her five children, each fathered by five different men. She got child support from each father monthly. Her kids suffered from one perceived emotional disorder or another. All psychosomatic in Stiv's opinion. The kids seemed fine whenever they came around but what did he know about kids?

The youngest was one, the eldest twelve. Jemena worked for Stiv at the pawnshop. He hired her pregnant with her fourth child even though she suffered daily nausea. She was smart and convincing. Did an excellent job in general with a spanking good sense of humor. Her first of many practical jokes on him came one day after lunch. Stiv walked from the backroom out to the sales floor to find Jemena crouching in the middle of the showroom, a wide puddle of red mess under her kneeling body. She was moaning loudly and saying, "Call 911, I need an ambulance, please someone hurry! Help me, please, it hurts so much!"

Stiv, never one to hesitate in an emergency, ran to her side asking, "How can I help, Jemena, what can I do? Is the baby coming? The ambulance should be here soon, don't worry, we're all looking out for you!"

Then another employee said, "What a mess, Jemena, you bitch, you're cleaning that up yourself!"

Stiv was shocked. Everyone in the room, eight employees and a few customers, stood around blank-faced watching, doing nothing. Jemena was moaning, holding her swollen belly, then dabbed a finger into the weak bloody liquid between her legs, put it to her tongue, and said, "This is sweet, I'm a sweet girl, aren't I? I taste so darn good, that's why all the girls love me."

She stood up with a half-empty bottle of Ocean Spray Cranberry Juice held behind her back. A practical joke and a nasty one. Everyone was in on it but Stiv. The room's laughter continued while Jemena mopped up the mess, glancing with her mischievous smile at Stiv every few moments until she was done. Then she downed the rest of the bottle, tossing the empty in the trash. He almost vomited, but a darn good joke.

One day Jemena gave Stiv some Reserpine, a children's tranquilizer. She explained how she regularly told her pediatrician his prescribed diagnosis was not working and she wanted to try a medication she read about. This was usually untrue; instead, it was an order from a friend she would sell the drugs to. If she could not sell them, she gave them to Stiv. A simple relationship.

Jemena was a five-foot tall, slim, gothically made-up Hispanic woman, not unattractive. Unfortunately, her make-up was garish. After five children she preferred the company of women, saying men were unable to handle her sexual workload. Plus, men could not be trusted. Basically she hated men. Stiv understood and admired her. She took care of five young children and worked a tough full-time job also expertly defrauding the government welfare system. He suggested on several occasions she write a book on how to con the government out of big bucks. One day she explained the con. Stiv was all ears.

They were eating lunch together in the breakroom watching *Seinfeld* reruns on the company TV. He was talking about how the new president might affect the old administration's policies. Especially giving away money and his staunch anti-socialism in general.

"Stiv, I'm a single Hispanic woman, a mother of five children from five different fathers. I'm twenty-five years old and on my own. I receive more money from the state and federal government than I make working here, and that's cash. I also get free medical, dental, and vision so don't pay into the company plan. My housing, daycare, and utilities are all paid for, plus I get two hundred fifty dollars per child per month in food stamps, loaded on EBT cards. I sell the cards for fifty cents on the dollar. I get twelve-fifty total on the EBT cards, after selling I have six twenty-five in cash. I sell to the same three people every month. We have seven free cell phones at my house and they all work. I rent them out to people for twenty bucks a day or until the battery dies. The chargers are proprietary and only I have them, plus they're untraceable. When the battery is dead, they get returned to me. I don't know what they're used for."

"That's amazing. So, you clear over ten grand a month with no expenditures? I hope you're saving money, sista."

"Not quite ten grand, more like eighty-five hundred. We have no bills except liquor and weed. I spend every penny on clothes and toys for my kids. I don't even save receipts because I don't bother paying taxes. Why should I?" she said, biting into an overstuffed Subway sandwich.

"How did you learn to score this dough? Who taught you?" he asked.

"I like to read, Stiv, and it's not rocket science," she responded, words garbled as she spoke through a mouth full of veggies and lunch meat. "That's all you have to do at the welfare office, or just ask. The people working there are happy to explain all the benefits available to mothers like me, or people like you. Job security for them, free money for us. There's a pamphlet covering every possible way you can get free money. I read brochures waiting to see my case-worker who is only too happy to approve my requests. You wouldn't believe how much the state is willing to give you. You just have to ask," she said.

"So you're saying if I go down to the welfare office, fill out a bunch of forms, they'll give me free money? It's that easy?" he asked half-joking and thinking about some upcoming bills he'd love the government to pay.

He took a bite of the steak sandwich he brought from home and waited for the intel.

"There's no guarantee, Stiv, but trust me. Fill out the applications for housing assistance, free cell phones, medical and dental care, transportation help, food stamps, child nutrition." She rambled."

Stiv studied her recent transformation from *not bad-looking, young mother of five* to a Gothic dyke with pale complexion, midnight black hair, black lips, and black clothes. She seemed to be putting on weight along with a new but lousy fashion sense.

"They give me a lump-sum check every month for more money than I make working here. How do you think I can drive that new Escalade? How do you think I can afford to take my whole family to Disneyland every other month? You don't know until you ask and what's the worst they can say? No? They'll most likely say yes because the welfare office is so backed up they don't have time to read through all the BS and Relief Paperwork. They just stamp Approved, and you get your check. Free money, Stiv, don't you like free money? I thought everyone did." Jemena looked at him again, her mouth full of masticated lunch meat and veggies. The shredded mouthful did not help her attempted new fashion statement, nor did her onion breath.

Looking at the TV, she continued, "I have friends beating the system for much more than me. I could get more too but what's the point in drawing attention? I'm doing okay, no need getting greedy, right?" Jemena took another bite, chewing in silent irony looking straight ahead at the flatscreen TV where Kramer was playing H. E. Penny-packer, a wealthy industrialist.

Stiv admired her. He wanted to explain that nothing was really free though, especially in a today's society. Someone was paying, and when the money ran out, you have chaos and anarchy like Cuba and Venezuela. Stiv was paying her way too, indirectly, of course. She knew this. He didn't want to break the bad news that the new administration didn't have the same mindset as the previous—quite the opposite. She might even have to give up her new Escalade and bi-monthly trips to the happiest place on Earth. He accepted the free mood-stabilizing drugs she offered and was pretty sure he wouldn't be going to the welfare office anytime soon.

Stiv rarely touched the other drugs in his cigar box except as trade for more pain meds. Only sixteen Oxycodone pills were left, a four-day supply by prescription standards. He could milk sixteen pills for twice the days if he cut them in half but depriving himself of the buzz. Nevertheless, he had an eight-day supply should times become desperate. In the past, he exhausted his thirty-day supply well before refill day. Those were panicked, anxious office visits. Running out of the drug was a physical and emotional horror and not an option in this lifetime or the next. Not ever again.

He tried to quit narcotics the year before; the Oxycodone that is. His wife was overseas visiting family so he decided to taste some cold turkey. He'd been feeling like a junkie and was bored with the proverbial monkey on his back. There was his wife's bitching too, which he under-stood, but man, could she bitch.

Stiv learned from an early age he liked drugs of all descriptions. It was very much how he felt about women.

He liked pills better than the powders or weed. Reefer was never his bag because he never knew how high he might get. He did not like the effects either way; his stoned mind asking too many deep and concerning questions. His rampant paranoia was shadowed by dark questions like who he was, who he wasn't, who he was supposed to be?

The cousins, as he called heroin and cocaine, were seductive scary entities offering too harsh an experience. Due to his adventurous nature and the fact these drugs were part of the roaring '70s, Stiv had to experiment. When he first tried the beautiful temptress, Golden Brown, he was fifteen. He loved her deeply and she loved him back blanketing him in a warm bond of loving intimacy. He even enjoyed the sting of the spike in his arm. A swollen purple vein popping, then mainlining the skag, pumping deep into his bloodstream.

Then a mooncalf reaction.

Golden brown, texture like sun, never a frown with golden brown

Brown was his most impulsive lover, both giving and sensuous. Golden brown was better than any orgasm so far. She loved him so good he was weak in mind and knees. He knew he loved her too deeply, too soon, too greedily. So he stayed away, jealous. She was like a good friend's beautiful overripe girlfriend. One who must be avoided and whose company must never be sought.

Thou shall not mess with thy friend's lover

Stiv played with the cousins when he could get away with it. He had a distinct bout with Cousin White. She was a lascivious inamorata, an insatiable lover. They partied hard on her rails whenever her lines were spread. This was often in the seaside town where he grew up. Everyone knew the town's beaches were often used for unloading boatloads of cocaine coming up from the south. A summertime blizzard.

For the record, a sound is a medium to large sea or an ocean inlet between two bodies of land. Stiv's condo sat on the edge of the Annalotus Sound. This is a place from where he stared at the blue-green waters with mellow thoughts dashing through his mind. The feeling was like a free breath of heaven.

As he reflected, the memory of a party popped in his head. This was early winter of 1977, just months before they lost Jack. The party was at a schoolmate's home, a mansion built in the shape of a giant crab, constructed with the illusion of hanging off the side of a cliff overlooking the Sound. Yet another cool house on a cool street in their cool town.

On Winter Hazel Drive, the Crab House was built in 1904, designed by McKim, Mead & White. The cover charge for admission was $100 per person unless you were on the VIP list. Stiv and friends never were. You could snort all the coke you wanted for a timed two hours. All night drinks, both soft and hard, plus snacks were provided. You could stay past your two hours but never make the mistake of breaking the stringent rules. Nefarious money was well spent in the form of unlimited nose candy, while rubbing shoulders with the town's elite and aristocratic types. There were affluent politicians, local mobsters, old money lock-jaws, and law enforcement including Feds. Beautiful males and females, both social and *working*. It was a good atmosphere for making new friends as all partygoers were filled with exhilaration. However, it was a fearsome place for making enemies. Only the foolhardy would cross the clearly marked lines of engagement. Rowdy, rude, disrespectful behavior was met with flashes of flames like lightning meted out by men who knew their jobs.

After Stiv's motley group paid and entered the inner sanctum, they sat at a large round wooden table with a dim light hanging low. Tobacco and reefer smoke drifted through the room like ghosts of dead parties past. An ornately framed mirror rested on the tabletop in front of each chair. A new razor blade still wrapped in brown protective paper accompanied each mirror. Aerosmith's "Toys in the Attic" played in the background, a suitable selection for party conversations and loud banter. The room's light was just dim enough to not identify faces unless warranted. People stood talking, some dancing, some couples sucking face. Stiv wasn't interested in bearing witness to anyone. Although everyone knew everyone else, a strict code of silence was always adhered to—or else.

Past the table and chairs, bay windows looked out over the dark freezing waters of the Sound far below. Distant blinking lights winked on the water like bioluminescent marine life, a crescent moon shimmered lazily in dreamy twoness with the indigo night sky.

Settled at their seats, they cut lines from the pile of fresh Peruvian flake. Stiv noticed their friend Michelle, who everyone called Mitch. She was sitting on the otherside on someone's lap just outside of illumination. Stiv waved, getting her attention, and said, "*Hey, Mitch.*"

She smiled her pretty smile, waving back, her young face shadowed slightly in the darkened room. Mitch was hugging and kissing the person whose lap she sat on. Stiv and Mitch were close friends unbeknownst to everyone. They'd known each other for years, sharing a secret bond and love affair. Stiv had steady girlfriends as Mitch had steady lovers both male and female. Neither would deny some form of jealousy, but expertly hid the fact from each other. Though Stiv was cool, he was also envious and jealous. Everyone loved Mitch and no one could deny sharing time given the opportunity. A tall wild-child with blue eyes, and blond hair. Mitch was a dreamboat always ready to party and jump in the sack after lines and a quaalude or two.

Stiv watched her lean forward, plastic straw to her cute nose, and snort up an industrial strength line of cocaine. Then she leaned back into the shadows, delicate fingers to her mouth. Stiv and his friends followed, leaning in snorting freshly cut rails of their own. The perfect, lightly cut coke entered their nostrils working its ancient magic numbing all senses.

Mitch moved slightly so the guy whose lap she sat on came into view. He snorted up his own thick line, erasing the powder, then vacuumed another into his other nostril, wiping the residue and pushing his index finger into Mitch's waiting mouth. This was done with intentional erotic tension for all to see. He rubbed the magic dust on her upper gum and tongue. Then holding his hand, Mitch salaciously sucked each finger, cleaning any and all remaining residue. Mitch was famously hot.

Stiv's group watched in stunned surprise, hoping no one noticed. They had to be careful because the room and its occupants were protected. But Mitch, the blooming young flower of youth and a part of Stiv's heart, was sitting on the lap of the town's newly elected mayor. Mitch was definitely not the mayor's wife. She was definitely still a minor, third year of high school, same as the boys. They were all snorting fat lines of cocaine together. It was a nervous, slightly panicked, eye-opening night. One for the ages. Stiv would ask Mitch about the liaison first chance he got although she'd probably deny the whole thing.

Chapter 3

A Ride by the Beach

8:55 A.M. Tuesday, July 4th, 2017

Because of the destruction he witnessed Golden Brown cause, Stiv kept his distance. As for Cousin White, he couldn't help but love and caress her. He saw the white pony buck off friends who hit the floor hard sometimes breaking bones. So Stiv rode her carefully, sparingly using a mental safety net and crash helmet. He was lucky to make it out of those drugged out years alive. Not all his peers did. Most notably and heartbreaking was Mitch. She drowned alone in the family swimming pool in August 1979. She was seventeen, had just been offered a fat contract with a famous modeling agency in the City. She didn't need to work but wanted to be seen on the cover of a fashion magazine. Instead, her beautiful body was found floating in cool morning water. Death by misadventure. The end.

When Stiv decided to kick the pain meds in 2016, he prepared the ritual with a case of Coke in cans, a fifth of good brandy, a pack of Marlboro Red 100s even though he no longer smoked, a case of Devil's Lake Lager, an extra-large bag of various mini-chocolate bars, Valium, and his cigar box of assorted pharmaceuticals. A half bottle of Oxycodone, just in case. He was sure he wouldn't need the opioids.

He stocked the freezer and bought extra vitamins and Milk of Magnesia. Called friends, informing them he was kicking his fourteen-year habit. They knew about the monkey and his addiction. Also, Stiv was generous when supplies were good. Everyone likes a hit of Oxycodone once in a while. Finally, he requested and received four paid days off. So along with his usual two, he had a week to get clean. No problem.

Stiv despised the TV commercials for rehab centers playing a hundred times a day, interrupting his classic movies and Seinfeld reruns. Twelve minutes of questionable entertainment, eighteen minutes of obnoxious advertisements. The douchebag actor looking you right in the eye, stating without hesitation or culpability:

"Narcotic pain medication is our country's biggest problem. A problem of epidemic proportions. I should know, I was a stupid fucking pain med junkie for ten years, but look at me now, I'm involved with hustling our country's opiate pain med addicts into spending their families' hard-earned money by sending them to our rehab facilities over and over again. A multibillion-dollar industry and we're raking it in, baby! And remember, it's impossible for you to quit an addiction without our help because addiction is a disease! You have a disease! Have your credit card ready! You can't quit alone

and you need our help. We also take checks and money orders! Call us before it's too late!"

"Wanker!" Stiv would yell at the TV.

He didn't need anyone, especially some talking head telling him what he could and couldn't do. Epidemic indeed.

He quit his long-term drinking habit after forty years, cigarettes as well. Sure it was tough, but quitting was mind over matter. There was no doubt he could and would quit his narcotic pain med addiction.

Being over fifty years old was a fact that never ceased to amaze him. Most of those years were spent in pain. He played ice hockey, lacrosse, soccer, and baseball through school. After graduation he moved to Japan for karate training at the source. He got his ass kicked but continued training ever since. A true testament to years of physical damage, pain, and punishment. He did not think of himself as a lethal weapon, more like a crash test dummy. In his younger years he never considered using pain meds for anything more than when he got his wisdom teeth yanked out, or after the frightful fiery car crash back in '77.

Demerol, Dilaudid, codeine, and morphine were not drugs Stiv experimented with for fun. Not until he was the victim of an industrial accident at work.

Fifteen years before, his crew was cleaning off upper racks in the warehouse—this was in the back of the pawnshop he managed—when a 150-pound pallet of plastic-wrapped metal goods fell to the floor, bounced once, and crashed into Stiv. The massive object pinned him against the steel superstructure. It was close, real close. Had the pallet hit him, he would've been a dead bloody pancake. He was not seriously hurt but the pallet jarred and wrenched his lower back. He capitalized on the opportunity. He'd been hurt worse on the ice, in the dojo, and trying to kiss his Gemini wife when she wasn't in the mood.

Paid time off, was his favorite song.

An ambulance sped him to the emergency room, sirens blaring. They called his wife. They took X-rays, probed and prodded every orifice. After two days of observation, he was released with a large supply of pain medication and paperwork. Vicodin, Percocet, and Oxycontin, the latter drug is time-released bliss. He also had a note stating one week off from work. Returning, light duty for one month. He found heaven in the drugs, almost as good as his first orgasm—almost.

His detoxification started fine. After the first ten hours he believed homemade cold turkey would be easy to digest. The first abdominal discomfort started about twelve hours in. To counterbalance the feeling, he popped 10 mg of Valium, chasing the pill with four fingers of brandy mixed with Coke in his Ringo Starr coffee mug. He followed the cocktail with an ice-cold bottle of Devil's Lake Lager. The alcohol and beer were wonderful. It was the first liquor he tasted in a year. Alcohol was so reassuring and delicious, like a deep French kiss from a long-ago lover. After the first bottle of beer, he opened and drank another, deciding after he was off the Oxycodone, he would start drinking immediately.

The alcohol made him dizzy, and sick. He drank too fast

or perhaps it was due to abstaining the last year. Soon his hands were cold and clammy; he felt chilled despite harsh perspiring. He sat on the living room couch, watching the sea birds and clouds roll past his window while the band Shadowfax played softly through his living room speakers.

Stark reality. He woke several hours later, then falling in and out of troubled sleep. Sick, he ran to his bathroom and did the technicolor yawn, all the contents of his churning stomach into the toilet. He felt the suffocating darkness closing in on him. Obviously—he needed more brandy.

Pouring a healthy jolt into the mug, he drank it down then popped two more V's chasing them with another beer. The booze and pills did not stay long. He vomited nasty stomach liquid into the bathroom sink, no time to reach the toilet. Putrid fluids splashed back in his face like the sea giving up its dead. His shirt and sweatpants were soiled.

Stiv cleaned himself then changed his clothes. He walked slowly back to his desk and popped 20 mg more of Valium. He chased them with a water glass half full of straight brandy and a bottle of Devil's Lake Lager. He glided to the couch, sat and waited. Joni Mitchell's soothing music lulled him dreamily into oblivion.

At nineteen hours, he got up after waking from a forgotten dream. In the kitchen he heated a frozen fried chicken dinner unfortunately passing out against the refrigerator. He woke slumped on the kitchen floor, the smoke alarms blaring, the room filled with burning fried chicken smoke. He set the timer for forty minutes rather than four minutes. He wasn't hungry anymore; the burnt food's sickening smell didn't help. After disarming the smoke alarms, he needed sugar so wolfed down six or seven mini chocolate bars. The super-sweetened delights made him feel even worse. Every injury he ever experienced came to life. Nausea bounced inside his stomach like the hammering of a sadistic blacksmith. He had cold sweats and a furious headache. In his blurred stoned mind, the world was finally coming to an end. No one cared where he was. Nobody cared whether he lived or died. No one cared while he gambled with death! Such gloominess overwhelmed him and he broke down.

Recovering, he spent the next five hours drinking eleven more bottles of beer, six more shots of brandy, and an additional 20 mg of Valium. The wasted daze turned him into a separate animal he did not care to know. In desperation, he opened the pack of Marlboros, hoping for burning redemption. Lighting up he drew deep inhaling in the middle of his living room, wasted or not, he knew this was an execution offense if his wife caught him. The cigarette tasted foreign and good. When the cigarette was spent his guts dry-heaved. He stumbled to the kitchen sink and barfed up his newly ingested stomach contents. It screamed from his body like insane snakes set free from a kill bag. Splashing back in his face again making him heave harder. His legs gave out, slumping to the kitchen floor again, where he decided to stay awhile.

Finally, he pulled himself up, he could barely stand without holding the counter for balance. His mouth tasted like he'd been sucking on a dead bird. The room spun and stank like fresh puke mixed with burnt frozen food. The dead air was like the hopeless stench of the violent, crowded Hong Kong jailhouse he once spent a week in one Friday night.

He waited for his confidence to returned. Then stumbled to the refrigerator, opened the door removing another Devil's Lake Lager. His brandy glass was right there so he poured a triple shot of brown liquid fire, drinking it straight and stumbling to his desk where his drugs were.

Oxycodone sat patiently waiting, expectant, like an old caring friend. Magic in a bottle like *I Dream of Jeannie*. Like a cool fresh stream on an impossibly thirsty day, or a gorgeous wanton slut to suck his cock releasing painful pressures in his body and mind.

Stiv knew with perfect clarity his remedy was there, right there waiting to help in his time of need. Salvation, the end of his torture, torment, and acute flu symptoms. Instead, he grabbed the bottle of Valium. He took out six blue bullets, 60 mg. This was a lot of diazepam, more than he ever took even back in the old days hanging with Mitch and Ribso. He knew this was a dangerous amount especially mixed with alcohol but whatever.

He popped the blue courage into his mouth, drunkenly counting the pills with his tongue, sucking down the dregs of the beer. His last inebriated thoughts were he'd have to go through this agony at least five more days.

When he awoke in the dark on the living room floor, the dark night traumatized his senses. He wasn't sure where he was or why he felt like black magic brought him back from the dead.

Was his awakening a stranger's only wish?

Dull light illuminated the room enough to gather his bearings and see his trusted surroundings. But mist and phantoms floated through his mind. Twenty-nine hours into Stiv's lame attempt at sobriety, he found himself in the land of lost men. A nightmare world of pain and plague. In this dreadful place his only sustenance was cold turkey, raw and bloody as birth.

He remembered the alcohol and narcotic-fueled noth-ingness he inflicted on himself. Afraid to move, he knew the pain was waiting patiently like a ruthless killer. Stiv's clouded mind played the ghastly shadows of the dream he woke from, just before consciousness. He did not want to remember the nightmare, but the sounds of the evil creature resonated as his memory...still hazy...forced him to bear witness.

He heard the shrieking stallion's cry, sounding like doomed beasts at a slaughterhouse. The screams were warn-ings not to enter the gates of regret. Stiv did not want to enter those gates, but his mind was bent on vengeance, so he entered. The dream played in color as he lay silent, his mind offering nothing but playing the dream like a movie on the screen in his mind.

The burnt smoking landscape was dark and forbidding, the galloping white stud a bloody-frothed mouth, eye sockets black and empty. Its enormous pink cock hung low with blood dripping and swinging between its hindquarters slap-ping, whipping side to side bright against its blood-streaked coat and filthy grayish skirt. The steed charged Stiv, teeth bared, shrieking threats of painful violence oozing from its chin groove and broken, blackened teeth.

The ghoulish stallion had to be a creation of his drug- and alcohol-fueled subconscious. Even though Stiv found being awake unbearable, he was glad to be away from the barbarous storyline in his mind. Dreams could be deceitful, mean, and terrifying. He refused to move from the floor for fear of waking the stallion until he noticed the cloud of stench strangling his nostrils. The stink of corruption clung and enveloped him like the foggy funk of a burning outhouse. Slowly sitting up, he saw dark stains of cooling piss in the front, warm slimy shit in back with foul puke down the front of his T-shirt. Most shocking, and perplexing, was he woke at all. He climbed to his feet and was completely done with the raw cold turkey. Forget about it!

Steven Huffam Baker walked unsteadily to his desk. He disregarded the tangible feeling of his putrid clothing. The new smell of three bodily functions added to the stench of burnt frozen chicken. He reached for his favorite bottle on the planet, his favorite substance in the universe. He poured 45 milligrams of Oxycodone into his palm, quickly transferring them to his mouth like a condemned convict's last meal. He chewed the pills into bitter paste, swallowing best he could while stumbling over to the refrigerator.

He opened and drank the magic elixir, chasing the paste down to his waiting stomach and central nervous system. Devil's Lake Lager was a liquid gift from the gods, forcing the narcotic mud down his dry throat to his stomach. This made twelve bottles of beer consumed.

Stiv did not care about his foul clothes. He did not care about the stench in the condo. He did not care if he stained the carpet or furniture. He didn't care about the piss, shit, puke, or anything else goddammit!

He only cared about getting straight—one of the worst characteristics of a junkie's selfishness. He did not care.

Slowly, he made his way back to the living room couch and sat. He looked out at the Sound and waited. Within twenty minutes, he was feeling okay. Thirty minutes later he felt good. A euphoric glow wrapped around him like a personal summer sun. All his aches and pains slowly, peacefully disappeared. The shit and vomit stench wasn't so bad, he wasn't so afraid anymore. His fear had been replaced by elation. He was going to be okay. This fact was absolute and he knew with stone-cold clarity his suffering was over and out. Stiv was certain his wife, family, and friends all cared and loved him completely. He wanted to call everyone, old friends and new, people from his previous lives, and thank them for their love, devotion, and understanding. He went to the sliding glass door and looked out at the pitch-black night, slid the door open, then walked into the cool, refreshing sea breeze. He breathed the Sound's briny smells, the light wind lovingly caressed his face like a newfound paramour.

"I love you, I love you all!" Stiv screamed into the pitch-black night sky.

"Hey! Shut up over there, do you know what time it is, asshole?" someone yelled from down by the beach.

Yes, he did. Stiv Baker knew exactly what time it was. He smiled an ear-to-ear grin knowing everything he needed to know. Especially how to maintain normalcy. No more shadows of confusion, no more denial, he was released from his tortures, unshackled, and set free into the world of narcotic pain medication addiction.

After cleaning the condo the best he could, glad to see he had not stained the couch or carpet, he washed his filthy clothes and showered in steaming hot water. Later, he called his wife, proclaiming his undying love for her, how he missed her completely and could not wait for her return. After, he pondered returning the detox supplies he didn't use and wondered if there was a cleaning service that didn't mind cleaning human shit, piss, and vomit off carpet and furniture if necessary.

Then Steven Huffam Baker sat at his desk, head in hands, and broke down like a wounded child. When he emerged from his self-induced confinement and failed detoxification, he told his inner circle he'd rather be a junkie for the rest of my life than go through that again. He spared the gory details, only saying he indeed, failed.

———

Before he left the condo for his doctor's appointment, he did some work in his soundproof drum room. His music sanctuary was a favorite aspect of the condo. On a table facing his three-piece drum kit, a powerful stereo system with two tower speakers stood waiting. He blasted music playing drums along with whatever tunes shuffled from his computer. Like most drummers, he amassed a collection of gear, forever searching for the perfect sound but rarely finding it. After fifty-plus years of drumming he still sucked. He was adequate enough to fool a novice listener yet not quite there to a trained ear. He made a meager living playing professionally in his younger days. Stiv never once did not enjoy playing his drums.

Ah, the sunny happy slopes of long ago.

Now he played out of love and devotion as a passionate drummer hitting hard and loud. Never a soloist but he could get by. Music was his first and very possibly his last love. The earth's bodies of water too. After fixing a cymbal stand he broke jamming to Slayer, he polished an antique Slingerland snare drum and looked through a stack of paperbacks on the floor. Some he already read, meaning to read again. Reading was another passion. Currently, and for the third time, he was reading *The Elements of Style* by William Strunk Jr. This short work on the principles of the English language was recommended by one of his heroes, Stephen King, perhaps the most brilliant writer of Stiv's lifetime. King mentioned Strunk's work several times in *On Writing*, a book on the craft that changed Stiv's life. He read anything that helped his writing.

He wrote dozens of short stories throughout his life. One in particular about the year his wife left him. The protagonist becomes a reclusive drunk going on to be a famous author ultimately winning her back. He wrote it during a dark, yet inspirational period of their marriage. They fought about his fondness for handguns and inability to drink like a normal person. One morning she was gone. Then 365 days later, she was back. She finally came to terms with the man she loved. They'd been together ever since. It was a sad, lonely time, but she did return. He needed to look at that story again real soon.

Finally, it was time to ramble. He peeked into his wife's studio where she often slept. Sometimes because of her late work, sometimes because she painted into the night and morning, sometimes when she was angry at him, and sometimes for all those reasons.

They originally chose this condo because years before, previous residents had broken down a wall leading to a space built into the superstructure of the building, unknown and unused. The former had used it as a nursery. It was a bit creepy, but perfect for her art studio and office.

The room smelled slightly of oil paints and canvas. They installed an excellent air ventilation system that eliminated paint and thinner smells. Her paintings adorned the walls and were abstract in the style of Kay Sage and her lunatic husband, Yves Tanguy. Also a brilliant surrealist. Stiv loved his wife's work and fortunately, so did the public.

She was curled up on the light blue daybed against the back wall, entwined with a paisley tan comforter. Her pretty face was pressed into a white pillow, making her look fairy-like. Long black hair splayed behind her head. Stiv never tired of her good looks. He spied as her long lean body gently moved with each breath. The room's air also kept the scent of his sleeping wife, the most floral feminine scent he knew; a scent that had unlimited power over him. To be near her immediately turned him on, feeling the familiar stirring in his loins and a distinct longing to taste her kiss. He wanted to wake her and make morning love, make her feel like she'd been mounted by the gods of love. His mouth watered envisioning fiery morning kisses. His wife, real and genuine, as textbook Gemini female as he'd ever known. She understood Stiv's needs but did not have the same. He could never get enough of her. A man cannot have everything in this life.

He was fortunate to still be so attracted to his spouse after all their years together. He still lusted after her daily, completely, and hopelessly. After twenty-five years together, making love to her was a gift from Aphrodite. Sadly, he adored this woman, sadly in the sense that he was powerless against her. A virtual slave to her and to this end, her bitch.

Her desk was always neat and organized with an illustration table to the left under one of the windows which offered excellent light for both her occupations during the day. There were different creams and aromatherapy bottles, jars arranged to one side. Her computer monitor was centered, an old picture of them smiling at the camera stayed framed and dusted watching her daily actions and work. The room was illuminated by the green light of the CPU. Stiv admired her good looks again. Reflecting on her nude body under the comforter making him shudder.

He felt a sudden profound guilt. The feeling overwhelmed him as he watched her sleep. Stiv spent a great deal of time contemplating the concept of true beauty. The first time he saw her, his future wife on a busy street in Osaka with a group of friends, became an end and a beginning for him. She was so beautiful he had to stop and stare. He'd never had a feeling of such totality before or since. Stiv knew then as he knew now, she was the only woman for him. She was his life companion.

He closed the door to her studio softly, composed himself, and left the condo in a dark, stormy temper. These feelings were not new, but almost clinical daily melancholy occurrences. Stiv frequently felt guilty about the way his life affected this innocent, beautiful girl he convinced to love him all those years ago when she was still a teenager. He was older by fourteen years and just persuasive enough to keep her interested. They were still a couple after going through rough times, the break-up, arrest, drinking and drugs, job and income woes, verbally violent fights, and arguments.

Yes, he was lucky. Stronger couples might not have survived those tempests, but they did. Stiv respected her honesty and Gemini spirit. Of course, she could be bloodlust honest and tightfisted, leaving out no negative detail, fact, or observation when needed as only someone you love can. He could not imagine life without her.

Dressed in new blue jeans, a white T-shirt with a loose navy-blue cotton sweater over, Oxford brown Sperry Topsiders he wore sockless, Stiv left the condo. On his right ring finger, he wore his gold skull ring. Even though it was early July, it was a cool summer day with the sun shining over all nature. He kept his chestnut brown hair short. His green eyes were more pronounced when he wore dark colors. He carried his Smith & Wesson Model 38 snub-nose revolver in his pants, secured by a wide silver-studded black belt. He put a speed loader with five extra rounds of .38 Special, Plus P Plus ammo in the left front pocket of his jeans where it nestled next to his balls, keeping the ordnance 98.6 degrees and giving him the look of two sets of testicles.

He carried a concealed handgun legally although not sure why. His ready-to-party Roscoe made him feel better because no one could argue with the one black eye of the Model 38. Working in the pawn business for so many years was probably the catalyst to always being armed, his perceived need for self-protection. Not every customer left his store happy, not every person on the street had a world-view of good intentions. One of the dangers of today's humanity.

Stiv carried a gun because he never wanted to be a victim or a hero, he just wanted a fighting chance in a hope-it-never-happens situation. Also, he compulsively carried a switchblade in his right pocket where it clipped steadfast like a well-trained guardian. He knew a lot about handguns and could discuss most aspects, from reliability to stopping power and ballistics. He admired the history of handguns and their use but did not completely agree with the obsessive need people had for owning and carrying them.

Nevertheless, he firmly believed it was better to have-

and-not-need than need-and-not-have. As for the switch-blade, or any of his knives he carried, having one in his pocket was about practicality and equally as important as bringing his wallet, keys, or iPhone. He never knew when he might need to cut a juicy corned beef sandwich in half. Aries are always prepared.

Handguns were as much a part of American history and culture as apple pie, the Stars and Stripes, and Corvettes. He also owned and collected eclectic jewelry, gold coins, and Rolex watches that kept the guns company in the safe. Working in the pawn business gave him the opportunity to purchase at low prices, a perk or a curse of the business.

———

He stood at the base of the four-story condo surrounded by lush green trees looking out at the Sound and its year-round icy-cold water. Stiv felt confident about his imminent doctor's appointment and about life in general. Why shouldn't he feel confident? He'd get another job. Everything would be fine. It had to be.

The melancholy mood faded as those thoughts always did, their love and relationship an endless enigma. He was confused by her, their marriage and life in general. Who wasn't? But that was okay; deep down he knew they were one. Time proved that.

As soon as he allowed his mind those simple innocent thoughts, reality crashed down like a cement mixer defecating a load on top of him. He had no job, no income, no medical insurance, and no prospects. His morning schedule was based solely on getting his monthly prescription of narcotic pain medication and nothing more. Such a depressing truth. But this was the labyrinth of his being.

The implications hit his questionable existence like a strait-jacket of desolation, a crippling sadness so immediately heartbreaking he popped and chewed two of the little blue 15-mg Oxycodone bombers from his pocket. The acrimonious flavor a reminder of his often-bitter life plus he wanted a nice buzz for the ride over to the doctor's office. He waited patiently for the drug to blanket those negative feelings. In the meantime he'd look at nature, the ships on the blue-green water, and wait like a coward behind a paid bodyguard.

Twenty minutes later, stoned, painless, and euphoric, he drove along the beach road in his 2015 Mustang GT, British Racing Green, another payment he soon could not afford. The road was lined with summer greenery and mansions on the waterside Stiv envied. The residential area ended and the road became a long line of shops and restaurants to his right, the Sound to his left; he was heading south. The beach and boardwalk were already crowded with summer people dressed in beach fashion fit for the cool holiday. The weather would improve, the news said, but he did not care. He had only one focus.

The shops and restaurants facing the Sound were over-priced tourist joints that were pretentious at best, lousy at worst. Stiv was a good cook and would challenge any one of the eateries to a cooking contest. Paying unreasonable prices for mediocre food was one of his top ten dislikes in life, right up there with bad music played loud, softcore porn, crap customer service, and middle-aged women shooting their mouths off. To his left, the city stood tall and shimmering across the Sound. He looked for jumping sea life as he drove closer to his destination. Fireworks would be bursting later that day and night. He wondered where he'd be. Stiv hoped to see a proud pod of whales or a school of rowdy dolphins, perhaps the family of otters that made this beachfront their home. Seals were always visible playing and chasing fish, making schools jump in frenzied escape attempts from the precocious canines of the sea. Of course, the masters of the sky were a daily sight. The extended family of bald eagles hunted and soared the coastline nesting in high evergreens in the park.

Toward the end of the road, the thoroughfare met a large bridge crossing over the East Waterway, allowing cars to travel to the downtown part of the city proper, or Chinatown, the baseball and the new football stadium next to I-90, a highway extending as far east as Minnesota. The Waterway was used by ships and boats heading north or south and had been in use for 125 years. Stiv turned right before the bridge entrance, up the summer greenery hill to the village of Admiral. This was where his doctor practiced medicine and wrote Stiv's prescriptions.

Chapter 4

Crystal Blue Persuasion and Sacrifices

9:48 A.M. Tuesday, July 4th, 2017

CRYSTAL, the pretty nurse, escorted Stiv into the climate-controlled examination room after taking his weight on the scale in the green-carpeted hallway.

"Good for you, Mr. Baker, you lost four pounds since your last visit," she chirped in her high-pitched voice.

He didn't mind the forty-minute wait in the claustrophobic waiting room because Crystal was so striking and Stiv was so high floating with the jet streams of the atmosphere. This was the seventh time Crystal took care of him that year. Ecuadorian, with smooth dark skin, she had dancing brown eyes that smiled with her expressions. She wore her deep brown hair pulled back in a loose ponytail, lips a sweet cherry red, high cheekbones accented with shimmery peach make-up. In her early twenties, Crystal smelled of floral arrangements and youth. He thought of complimenting the cheap engagement ring on her slim left ring finger but did not.

Stiv considered his knowledge of the Inca Empire, their conquest into today's Ecuador. He didn't know much, but thought of human sacrifice, mountains of gold, and the Spanish Conquistadors. Then the slaughter of millions of Indigenous people in the name of plunder and the Catholic Church. He wondered if her bloodlines were royal, soldiers, farmers, or slaves. Were her ancestors victims or participants in the blood-letting orgies her descendants were infamous for. His mind often wandered to the history of people he met. Did she even know…did she want to know?

"Please sit on the examination table, Mr. Baker, and let's get your pulse and blood pressure."

Crystal had a wonderful habit of wrapping her arm around his when attaching the blood pressure tester on his bicep, his forearm lightly touching her firm left breast. Pretty cool. Not exactly a happy ending but pretty cool all the same.

Crystal looked at her watch as she pumped the bulb of the apparatus. Stiv thought of Led Zeppelin's "Lemon Song," silently admiring her pretty profile and appreciating her light green scrubs. He had to wonder if she wore a thong or not.

Refill day for Stiv's Oxycodone prescription was a mixed bag of spinning emotions. There was exhilaration, excitement, and delight paired with dread, anxiety, and extreme paranoia. Sixty minutes earlier he chewed two pills, plus the one earlier, three-fourths his daily dose. He was high, happy, and confident. The drugs made him float in a peaceful narcotic euphoria. Three hits, 45 mg, twice his normal every-six-hour dose, but who's counting?

He was happy and stoned in the knowledge he would have 120 hits of Oxycodone later in the day, a new month's supply. The serenity was short-lived though. A jolt of electric terror ice-picked his cranium. The what-ifs—the goddamned what-ifs. *What if something goes wrong with your new prescription and supply?* This paranoia happened every month, every thirty days like any junkie's alarm clock.

Stiv's life was based on doctor's appointments and pharmacy runs. This of course, limited his scheduling ability for anything. Travel plans, getaways, or family events had to be carefully planned around his doctor's appointments and pharmacy visits. Perfecting his appointments over the years, everything was calculated in mathematical sync and harmony. The planning and execution of these monthly office visits had been ongoing for almost a decade and a half causing plenty of problems. But to his credit, he always had his timing close to perfect, even with long overseas trips and cold, accusing questions from his wife. He was proud of himself because his drug runs every month were works of precisely timed calculated art.

"Your blood pressure is one-twenty over eighty-two, Mr. Baker, excellent," Crystal exclaimed.

She was so upbeat in youth and Stiv was surprised her presence did not make his blood pressure rise.

"The doctor will be right in," she said, documenting his chart before heading for the door.

She had a perfect body for exits.

Sitting alone in the examination room, Stiv looked at the antiseptic-smelling space hoping for something useful to steal. There was nothing. Only a metal sink, trash bucket in a corner, and toxic waste container attached to the wall, half-filled with old syringes teeming with germs and gnarly infections.

He quickly moved to the chair in a corner. The alien-looking examination table waited in the middle of the room for victims with its leg-stirrups folded to the sides. He imagined examining Crystal on the table and thought about what he would do with her. Stiv never considered himself good-looking, though he never had trouble attracting women of all ages, men too. He had no use for men sexually, although he had been in love with different guys throughout his life. He just didn't want sex with them. The obvious difference between hetero and homosexual. He felt intense infatuation for different men during his life, but Stiv adamantly believed men had the right backs, but unfortunately, the wrong fronts. As long as women were available, he had no use for men. Not that there was anything wrong with it.

He had the gift of gab also a spanking quick sense of humor. He learned at a youthful age females love to be entertained, laugh, hear stories, eat and drink; this was one of his many hooks.

No one believed Stiv's age including himself. He'd be sixty the same year as the next presidential election. Sixty was a big number. At 5'10" and fit, his sparkling green eyes helped attract women. His face showed minor damage from excessive exposure to the sun, he'd been a beachcomber all his life. His wrinkles were still underlying as a result of the meticulous care he took with his facial skin. When he was drinking heavily, he ballooned to over two hundred thirty pounds. However, always strong and fast, he could take a punch and deliver a strike with serious energy. He felled many an opponent on the ice, in the dojos throughout his training career. In his younger bar haunting days, Stiv had a bad reputation for starting fights with the biggest brawlers he could find. His philosophy was no one ever messed with the big guys, so he figured they couldn't fight. This thinking was wrong of course. Over his drunken years, he was infamous for fighting goons, inflicting damage while taking serious punishment as well. Some muscle-heads were excellent fighters and

Stiv was not as tough as he thought. Sometimes he won, sometimes he got his face kicked in, but he never backed down.

The walls of the examination room were decorated with framed pictures of foreign lands with bicyclists riding through the countryside scenery, mountains, and forest roads. Accredited medical school diplomas hung in ornate frames Stiv paid zero attention to. As far as he was concerned, Cyclops's degree could've come from Joe's Bargain Store on 5th and Union. So long as he could write prescriptions.

Stiv referred to his doctor as Dr. Cyclops because he was a much older man in his late seventies. Quite large and pockmarked with gray thinning barcode hair that stuck to his flaky scalp. Red-rimmed eyes, horn-rimmed glasses always dirty and fogged over. He resembled the 1940s movie character of the same name. That mad doctor had a creepy laboratory deep in the South American jungles and performed bizarre, unnecessary experiments on Indigenous people.

Cyclops had the dubious habit of picking his nose while he spoke, advised, diagnosed, and prescribed. He would then eat whatever matter the probing finger found in his particle-filled nasal cavity. Yes, he was nauseating in general, but he wrote Stiv's prescriptions every thirty days, had been for almost fifteen years. Stiv platonically loved the man. His own personal version of the Stockholm syndrome.

Well, sort of.

The door opened and the doctor entered grandly knocking Stiv out of his reverie.

"So," he bellowed into the room. "How we feeling today, my friend? Any gout flare-ups?"

"No gout since I quit drinking, sir. I told you that last month. I've lost some weight and I haven't had a drink in over twenty-two months. How about that?" Stiv lied.

"That's good," the doctor said, unconcerned, putting his left index finger into his left nostril where he began to pick and pull at nose hairs, the latter looking like mini party favors.

"So, Mr. Baker, what are you here for today?" the doctor asked.

His voice was altered by one plugged nostril. And Dr. Cyclops knew exactly what Stiv was there for. The same as every month, 120 15-mg Oxycodone baby-blue bombers. What a stupid question.

"I just need my pain pills, sir. My back is killing me," Stiv said dramatically. "I'm out of Valium as well. Can you change the five mg to ten mg pills? I can break them in half."

"No, I can't," Dr. Cyclops snapped much too sharply for Stiv's liking. His voice still faltering from his nose digging.

Stiv thought the doctor's reaction was unnecessarily strong, as if Valium was a Schedule II narcotic rather than a Schedule IV.

Oxycodone, a Schedule II drug designated so by the FDA because of its high probability for abuse and addiction. Stiv could vouch for that. But Valium? No way. Then again, Stiv knew some benzo freaks, so maybe there was a point.

"Five milligrams is fine then," Stiv said, more concerned about his Oxycodone anyway.

"I should say so," Cyclops stated, looking at Stiv's chart.

Oxycodone, an opiate synthesized from codeine methyl

enol ether, also known as Thebaine, an opioid alkaloid found in the Persian poppy and one of the many alkaloids found in its flowers. A potent pain pill generally prescribed for relief of moderate to severe pain. In 1916 German scientists developed Oxycodone, which packed a blitzkrieg buzz. Also the most abused drug in America. Stiv could vouch for that too.

"You know you have to get an MRI for me to keep giving you the pain medication, Stiv. They're putting doctors out of business and even in jail for overwriting this stuff. Have you heard?" Cyclops asked, nasal voiced.

Of course Stiv heard, everyone knew, especially pain med junkies like him, how could he not know?

"No, I've not heard that," Stiv lied. "Sounds like a few bad apples had to go and spoil it for legitimate pain medication patients. And I got that MRI five months ago as I told you I would. They charged me five hundred dollars even though *you* said my insurance would cover it. Remember, Doctor?" Stiv was annoyed at the memory of his out-of-pocket expense.

"Well, what do I know about insurance coverage? What do you have anyway, that Affordable Care Act crap? That nonsense won't pay for anything and I'm a doctor, not a health insurance adjuster after all," he said absently, staring at Stiv's chart. "Anyway, your blood pressure is good. Are you still taking Lisinopril?"

"Doctor, I told you about three months ago I stopped taking that medication after I stopped drinking, it was making me nauseous. I know I told you. My blood pressure is fine without it, right? And when I got the MRI, I had Health Shield, the best."

"I can see your blood pressure is good, Stiv, these glasses work, you know, I read the English language pretty well,

Latin, too," Dr. Cyclops said condescendingly, taking out his prescription pad with the same hand he used to pick his nose. This was Stiv's favorite part of the visit aside from the biohazard snot and greasy nose residue.

What he got was 120 hits of 15-mg Oxycodone, four per day, one every six hours for pain, anti-depression, euphoria, boosted energy, happiness, and an all-around kick-ass perspective on life. If he were still a drug dealer his monthly push would earn around $3,600 a month on 120 hits, $2 per milligram, $30 a pop. Not a bad source of income, especially considering his current situation. However, selling Schedule II narcotics is a felony offense with guaranteed jail or prison time if and when caught.

And both places of incarceration have the wrong kind of bars.

Unlike Oxycodone's attractive cousin Percocet, Oxycodone has no acetaminophen, aka Tylenol, or *cut* in junkie-speak. The pure form of the semi-synthetic opioid is highly prized in the world of drug abuse and valuable on the street. Oxycodone can be crushed and snorted, cooked like heroin, and injected, chewed for faster effect, smoked in blunt form, or burned for inhalation purposes. Yes, a versatile drug for sure. As Dr. Cyclops wrote out his prescriptions, Stiv watched with his usual sense of junkie urgency. Giddy, elated, nervous, and anxious; no pill could quell until he scored. His prescriptions would get written in this tragicomedy, Act One, he knew that, but the what ifs always ran through his mind like shrieking Harpies from Greek and Roman mythology. They greedily called out doubt especially at the moment of collective truth.

Then there was Act Two, pacing the pharmacy floor waiting, waiting, waiting. Junkies hate to wait. The pharmacist would either fill or not fill the prescriptions, that was it and the question. Both acts were equally important and the Harpies never tired of shrieking what-ifs in his head. The birdlike creatures, their ugly maiden faces and long bony claws, were in a constant state of hunger for harassment in Stiv's head. They would only fly away when pills were in pocket, bought and paid for.

But—what-if?

Stiv watched the doctor scribble crude doctor scratch on his prescription pad, doctor's name at the top. The linen-cotton paper was specially lined and inscribed with intricate watermarks to help against patient prescription forgery and/or counterfeiting. US currency used similar paper for similar reasons. Everyone knew it was a waste of time, where there's a will, there's always a way, but whatever.

Stiv hoped his anticipation wasn't too obvious as Cyclops wrote out the two prescriptions, a process that made him feel like a child waiting for a treat. He rarely touched the Valium but enjoyed building up his massive stash, an act the FDA deemed hoarding, another felony.

Dr. Cyclops handed Stiv the prescriptions containing chicken scratch and snot residue, saying nothing. Stiv checked both for accuracy and signature. Valium meant little to him; the 120 15-mg Oxycodone meant Stiv's entire world for the next thirty days.

Moving toward the door, Dr. Cyclops said, "Be sure to get that MRI, Stiv. Don't disappoint me."

The visit was over.

"Don't disappoint me, motherfucker," Stiv involuntarily mumbled.

"Wha...what's that?" Cyclops asked, turning back to look at Stiv.

"Nothing, sir. I said, *thank you*."

"Well then, you're welcome. See you next time, Stiv."

Cyclops was gone.

Stiv walked out of the examination room down the hall past the scale. He was hoping to see Crystal for some future mind-movies but no such luck. Instead, he went to the front desk's sliding glass window where the old crone receptionist parked her withering parts. The exact opposite of Crystal with goblin like features and a voice to match. She had the chronic smoker stench of stale cigarettes and old lady perfume. Nauseating.

Because the prescriptions were both scheduled narcotics, the receptionist had to make photocopies of each. Big Brother was always watching, he joked to the administrator every month, who never seemed to get it, ever month, or she did but didn't give a damn. She was never friendly anyway. Stiv considered her a low-level gargoyle. She was not his fan either as they'd had words in the past about appointment scheduling and mistakes on his co-pays. They were always her fault, or so he believed. She could jump in a lake either way.

Chapter 5

What-ifs and the Harpies Return
10:46 A.M. Tuesday, July 4th, 2017

ANOTHER CONVENIENT ASPECT of Cyclops's office was its proximity to the National Chain Pharmacy four doors down. One-stop shopping. Back in his drinking days, Stiv would score a half rack of whatever beer was on sale and a fifth of cheap booze. In those bygone drinking days, *cheap and plenty* was his philosophy. He'd been going to this pharmacy for a long time; a pill junkie must be loyal to his drugstore. A good pharmacist will save your prescription meds every month if you establish yourself as a regular and not a troublemaker. At least he was a regular; the trouble part was a different story. A doctor can write your prescription for narcotics before the thirty days are up, but the prescription cannot legally be filled. No pharmacist in the country will fill your Schedule II narcotics before the documented due date. Not legally.

Stiv got into arguments with pharmacy workers as well as pharmacists and store managers when they gave him incorrect Oxycodone refill dates. This was never their fault. Stiv knew it too, but it was his bad habit depending on other people's information. Ultimately, it was his responsibility to know when he could pick up his drugs, but that did not matter. He took it out on them because he could be an ass, like most junkies when it came to narcotic pain meds.

He'd told off several employees at both the store and corporate level. But he always came back to this location. Stiv did not want to build a new relationship at another pharmacy. The store staff hated him, that was true, but he didn't give a crap. When it came to narcotic addiction it was always better to dance on the side of absolute. Stiv walked into the store, seeing the nice female manager who was always there. She greeted him with a smile. A lovely dark-skinned woman, friendly and professional to a fault who hated him. He told her off quite viciously in the past. He even spoke to her boss, the district manager, telling him she was unprofessional, incompetent, and rude. None of the insults were true, but junkie-panic brings out the worst in people so blaming her came naturally.

Stiv knew she was a puppet of the corporate system. His recent termination proved once again he was unable to inhabit that world. This stylish manicured woman was one of those unfortunate salaried middle managers who had to put up with a ton of crap from both the customers who abused them and the company that offered little or no support. Overworked and underpaid, forced to compromise family duties. Middle corporate management in America at its worst. Then again, he was recently unemployed from middle management and would give dearly to have that job back. Plus, he was fired, so who was he to think like that?

Stiv nonchalantly walked through the dental care aisle, taking in the bright colors and minty pleasant smells, straight to the pharmacy drop-off window. He expected to see the slatternly pharmacist who never gave him notice except to curtly answer his questions then go about her business. Always sharply dressed in dark-colored slacks under her long white scientist gown never buttoned. She wore tight-knit shirts and horned-rimmed glasses, her onyx black hair loose and flowing. Expensive-looking high-heeled shoes that looked uncomfortable so added to her foxiness. She radiated cruel dominance, and dungeons, restraints, and whips, leather, and wonderful, merciless orgasmic pain. Her nametag said, Maria but who knows.

The slattern was missing—the Harpies shrieked.

In her place was a brown-haired, dark-skinned woman in her mid-thirties. She looked Persian with fierce green eyes, orange specks sparkling in an exotic Caspian way. But when Stiv approached what was obviously *her* counter, there was no smile on her attractive face. This was the second moment of truth for his medication refill exploration.

What-if? The Harpies shrieked and laughed their high-pitched, callous cackle.

Disquiet screamed in his mind. This new pharmacist set off Stiv's internal security alarms, compounding his regular paranoia.

The Harpy's mocking what-if questions were as follows:

Is the pharmacy out of Oxycodone, Stiv?

If they send you to another store, will they have your meds, Stiv?

Will this new pharmacist fill your prescription, Stiv?

Will she give you a hard time about insurance, Stiv?

Why is she looking at you like that, Stiv?

Can she see what a loser you are, Stiv?

Stiv!

What-if, Stiv? they shrieked.

He was worrying too much. Everything would be fine

like always. Just be polite, smile, receive, and pay. Then get the hell out of there.

However, if they were out of Oxycodone, which often happened, he would have to drive all over town to different pharmacies because they will not tell you over the phone for security reasons. There was a new trend of strong-armed robberies perpetrated by junkie-bandits who would not take no for an answer. Stiv could understand but these idiots made legitimate junkies incredibly frustrated.

He did not like the way this new pharmacist looked at him, although he did indeed like the way she looked. He was well-dressed and groomed, wearing nice jewelry including his diamond-eyed skull ring and one of his handsome Rolex watches, his personal presentation was neat and professional by any standards. He was above reproach. However, the look in her eyes told him she was going to be a regular pythoness. Of course, he always felt this way on med refill days.

The second moment of truth.

"Hello, and Happy Fourth of July," Stiv said to the woman who held his fate with her razor-sharp perception. "Where's Maria today?" he voiced with attempted familiarity. He spoke in his friendliest refined East Coast private school greeting.

"Maria was transferred. This is my store now and I don't celebrate the Fourth of July but thank you anyway," she monotoned, with a Middle Eastern accent.

Her name tag read *Azar*.

"What can I do for you, sir?" she asked, her voice confident.

She looked fresh out of the *Arabian Nights*.

"I'd like to fill these two prescriptions, please," Stiv said cheerfully, sounding equally confident, but hardly feeling it.

He handed her the two squares of paper feeling like Oliver Twist.

Please, sir, may I have another?

"Insurance card and ID, please," she demanded in a voice shaking Stiv's confidence.

He pulled out his wallet and removed his driver's license, handing it to her.

"I'm between insurances right now. I was laid off recently, so I don't have insurance at the moment. I'll pay out-of-pocket," Stiv lied, having been fired, not laid off, smiling his most agreeable smile, a tooth or two.

She stared at the prescription papers then punched information into her computer. She looked at the papers again, looked up at Stiv, glared, looked back at the computer screen, punching more data. She looked hard at his ID, looked at the back of the document, then looked back at her computer screen. She was reading something on the screen apparently, typed something more, looked back at Stiv, and said, "I am sorry, Mr. Baker, but I do not feel comfortable filling these prescriptions for you today."

His heart and the Earth stopped at the same time, giving him a minor whiplash. In his second ever out-of-body experience, he saw himself from above standing at that pharmacy counter with the Persian woman on the other side. Her words were a flamethrower roaring in his face charring his flesh, a dirty bomb filled with jagged nuts and bolts, sharp-pointed screws, shards of glass, and different lengths of nails all ripping his skin down to the bone. Stiv could feel his blood pulse-rushing from the vicious wounds, pouring down his face, dripping off his chin with the explosion's heat like a blast furnace incinerating his eyeballs. His out of body experience lasted the same amount of time it takes light to travel one inch, approximately 1/12th of a nanosecond, and he said softly, "Pardon me?"

"I am sorry, Mr. Baker, I simply do not feel comfortable filling these prescriptions. According to your records, you've been taking these medications for far too long. I would need a concise diagnosis from your doctor before I could fill the Oxycodone. I will fill the Diazepam as a courtesy, but I will not fill the Oxycodone. I'm sorry for any inconvenience," she said, with a slight orange sparkle in her fierce green eyes. Her green eyes were cold, very cold.

"Um, what do you mean, you don't feel comfortable? Who are you to feel comfortable or not with what my MD, that's right, my *medical doctor*, prescribed me. I don't care how you feel. Do your job and fill my prescription before I get upset, please."

"I'm sorry, Mr. Baker. I have every right to refuse to fill your prescription if I feel it is warranted. I am not required to explain my decision but as a courtesy to you, I have. Again, I do not have any information on your condition or why you are taking this medication. Your doctor has been prescribing it for too long and he is overprescribing the dosage. If you do not have a chronic illness, the amount of time plus the dosage is out of prescribed guidelines."

"Excuse me?" Stiv said to the green eyes, his panic rising.

"This medication is highly addictive and stringently controlled. Honestly, I cannot believe you've been taking this drug as long as you have. Are you not following the national news on this crisis, Mr. Baker?"

"*Crisis?*" he repeated sarcastically. "What does some crisis have to do with me?"

"Yes, Mr. Baker, narcotic pain medication crisis. And I

for one will not contribute. I hope these reasons help you to understand my decision to not fill your Oxycodone today. If not, you should speak to your doctor. Now, I have explained again. That is all I am required to do by law."

"Fine then!" Stiv shouted. "I'll just go to another pharmacy where the pharmacist isn't so rude and unprofessional! You have some nerve judging me, lady. That's what you're doing, right? You think I'm some kind of junkie or drug dealer?" Stiv barked, losing his cool.

"Mr. Baker, please tell me what your ailments are. There are no notes in our system about you. What pains are you having that would justify this amount of such a strong pain medication?"

"Why do I have to explain myself to you? You're not my doctor, just some arrogant self-righteous pharmacist with a piss-poor attitude!" Stiv yelled with the voice of the righteously indignant. "As I said, just fill my prescription, which is your job, and you'll never see me again, I promise. Your job is not deciding what medication I should or shouldn't take, Azar! And if you feel so medically inclined, you should've stayed in school and become a doctor. I'm sure Affirmative Action would've made room for you over a more qualified person somewhere," Stiv croaked, sure he would get his way.

Well, sure but not positive.

"That is where you are wrong, Mr. Baker, because that is precisely my job. As it states on my pharmacist license, I have the right to refuse filling any medication for any reason I deem reasonable and rational. I am sorry you are ignorant of this FDA law, but I suggest you do your research. It is not necessary to be angry with me. I am only doing my job and what is expected of me. Perhaps you can understand a bartender cutting off a drunk customer?" Azar paused here, looking back at her computer screen. She madly typed for a moment, then looked back at Stiv's shocked face and said, "Also, I have entered your name into our national database as a person whose narcotic pain medication prescriptions cannot be filled by our company or its affiliates until further notice. Please know that we share this information with all the major pharmacies in the country. Are you set up for our text messaging system, Mr. Baker, to alert you when your other medication is ready?"

"What does all this mean? A drunk bartender? What are you talking about?" Stiv screamed in panic-overdrive, continuing to stand his ground as he glared at this woman.

Several people waited in line behind him, but he didn't care. He wanted to jump over the counter and thrash this Persian bitch! Rip her goddamn clothes off and cane her bloody, humiliate her and take whatever pills he wanted from the pharmacy. Fuck that!

Then in an instant murderous trance, he remembered the Model 38 in his belt. Five rounds of .38 Special Plus P Plus ammo! He could kill her, right there and then, why not? Two in the chest, one in the forehead, tap tap, tap! Forget prison and all these losers!

Instead of greasing her, he forced his panic into damage control, and knowing it would be short-lived, he said quickly, "Why are you doing this to me? I've never had a problem filling my meds before. Do you have something against me personally? We've never met."

"Well, Mr. Baker, I know this doctor of yours, all local pharmacists know him, I will tell you he should not prescribe this much narcotic pain medication for this long without a great deal of documentation we can see in our system to justify his diagnosis. I am sorry."

"So, because this pharmacy hasn't been keeping notes

on me to your *Azar* standards, you're refusing to fill my prescription based on your own judgment? And now you're slandering my doctor's reputation and practice as well? Not to mention you blacklisted me? What does that even mean?" Stiv hissed. "You got nerve, lady! I'm gonna mess your life like you're screwing mine! I'm calling your corporate office and making sure they know what kind of employee you are. I hope they revoke whatever fake visa you have and deport you back to whatever shithole you came from!" he spewed through clenched teeth.

"You did not answer my question, Mr. Baker. Do we have you on file to receive text messages? We want to be sure you get the medication we can fill in a timely manner," she said sweetly, eyes wide with fake concern as if speaking to a petulant child.

Stiv could not answer. He could feel his face reddening.

"If you don't mind, Mr. Baker, people are waiting behind you. May I please help them now? We will text you when your prescription is filled. Have a nice day."

Stiv was frozen like a human popsicle. Did his life just flash before his eyes? He turned to walk away but remembered Azar held his prescription for his Oxycodone refill. He quickly turned back, crashing into an old, crumpled woman wearing a winter coat and bedroom slippers. She smelled of an aged human in need of a bath. Her multicolored makeup applied in obvious half-blind haste; a wilted white lily attached to her coat made her look like a *Night of the Living Dead* extra. She had been next in line and one of the voices Stiv ignored earlier. Now it appeared she had been speaking to herself.

To Azar she was saying, "My bunions been killing me these days and the skin on my feet smells rotten and been flaking off in pieces, my toenails are sharp as razors, what kind of cream do you re..."

Stiv rudely pushed past the grisly old woman, cutting off her disgusting question and knocking her away from the counter with a solid frontal hip-check.

"Well, I never in my life, such rude behavior!" the old woman cried. "Where do these boys learn their manners? What kind of mother do you have? You're lucky my Wallace isn't with us anymore; he would trounce you! He was a steel worker, you know, in the USW Union Number Forty-Six for thirty years!" she yammered with a vulturous screech.

Stiv turned to her and said, "Yeah, I know who they are, lady, they backed Hillary last year, smart move. Now, if you don't mind, I'm not finished with the pharmacist here," Stiv said, turning back to Azar's counter ignoring the old woman who was mumbling something. He considered telling the old bat to shut up, or even better, introducing the Model 38. She immediately began lurching around in a tiny circle mumbling. He had no idea what she was saying. He was too focused on Azar the Wicked.

He stood erect, filled with bloody passion, staring at this new nemesis at *her* counter. Why did she have to be good-looking? He hesitated, gathered his thoughts. She stared back, arms crossed and tensed, thoughts decided, ready to attack or defend, prepared and definitely angry at Stiv's rude behavior.

He was pissed and ready for a fight. Also terrified at the possibility of not getting his narcotics. If that were the case, *cold turkey* would fly into his life to torture him again. He was starting to believe Azar knew this. He could hear people in line grumbling but he didn't have time to worry about that. Then again, had he been witness to some dipshit guy disrespecting an old woman and a female pharmacist, Stiv would say something too. Not this time though as he was the perpetrator.

"Can I please have my other prescription back? You still have it," Stiv requested politely.

"Oh, Mr. Baker. I am sorry, but I must keep that prescription request until we hear back from your doctor's office. We will put a call in after lunch, and then we have some paperwork to process because of your blacklisting, so perhaps you can call us tomorrow to see if we can release the prescription to you."

"But that's my prescription, Azar, written to me by my doctor! Please, give it back to me now," Stiv said again, squarely with a faint hint of fear he tried desperately to hide.

"I am afraid I cannot do that, Mr. Baker."

"Azar, I am out of my meds," he lied. "I understand I was rude to you and the nice lady behind me who I'll apologize to, but I'll take my prescription to another pharmacy. I'm in great pain," he lied again. "I can't wait till tomorrow to get my prescription back from you. Please, just return it and I'll go quietly."

"Okay," Azar said. "If you get back in line so I can help these other customers who have been patiently waiting, I will see what I can do. But I promise you nothing, Mr. Baker. And for your information, I have been an American citizen for over ten years and this is my country and my homeland is no shithole." Azar hissed the last words, eyes narrowed to angry slits, leaning toward him.

He smelled an unfamiliar intoxicating scent coming from her like vanilla, cinnamon, and freshly cut wood. "Take a good look around you, Mr. Baker, *your* America is quickly becoming *everyone's* America, people of color's

America. Look what the white man has done to this continent with five hundred years of violence, slavery, and destruction. Do not talk to me about homelands, especially ones you are ignorant about."

Stiv stood staring at Azar, wondering how he got himself into this mess. First, she refused his badly needed anti-withdrawal medicine, now she was giving him an American history lesson. He had no choice but to listen because she still had his Oxycodone prescription.

"I am sure your ancestors had homelands too. Are they from shitholes, Mr. Steven Huffam Baker?" she asked with defiance. "I will help you with an added condition; apologize to Mrs. Kern, she is one of our best customers," Azar stated ominously. "And I doubt you would know, Mr. Baker, that *Huffam* was Charles Dickens's middle name, or did you know? No matter. Please apologize to Ms. Kern," she said condescendingly with victorious ice-cold irony.

Stiv stared at her. She stared back. *Huffam* was chosen for his middle name by his Pops specifically as an ode to Dickens and Stiv loved the name. This was the first time in his life any person had acknowledged the fact outside of his family. He did not think even Zander knew and was tempted to say something supercilious to Azar but bit his tongue, in dire straits.

Another pharmacy tech was helping customers so Azar could focus on destroying Stiv, and fine focus it was. The people in his line stayed there as did the old woman he bashed, probably enjoying the show, or like a stunned deer in the headlights.

He continued staring at Azar, very sorry he argued with her. Not compassion nor a chivalrous level, but on a junkie denied his fix level. Now at a loss for words which was ridiculous for him.

Stiv silently turned and faced Ms. Kern, who stood so close he could smell stale beer, cooking grease, rotting vegetables, and moldy books. It did not help that her face was contorted in anger, jaw moving side to side with thick yellowish gunk at each corner of her off-centered red lipstick giving her a jack-o'-lantern grin. Stiv thought he might puke.

"I'm sorry I was rude, Mrs. Kern," Stiv said with zero enthusiasm inches away from her grimacing face.

"Don't talk to me!" Ms. Kern bellowed then belched loudly spewing some yellow gunk on Stiv's navy blue cotton sweater. Then pushing past him to Azar's counter she started mumbling incoherently. He picked up a few words like schooling, manners, rudeness, and police. All demented senile talk as far as he was concerned. He began his disconcerted trip down the Walk of Shame while flicking the yellow gunk off his sweater past six men and women of varying ages and stature.

Azar had him by the balls. She was a power-hungry wench Stiv should not have messed with. But he did. The Harpies were waiting for him.

Chapter 6

The Little Bighorn and Blacklisted
11:30 A.M. Tuesday, July 4th, 2017

STANDING at the end of *her* line, Stiv was not finished with Azar, oh no, not by a far cry. He would wait in *her* line, play *her* games, then get his prescription back. Then, like the calm before an F5 tornado, he would call their customer service line and light the bitch up like a gasoline-drenched mob of sheep set alight with a Jet 531 SuperTorch. He imagined the flaming, shrieking mob running down a grassy tree-lined night-scape incinerating, smoking, cooking together in tight hierarchy formation illuminating the night.

Or at the very least, he could find out where Azar lived and throw a cinderblock crashing through her living room window. That would be a nice how-do-you-do. His mind-movie played in the part of his brain housing vengeance, memory, and selective attention, probably his dorsolateral prefrontal cortex. But he wasn't sure and didn't give a crap anyway.

So he waited in *her* line, very high, very shaken, and very angry. His revenge plot, his only company. If this maddening day didn't start going his way, his anger would turn dramatically to fear, neither emotion easy to control without a solid crutch.

Staring at the streaked linoleum floor, he started hearing the sounds he'd not noticed before. People were talking in an arrangement of voices on different insignificant subjects while Billy Joel droned out one of his exhausted tunes. At least "Piano Man" was not blaring. Bad music played loud, the freaking pits, man.

Blocking out the clamor, lost in blank thought, he took out his iPhone, and looked up the meaning of AZAR. It sounded like an Orc name out of a Tolkien story. His reasoning was not far off. *Azar* had two meanings in Farsi:

1. The ninth month of the Persian Calendar.

And more ominous,

2. Fire.

That figured. He had to admit he was totally attracted to her and with that thought his mind pictured her in Cyclops's gyno chair completely nude with false erotic fear in her green eyes saying, "Please don't hurt me, master, I know I've been a bad slave, please don't punish me..."

Oh my, now that would be interesting. But the thought died like mayflies. Instead, he wondered if Azar was a Gemini. A fiendish thought considering his past masochistic loves for women under that frightening zodiac sign.

Azar skillfully ignored him as if he were an invisible germ. The life-sized statues standing in front were wearing human clothes moving stiffly. Time halted. He was doing the junkie two-step only in limbo form. Waiting for what felt like a thousand centuries, Stiv felt a strange peace and calm. Everything would be okay, the universe would guide and protect him.

For reasons he could not explain, the story about Custer's 7th Cavalry galloped into his mind. Probably because of Azar's immigration speech. The battle took place a hundred years and twenty-one days before and almost to the hour. Talk about a bloody coincidence.

Yes, the story as Stiv heard it from his Pops, who hated Custer's memory, calling him a "baby butcher," featured General George Armstrong Custer telling his troops on the sunny morning of June 25, 1876, at the Little Bighorn River, "Don't worry men, those are friendly Indians over them hills!"

This was a history joke, of course, but joke or not, legendary famous last words because General Custer, a military strategist genius, was wrong. Dead wrong. The four combined Native American tribes were not friendly. These warriors, whose ancestors inhabited those lands now known as Montana for the last 15,000 years, were bloodthirsty and angry. The American soldiers, predominantly white and armed with Springfield Model 1873 single-shot carbine rifles and Colt .45 revolvers, were outmanned and outgunned.

Indeed, these innocent Native American Indigenous people were pissed, now hostile and ready for war. They were armed with Henry and Spencer repeating rifles, bows and arrows, spears, lances, tomahawks, belt axes, and war clubs. They were ready to fight to the death against the white man trying to steal their land. These original American people were exhausted from the lies and having their homes and families destroyed. Who could blame them?

Azar's comments went through his head like a sharp ice pick and he did not disagree with her. As far as Stiv knew, for the length of recorded history the white invaders were like locusts throughout the world, basically annihilating everywhere they went. Robbing, pillaging, raping, and slaughtering innocent Indigenous people since the beginning of time. Stiv thought he read Paleolithic Homo Sapiens, aka, early white humans, killed off the Neanderthal 45,000 years ago. And everyone knows the Neanderthal were here first.

Waiting for Custer on the other side of the hills were not helpless, defenseless women and children as Custer hoped, but approximately 2,500 well-armed, well-trained, determined warriors. Chiefs from the Lakota, Northern Cheyenne, Arapaho, and Blackfeet tribes waited in a bloodlust frenzy for the unknowingly suicidal 7th Cavalry.

Azar was waiting too, waiting for Stiv Baker. She was armed with her knowledge, accredited diplomas, and pharmacist license. She waited like the five war chiefs waited for Custer in their finest, good day to die battle gear and war bonnets. Custer and his host met their fate on the afternoon of June 25, 1876. Massacred to the last man. Sitting Bull, Crazy Horse, Chief Gall, Lame White Man, and Two Moons sent Custer and his men into hell, bloody vicious *take no prisoners hell*. In his blind egocentricity, General Custer was ignorant to the overpowering odds against him. He sent his men over those hills and the Plains were awash with crimson 7th Cavalry blood and entrails. Stiv's turn now, and he did not know the overpowering odds against him either. No expression, no words, only a means to an end.

Manifest Destiny

Azar's face gave away no emotion. Stiv waited to hear his fate. Not the slightest *tell* did she offer, and this pissed

80

him off even more. Fortunately, he caught himself because he knew she held the dull gelding shears to his balls.

"Thank you for your patience, Mr. Baker," she said coldly, the slightest accent to her educated English.

What the hell made this dumb bitch think he was even remotely patient? For fuck sake!

Azar began his death sentence. "We contacted your doctor's office and they informed us the Oxycodone prescription should not be filled now, but instead, for us to shred and destroy the prescription paper, which we did. Furthermore—"

"Wait a minute!" Stiv interrupted with a flaming tongue.

"Furthermore!" Azar interrupted Stiv and continued in a louder voice. "They told us to inform you that this doctor and his office, as of today, will no longer treat you for any ailment. They said you will receive a registered letter from this office notifying you officially. Lastly, the only contact you may have with that office is to request a referral. Do you have any further questions for me?" Azar asked, staring at him, waiting, arms crossed and ready to rumble.

"Well, that's just great!" Stiv thundered. "What am I supposed to do now? I'm out of my medication and I'm in terrible pain," he lied to Azar for the third time. "Don't you care about that? Isn't there some *oath* you take to help people? That prescription was my property, you shredded my personal property, Azar, you arrogant bitch!" Stiv shouted, now officially out of control.

"Mr. Baker, you never told me if you are set up for text messages," she asked, pleasantly deescalating.

"Can I have my other prescription back, please? I'll go to another pharmacy, Azar, although I must say I'm really glad we met today. You have especially good customer service skills and should consider teaching a class. You've really messed me up. Thanks a lot!"

"I wish you no ill will, Mr. Baker. I am simply doing my job. You are the one who did not want to cooperate when I inquired as to your particular ailments. And technically speaking, the prescription paper and codes written belong to the prescribing doctor until filled at a pharmacy, at which time the prescription becomes the property of the pharmacy, and ultimately the pharmacist who filled the prescriptions. In this case, Mr. Steven H. Baker, me," Azar said with a smile.

Stiv did not know whether to scream, laugh, or cry. Azar was good; he admired her subtle torture techniques.

"This is totally unacceptable. I don't know what to say. I've never had a problem before. I just show up, wait a bit, and get my meds. This is ridiculous!" He yelled. "And calling it your job doesn't make it right, Azar. You know exactly what you're doing," Stiv said, trying not to sound beaten.

"Nevertheless. As far as your pain medication is concerned, I have no advice. As a licensed pharmacist it is my job as well as my responsibility to evaluate the medications I fill as well as to evaluate the patient and the reason for the medication the doctor prescribed. I evaluated you and this is the result. Perhaps you should seek out anger management classes, Mr. Baker. You seem extremely tense and full of rage. Here is your written prescription for Diazepam. Have a nice day," she said, nostrils flaring.

He was in shock—did this really happen? Stiv took the little piece of blue paper noting the Diazepam refill, balled it up in his hand, and threw it on the streaked linoleum floor as he mad dog eyeballed Azar before turning and heading out. He was dazed and confused.

Stiv slowly walked through the large colorful store, noticing different aromas he had not noticed before. His usual helpful brain was now panicked and no help. When he looked towards the exit, he saw the store manager looking at him from across the room. She must have known what happened. Stiv understood he'd been defeated...for the moment. He considered telling the manager off again for good measure but knew it would do no good. There were more ways to score Oxycodone if one had a mind to.

First, he had to organize his thoughts. The Harpies were back, now accompanied by screeching cowboys and Indians. He could not let Azar get away with this. She must be reported to her corporate office at the very least. He needed to make as much trouble as possible out of general principles. Then he remembered Cyclops's office was almost next door so he hurried out and over, certain speaking with his doctor would fix this problem. Stiv was twenty seconds too late, arriving just in time to see the rear end of the black R-Type Maserati driving out of the office parking lot. Behind the wheel, Dr. Cyclops.

Stiv went straight to the receptionist window, pushed opened the sliding glass scaring the old goat sitting at the desk. He ignored the other patients. No sign of Crystal.

"Why did that ridiculous pharmacy just tell me this isn't my doctor's office anymore? What was this decision based on? Why did that pharmacist confiscate my prescription? Why did that idiot pharmacist refuse to fill my prescription the doctor wrote for me?" Stiv demanded.

"Mr. Baker, I have no idea what you are talking about," the old crone lied...she had to know. "Also, please refrain from speaking to me like that, I have done nothing to you. I would suggest calling back tomorrow and speaking to the doctor's assistant. I have absolutely no information for you. I'm sorry," she said, staring.

For the second time that day, second time that hour, Stiv's panicked mind thought about pulling the Model 38 and blasting this lying bitch to the other side of fuck all! He was in trouble and knew it, real trouble. And a junkie out of his fix was in a world of trouble. The panic was coming straight at him like a vicious cornered animal attacking to retreat.

Stiv glared back at the woman, turned without another word, and walked out of the doctor's office for the last time. He never saw Crystal again. This sad fact was yet another casualty in a day directed by diabolical absurdities. He was so depressed he was sure he would collapse...but he did not. Instead, he turned what mental energy he had left into payback. He had a few days' supplies and several other possible ways of getting his drugs. All was not lost.

Chapter 7

Rep Boy and the Hits Just Keep On Coming

11:58 A.M. Tuesday, July 4th, 2017

STIV SAT in his car with the engine running, AC on. His yellow stained sweater was discarded to the passenger seat. The butt of his Model 38 was now sticking out of his waistband like an angry black snake. He searched for the National Chain Pharmacy customer service phone number. He should have had the number on speed dial. He tapped the number, hit the speaker button, and waited. "Muskrat Love" played torturously while he nodded off in narcotic vaporous oblivion as dopamine flooded his bloodstream. In a euphoric semi-conscious trance, floating down a comfortable river of warmth, he was brought back to the cold reality of the day by a strange man's voice saying, "Thank you for calling the National Chain Pharmacy customer service hotline. All calls are recorded for training and accuracy purposes. This is Rod speaking, How may I help you?"

Stiv was expecting the automated artificial intelligence bitch prompting him to listen to a bunch of bullshit options before he got a live human. He was fully prepared to take his aggression out on the alien as a warmup, but now he was up to bat with some rep boy on the line waiting to hear his story. The friendly male voice caught him off guard and he hated that.

"Um, yes, um, hello, um, I'm calling to make a formal complaint about one of your pharmacists. She was rude, unprofessional, and caused me terrible stress and anxiety today, just a few minutes ago, in fact. Is it the practice of your pharmacy staff to make judgment calls on customers? I've personally never heard of such a thing. Can you explain to me why I was abused and mistreated this way?"

"I'm sorry, sir. What zip code are you calling from?"

"What the hell difference does it make what zip code I'm calling from?" Stiv shouted.

There was a long pause from Rod, the Rep Boy, wherever he was working.

"Sir, I am here to help you to the best of my ability. Please help me to help you and I'd appreciate it if you do not raise your voice during our conversation." Rep Boy paused, then continued. "I need some information before I can log your grievance. You do have a complaint, right?" he asked.

The helpless feeling was creeping in again. So Stiv relented, having been rude first, and yes he did have a complaint, a serious complaint.

"Fine then," he said grudgingly. "Ask your questions."

"May I have your name, day, and month of birth please?"

"Stiv Baker, April, that's all I'm telling you."

"Is that your real name sir?"

"No, it's someone else's," he said, sarcastically.

"I'm sorry, sir, Stiv is a unique name, I've never heard it before and I like the sound," Rep Boy lisped.

"How nice. Perhaps you can name your child Stiv, boy or girl."

"Ha! That's a good one, Mr. Baker," Rep Boy said, giggling like an annoying child. "I doubt very sincerely my partner and me will be having children anytime soon, but thanks for the suggestion."

"Wanker," Stiv mumbled.

"I'm sorry, sir?"

"Nothing."

"Mr. Baker, do you have a National Chain Pharmacy rewards card and if so, may I trouble you for the ID number on the back, please?"

Stiv was not sure how many more questions he was going to answer before lighting this douchebag up. Just doing his job or not. He pulled his wallet out of his back pocket, then fished around in his knife pocket, fingertips touching one of five 15-mg Oxycodone he stashed there earlier. Pulled one out between index and middle finger, popped it in his mouth, chewed it up, swallowing best he could considering how dry his mouth was. He actually liked the taste. He could not describe the flavor except to say it was bitter, a bitter pill to swallow, but not at all unpleasant. He could've used a fat double scotch on the rocks with an icy-cold Devil's Lake Lager chaser to wash the chalky narcotic paste down. He took his rewards card out of his wallet and gave Rep Boy the number.

"Thank you for that information, Mr. Baker. Now would you please explain your negative experience and please be as detailed as possible. And I remind you, all our phone calls are recorded for accuracy and training."

Stiv began using his righteous voice of the wronged. "As you can see from the information you've gathered on me, this is not the first time I've called your company's customer service hotline and—"

"Yes, I do see—"

"Excuse me! Please don't interrupt me until I'm finished, I hate when—"

"Yes, but—"

"There you go again! Can I just get my goddamn complaint out without interruption? I talk, then you talk, I talk, then you talk. That is known as a conversation, so can I talk now, or do you want to continue?"

There was a long pause over one of the millions of land-lines in the United States; both Stiv and Rep Boy waited.

Then Rep Boy said slowly and sullenly, "Please, Mr. Baker, go ahead."

"So, as I was saying. I've had problems with your company in the past, as you can see." Stiv waited, testing Rep Boy, but got only silence.

"I've been using this particular pharmacy for many years, ever since I had disagreements with another of your company's so-called managers at another location. That man is an idiot. So I started coming to my current pharmacy. After a few minor issues with the store's management team, we started getting along for the most part. Some incorrect information from some of the pharmacy workers you employ, but nothing too serious until today, about forty minutes ago..."

Rep Boy was silent so Stiv continued, "...And then the pharmacist confiscated my prescription. Just took my property and shredded it. Got me blacklisted from my doctor's office and blacklisted from filling pain medication at the National Chain Pharmacy. Where the hell would a pharmacist think they have that kind of power? That was my property, I can't begin to tell you how much trouble she's put me in, not to mention I'm out of my meds. What am I supposed to do?"

There was silence on the other end of the line. Stiv figured Rep Boy was either reading notes or taking them. After what seemed like an excessive amount of cold silence he said, "Mr. Baker, first, I want to apologize on behalf of myself and my company for the bad experience you had. We are very proud of our long-standing positive customer service rating as well as our five-star rating with the Better Business Bureau—"

"—Please!" Stiv blurted out.

"Excuse me," Rep Boy stated, "I thought we weren't interrupting each other, sir?"

Stiv could not believe his ears. He wanted this problem fixed, not a bunch of bullshit. He was in shock at how badly his day was going.

"Sorry, go ahead," Stiv said, ready to freak out.

"Like I was saying, Mr. Baker, we have a five-star rating from the Better Business Bureau, or BBB, as we like to call it."

"Give me a break," Stiv muttered miserably.

"Excuse me, Mr. Baker?"

"Nothing."

"Well then, after everything you've told me, please let me inform you that the pharmacist who helped you today added her own notes as well as witness names and statements. There is written mention of video surveillance of you allegedly, and I say *allegedly* because I haven't seen the video myself, nor will I. But allegedly, you can be seen making threatening gestures toward pharmacy staff."

He let that sink in. Stiv did not take the bait.

Rep Boy continued, "They almost called the police, apparently. Lastly, I must inform you that it is the responsibility as well as the duty of every licensed pharmacist in the country to make judgment calls on filling customer prescriptions. Your information has been entered into a national database as blacklisted from filling pain medication at this company and all of our company's affiliates." Rep Boy let this ring in the air too like slow-burning acid on Stiv's flesh.

"Have you known all this and the conclusion of this call the entire time we've been on the phone?" Stiv asked miserably.

"Yes I have," Rep Boy answered without emotion.

And Stiv knew in a word, he was *screwed*. Now it was absolute.

"So you could've saved me all this bullshit dialogue from the start? Why did you put me through this, is this your idea of good customer service?"

"Mr. Baker, like the pharmacist you dealt with today, we have policies and procedures and SOPs, or standard operating procedures, we have to abide by. I was simply doing my job, like the pharmacist. Was there anything else I can do for you? Do you have any further questions I can answer?"

"Well," Stiv began slowly, his voice shaky low in pre-panic mode. He was sweating, and his stomach hurt.

"What am I supposed to do? Does your company want me to purchase drugs illegally? Forge prescriptions, doctor-shop, obtain prescriptions through unethical doctors and dentists at so-called pill-mills? I can, you know, but why should I? Why did that asshole pharmacist decide to pick on me?"

There was silence on the other end. Rep Boy was waiting to be sure Stiv was done speaking. Rep Boy had no idea how done Stiv really was.

"Mr. Baker, I empathize with your *issue* and situation, I wish I could help, honestly, but there is absolutely nothing that can be done by my department, by me or my supervisors. I am sorry, sir. Do you have any other questions for me?"

"Yes, I do, you scumbag, can you help me score some Oxycodone, motherfucker?" Stiv shouted into the phone, hitting the red kill button ending the call and slamming the phone down on the passenger's seat. He sat staring at the dashboard, wondering what the hell he was gonna do.

Chapter 8

Reflections in Her Eyes
12:25 P.M. Tuesday, July 4th, 2017

THE INTERIOR of Stiv's car was deafeningly silent; he was unaware of anything going on around him. His mood was murderous and mean, stoned, numb, and scared. Stiv believed the three most troubling human emotions were love, guilt, and regret, not necessarily in that order. He liked hate and considered the emotion useful and had made friends with the feeling years ago. He did not find hate troubling at all. Though hate took a lot of energy, it was energy he could channel into other more positive issues like finding a new job or scoring drugs.

Going home that early in the afternoon was not an option. His super-perceptive Gemini wife knew him too well. He could not hide his frustration, sadness, or anger from her. She would question then bait him, then they would argue, an argument he could never win. Her Gemini spirit was far too powerful; he never knew which twin was waiting for him. This was part of the package when you married someone born between May 21 and June 21. Stiv had a long history with Gemini women in his life and for the record, zero regrets; he could not help being a masochist regarding this particular zodiac sign.

He wanted a drink of booze so badly he could not classify the want. The Earth might stop spinning if he did not get a shot of something alcoholic, and quick. This included but was not limited to aftershave or cooking sherry. But he would not drink and he knew it. Not yet. He was already high as the billowing clouds, having taken a full day's supply of Oxycodone in three hours. He did this as any giddy junkie would, confident in the knowledge he would have a brand-new prescription to take home later.

Big mistake.

Everything was going wrong. His emotions were a train wreck. How could he have predicted his terrible luck? Azar, the Persian Beast, had suddenly entered his life and just as unexpectedly, turned him upside down. His brain daydreamed a scene of overtly sadistic dread with Azar lovingly torturing his bitch ass.

Suspended by rope tightly tied to his ankles, his hands were lashed painfully behind his back. He was helpless. His head was a foot above a slow-burning bed of red-hot coals strategically laid beneath him. Flames licked slowly baking the cranium protecting his brain. Azar's green eyes sparkled, reflecting the firelight while gently, tenderly stoking the fire, keeping the flames low. She smiled a sadistic radiant smile as she watched his brain slowly cook inside his head. A circle of burnt flesh appeared where his hair used to be while his brain boiled. Azar whispered incomprehensible words of hate in the middle of his mind's darkest desolate landscape.

Stiv knew a doctor who did not believe in the current social restrictions of prescribing narcotic pain medication. This medical practitioner would write anyone a prescription for anything so long as cash was paid. But the visit alone would be a painful $500. This doctor did not take health insurance, no check, credit card, or wampum. No receipt of the visit nor a paper trail would be available. Cash or forget about it! The 120 pills would be another $120 if he could find a pharmacy that would fill it for him.

Blacklisted indeed.

He had the money, sort of, but more pressing bills were forthcoming soon. Then there would be the *guilt*. Guilt because of how his perpetually innocent wife would feel if she knew her husband was going to a crooked doctor who only took cash. Honestly, he did consider her innocent and somewhat abused as well. Spending money on his drug habit after being fired was pretty darn desperate, embarrassing, and he *loved* her. He *regretted* ever starting the narcotic pain medication way back when and not stopping before he got dependent. His three most troubling emotions were tied directly to his weaknesses, and he *hated* himself for it.

Stiv could not let the idea of a new thirty-day supply escape his head. Like a comforting life jacket on the high seas of addiction, he would go see the expensive quack. Love, regret, and guilt be damned. The narcotics were just too good and the withdrawals so damn bad.

Chapter 9

The Hard Love World of Zander's Wisdom

1:45 P.M. Tuesday, July 4th, 2017

STIV SNAPPED AWAKE, reaching for the Model 38 in his belt. He relaxed as his surroundings became familiar. He nodded off in the pharmacy parking lot. Oxycodone had that effect. When he drank with the pills, he would catch himself nodding like some poor street junkie sitting on cold pavement in a filthy alley. The wife caught him a few times too, offering concern, scorn, and cold-blooded accusations.

Nodding out and falling asleep have very different looks. Falling asleep, one generally gets comfortable, slowly reaching REM.

Nodding out is a slow-motion attempt at staying awake. Snapping awake, eyes darting, left and right. Then eyes start slowly closing again while making strange faces because you do not want to sleep, you just cannot help, nodding out due to the narcotics.

His first thoughts were murky, a foggy veiled semi-light recollection, a dream of the living dead. Stiv knew the nightmare was real, his worst junkie fears and paranoia finally materializing. The biggest, meanest, scariest what-if crashed into him like a speeding locomotive colliding into a gasoline-loaded suicide-jockey's tanker.

Stiv jumped out of his car and stormed back into the National Chain Pharmacy, the Model 38's hard rubber-grip sticking out of his belt like a venomous snake directing Stiv's forward motion. This reckless exhibition of handgun carry was completely legal but intimidating and against all Stiv's personal gun-carry rules. He didn't care and went straight to the beer cooler staring at all the delicious possibilities. He tried to recall different flavors since he did not see a brand he hadn't tried. Instead, he grabbed a liter-size bottle of Coke and a Big Grab Bag of Swivel's Chips. After he paid and was about to leave the store for the second time that day, he looked back at the pharmacy. Azar was looking right at him, her arms folded across her chest, a sly knowing smirk on her dark-featured face.

The boiling brain vision screamed.

Stiv waved a big half-moon wave like a metaphoric SOS signal. She waved back, smiling her evil smile. Stiv walked out of the store mumbling obscene curses and oaths on her and her ancestors with the very real intention of destroying the bitch.

The Mustang lurched from the parking lot like a drunken old man stumbling from a dive bar, pointed toward the beach, a little-used water park on the edge of the Sound. He drove slowly down the summer-green tree-lined street listening to Samantha James's beautiful mellow voice singing, "keep moving," trying to quell his mind while also killing time.

Entering the compact park, he drove to the boat ramp

down to the Sound's tiny waves licking the asphalt launch. He was on a slight decline angle pointed into the water. He stopped just short of his front tires touching the water's edge, then ripped open the package and wolfed down fists of salty chips, chasing the saturated fat with cold Coke. The food made him feel better, as did the 180-degree view of the city across the Sound's north and south. But even the comfort food could not quell the Harpies. They shrieked in his head, warning of his looming failure! That he better come up with an idea quick.

Time to call Zander.

Zander owned a law firm in Manhattan, his offices occupying a portion of an office building in the heart of Midtown, Manhattan, with panoramic views of the City. It was a stunning and obscenely expensive office. Stiv was sure Zander could help. They had been in bro-love for forty-plus years, through thick and thin. Zander would know what to do.

Stiv called Zander's unlisted cellphone only family had, his cavalier cohort answered on the second ring with one of his annoying salutations alerted by caller ID.

"What's up, asshole? Why aren't you out looking for a job?"

"Well, I've got a bit of a problem," Stiv said.

"For a change, you mean?" Zander asked, in his irony laced voice.

"Well, yeah—huh?"

Zander was silent so Stiv continued, "I was hoping you'll help me out. And who looks for a job on a national holiday?"

"If you're having girl problems I feel bad for you, son, I got ninety-nine problems but a bitch ain't one!" Zander sang dangerously out of tune.

"You should never sing again, I've been telling you this for years, not even a crap song like that. No charge for the advice," Stiv said, thinking of a new metaphor for his repertoire of major dislikes. Bad music sung badly.

"Do you need help screwing your girlfriend, I'd be glad to help and no charge. When will you be needing my services?"

"You know I don't have a girlfriend Zan, my wife's kind of funny about that."

"Yeah I know, everybody funny, now you funny too," he imitated George Thorogood. "When you get a girlfriend let me know," Zander stated in Thorogood's accent. "I won't hold my breath though, no-job dickheads like you don't attract women..."

"Thanks, are you really gonna bust my balls like this? I shouldn't have been fired. They should've let us go behind the building and fight. I would've kicked that geezer's ass even worse!"

"Yeah, Stiv, and you're not a geezer? And large corporate HR departments aren't real big on employees fist-fighting to resolve disputes. Did you call for a particular reason? I'm kinda busy here trying to finish early. I hope you've taken the three-hour time difference into consideration. I'm taking the family to the annual Fourth of July party at the beach club tonight."

"That's nice," Stiv said, half meaning it, having no club to attend. "I need some legal advice if you have a moment. Is that cool?"

"Sure, why not, it's a national holiday and a free country, why shouldn't I give out free legal advice and services. Let me know when you get a girlfriend though."

"Yeah, I'll do that, but look, bro, I just got into an argument with a pharmacist who refused to fill my pain medication prescription. We argued but of course I was polite and professional as always," Stiv said sincerely.

Zander knew better but said nothing.

"She calls my doctor's office; they tell her to tell me my doctor won't see me as a patient anymore for any reason. Then she says I've been blacklisted in their national database tied to all major pharmacies in the state. Have you ever heard such a situation? Can the pharmacist treat me like that?"

"I've heard all three, what do you think I do here all day? Did she give one?"

"One what?" Stiv asked yawning.

"Stiv, what are you stupid? A reason, asshole. Did she tell you why she refused to fill your prescription, why she called your doctor's office or why your dumb ass is blacklisted?" Zander asked, waiting.

Stiv was silent so Zander continued, "Did she tell you why she treated you like some creature from the dark, Stiv?"

"Creature from the dark?" Stiv repeated, having momentarily blacked out.

Zander was silent so Stiv went on, but he was getting bored already with Zander's psychoanalysis and did not want Zander to know he was very stoned.

"Well yeah, she said I've been taking the meds too long and my doctor's overprescribing me. Said there's no documentation why I'm taking Oxycodone at all. I've never dealt with this bitch before. She's from some Middle Eastern shi... country," he corrected himself. "Who by the way is a total piece of Persian ass but what a bitch, she punched my number, bro. Who is she to judge my doctor's diagnosis? What's up with that?"

"Yes, she can and apparently did refuse to fill. I'm pretty sure when she called your doctor's office, she accused them of overwriting. It freaks doctors out these days when someone points the narco finger. You're the sacrificial lamb, Stiv. That pharmacist can cause your ex-doctor a lot of trouble, I'm sure he knows that. So the guy took the path of least resistance firing your bitch ass, now he has your blood in his books showing he cut you off. A damn shame," Zander said. "And that's a reason alright, several actually, and here are the facts as I see them," he said over dramatically. "Yes, she can and did refuse to fill your prescription. Yes, if she tells your doctor and/or his office you're a troublemaker, which I'm sure you are, and I'm sure she did, they can and will fire you as a patient. They do this more to protect the doctor because frankly they don't give a shit about you, especially if you make trouble, which you did. Apparently, Stiv, your new pharmacist told you in no uncertain terms to go fuck yourself," Zander guffawed.

"This kind of crap counsel and advice should be free. I should apply for legal aid at the welfare office. From what I understand they're giving away free money down there."

"Welfare sounds about right for you and my services ain't free, fool. I get five hundred fifty bucks an hour with a one-hour minimum. You wanna use a credit card or should we bill you?"

"Put it on my tab and please tell me I'm not fucked?" Stiv asked, downtrodden.

"I can't do that because you are Stiv, in more ways than one."

"Yeah, I know. That blacklisting might be a real problem, finding a new doctor too. I can't believe this shit, Zander," Stiv whined into the phone.

"You might be missing my point, Stiv."

"No, I get it. It's hard to find a new doctor, especially one who'll write Oxycodone. But I'm cool. I got a doctor here in town who'll write anything I want for five hundred bucks cash. Doesn't even take insur—"

"You're one dizzy dude, you know that, Stiv?" Zander interrupted.

"Why?"

"For one thing, you're stupid. Also, your priorities are all screwed up. You got fired by your doctor, do you have any idea how hard it's gonna be to find a new one? Especially since you've been blacklisted. Also, you've been blacklisted, whatever the fuck that means, and, you're a walking talking junkie and apparently you don't even know it. That's your biggest problem, Stiv, not where you can score more drugs. You gotta get off that shit, bro. Do you like being a junkie?"

"How am I a junkie? I take the pain meds for my back, you know that," Stiv said defensively.

"Tell it to someone who doesn't know you, bro. We've been friends a long time and I love you, you know that, but maybe this pharmacist did you a favor. Why not stop taking the pills? Are you even in pain?"

"I think so, but I haven't stopped using the pills since I tried cold turkey last year. Messed me up good, damn near killed me, remember? And why do you have to call me a junkie?"

"How could I forget? Didn't you shit and piss your pants then puke all over yourself? I don't know too many people like that," Zander said.

"Yes, I did. It was pretty bad, I never want to go through that again. You shouldn't break my balls about it, Zan."

"Too bad, I'll always break your balls because you proved then and there you're a junkie, you couldn't stop the pills, right? You've been on them ever since and twelve years before that. How are you not a junkie, son?"

"Because I'm not," Stiv said, a little hurt.

"So let me get this straight, you want me to pretend my best friend's not a pain med junkie, even though he's been taking a high daily dosage for over fourteen years, went through life-threatening withdrawals a year ago, is that correct?"

Stiv was silent so Zander continued, "That's why I called you a junkie. You don't think much of what I do for a living, do you?"

"Of course I do."

"Then why would you think I didn't know you're a junkie?" Zander yelled.

Stiv was silent again, thinking about slamming the phone down and going for a long one-way swim.

"Make sense now? Or are you too stoned to get it? You're stoned, aren't you?" Zander demanded.

"I get it already. And no, I'm not stoned," he lied.

"That's a good boy, Stiv, now man up and quit the pills. You don't have to be a pussy all your life. You quit drinking after forty years of being an obnoxious pain in the ass drunk. You should be able to kick this annoying pill habit too. Do you like being a junkie?"

"Backoff, Zander, will you?" Stiv yelled for the first time.

"Will I what, Stiv? Hey, you called me, remember, or are you too high?"

"I'm not high," Stiv yelled, lying again.

"Yeah—sure you aren't. Look, Stiv, I love you, always have, always will, you know this too. But you got a prob-lem, bro. Deal with it. I'll do anything for you except help you convince yourself it's okay to be a stupid pain med junkie. It's not and you're better than that. It's time to quit, bro. You can do better. And speaking of doing better, how's the wife? Not too rough on you getting fired again, I hope?"

"Not as rough as you and we don't talk about my ex-job, it only gets ugly."

"She knows you're a junkie, Stiv," Zander said with conviction.

"She knows I take the pills for my back and what junkie? She doesn't care anyway."

"Yes Stiv, she does. How can you say that? She's stayed with you all these years because she cares too much. A woman loving you less would've quit your junkie ass years ago, especially a class act like your blushing bride. I'll never know how you tricked her into loving you anyway. She's a good woman, Stiv, do whatever it takes," Zander said prophetically.

"I think you love me more than she does, faggot. And the answer is still *no* and I'm so glad I'm not paying for this legal consultation," Stiv said.

"You're gonna pay, buddy, *you're gonna pay the man, big time*. Get your shit together, Stiv. Read *Diary of a Drug Fiend*, Aleister Crowley's fall into cocaine and heroin addiction. Your life is all sorted out in that book, Stiv. He penned it in the 1920s, about a World War One Sopwith Camel pilot and the secret society he belonged to. Describes you clearly."

"I read the book in the eighties and I gave it to you, remember? And how does the book describe me?" Stiv asked.

"Yes, I remember you gave me the book but did *you* actually read it? Because if you did, we wouldn't be having this conversation."

"I read it," Stiv said. "And do you have to talk in riddles?"

"Good boy, then you recollect the narrative's message to society, which includes you. Think about it. And what I'm saying sounds like riddles to you because you're stoned, Stiv Baker, think about that too. Ring again anytime and keep me posted. I love giving free legal advice to junkies on national holidays. Thank you very much for calling, tell your wife she can do better and that I say hi," Zander said in his irony-laced, hard love voice then hung-up.

Stiv stared at the choppy blue water while taking a few pulls from his bottle of Coke, then burst into tears, spitting cola on his jeans. He sobbed for a while, not because of Zander, that was a standard conversation, but because the day's trials finally caught up with him. He blew his nose in his pocket handkerchief, feeling a little better. Pulling the Model 38 from his belt, opening the wheel, he looked at the five pristine .38 Special primers before closing the wheel again. Hefting the snub-nosed around, he hit the play button on the CD player. Joni Mitchell's *Court and Spark* album began to play. One of his favorites.

He put the bad news end of the Model 38 to the bridge of his nose, index finger of his right hand on the trigger. Applying the slightest pressure, he could see the shrouded hammer moving back slightly. He thought about his wife, considered how beautiful and desirable he found her after more than twenty years together. He pulled slightly harder on the trigger, the revolver in double-action mode, a twelve-pound pull, the wheel moving again slightly.

A pod of dolphins were swimming two hundred yards out in front of him. He watched their dorsal fins break the surface when they came up to breathe the same air as him, the Model 38 still at the bridge of his nose. Stiv did not think it was fair the dolphins could breathe air but he could not survive underwater. Life was never fair. Looking up, he watched a colony of seagulls soaring in the breeze. More unfairness. Why couldn't he fly? He applied slightly more pressure to the trigger so the wheel, like the Earth, slowly turned.

The gulls dived, dancing near the pod of dolphins, hitting the water and scavenging chopped fish bits from the dolphins' leftover lunch. He maintained the same pressure on the trigger, the shrouded hammer slightly off the firing pin.

Suddenly from behind his car appeared a murder of crows from up on the hill of houses. They began attacking the seagulls in a dogfight of sky acrobatics for the free lunch. It was a fracas the gulls could never win, and they retreated to circle the dozen or so highly intelligent, territorial, dive-bombing black Corvus Brachyrhynchos, or American crows.

The next jacketed hollow point in the revolver's rotation, a .38 Special, Hydra-Shok Plus P Plus 127 grain hollow point bullet, waited to take flight at 1,150 feet per second.

Chapter 10

The Hemingway Out
2:30 P.M. Tuesday, July 4th, 2017

STIV WOKE, the dolphins singing and dancing like in a deep blue oceanic disco. The murder of crows was gone but the gulls still soared, imitating slow-motion riders. Stiv thought about the Octopus's Garden in front of him, the seadogs beckoning him to join their sea mammal games. He knew they were tempting him when their bottle-shaped noses broke water to breathe the oxygen they shared with appetency. It was fair, how could he deny it?

In a gathering of last exit thoughts, his recent termination was most prevalent followed closely by the demeaning loss of all the other jobs over the years, health insurance and income. Add a large amount of shredded pride to that list. Stiv might finally have to admit to himself: he had a problem, he was a pain med junkie. This observation was a crushing source of turmoil. There might be the glaring possibility he had anger issues too. Were these sufficient reasons to exit through the last permanent passageway? He wasn't quite ready for the secret unknown on the other side. Though there wouldn't be any guilt, love, or regret, these facts were something to consider. But how could he be sure? Probably only the lonely abyss of total darkness awaited. He liked the darkness, could rest in her quiet patient eternity because there's nothing quiet or patient about the assault of narcotic dependence and withdrawals. And he believed the only truth the dead know for sure is it's better to be alive in the light.

Stiv told anyone listening on the subject, his ideal way out of this world aside from healthy old age or dying in the *saddle* of a hot woman was the ocean and her jagged sharp timelessness, adrift in last disoriented thoughts. A bullet to the brain was messy and cliché. He called that particular form of suicide *The Hemingway Out*. Fortunately, his life insurance paid if that were a course of action; his wife was his only beneficiary. Everyone needs money.

He nodded out again but snapped awake dehydrated, cotton mouthed. As he finished the last of his now warm Coke, the silent reckoning Model 38 remained in his right hand, waiting at his side like a loyal minion. He wondered how long he crashed out comatose. The dolphins were still waiting for him to wake, like swimming phantoms whispering for him to hear. That was so thoughtful of the playful pod.

Stiv held the revolver up, waving, not pointing the roscoe at them but presenting and showing the pod he finally surrendered to their counsel and amphibious wisdom. Knowing their charitable mission was complete, they suddenly and in perfect synchronized family bond swam off into their unfathomable worlds.

Stiv wondered if the group of dolphins, the colony of gulls, and the murder of crows knew each other or saw each other regularly. Could they communicate?

Stiv grabbed his iPhone, paused for a moment to think about the sudden departure of the sea mammals, wanting to know everything about the species.

He decided to ring Zander again. Regardless of how annoying Zander was with his regular course of cynicism, he was a pragmatic genius, always had been. No matter what though, he'd loved the man for almost five decades. With everything flooding Stiv's mind that day, he forgot to wish Zander a happy anniversary.

———

They first met July 4th, 1976, America's Bicentennial, exactly forty-three years ago almost to the hour. Stiv was babysitting a very wasted young lady classmate he shared time with that long-ago summer holiday. They dropped acid, she took too much, end of story. Stiv was able to keep her safe for the most part, controlled while trying desperately to get into her pants. It had been an adventurous odyssey to say the least. While they were walking toward the neighborhood country club, they bumped into an arrogant townie hooligan on the train tracks where their remarkable *trip* began.

He and Stiv talked shit at each other. The hooligan insulting him also flirted with Ariel. Complimenting her fine ass right in front of Stiv, really pissing him off. Both were trying to impress the stoned, raven-haired, green-eyed doll. As life's fortunes sometimes have it, they walked away from the confrontation, luckily for Stiv. The hooligan was a tough street brawler from a proud family with a group of psycho-thug friends. Walking away was rarely the case in their rowdy little East Coast town, but fortune shined on Stiv that day.

Stiv knew none of this at the time as they went to different schools. He definitely recognized him and the dangerous look in Zander's eyes that day. Neither knew why they did not jump, fate, a mischievous calculation. But they did not or the future would have been altered. Ironically, ever-present influences guided them to meet again completely by chance weeks later at a keg party of a mutual friend. Zander's cousin. Destiny brought people together, as did synchronicity. Zander approached Stiv first, asking if they met before. Stiv did not remember until they started talking, then the previous 4th of July came up and all clicked into place. Laughing, handshakes, and a new inseparable friendship began. They were brothers ever since, mixing their blood at some point after a messy brawl with another group of rowdies they pounded the shit out of. They became equally dependent on each other for different reasons.

That Bicentennial Stiv spent hallucinating, chasing the beautiful sixteen-year-old minx from one end of his neighborhood to the other, trying but failing to score. When Stiv moved overseas, Ariel somehow hooked up with Zander, the bastard, just before the two went off to their own respective lives. It had been a one-time gig, but Zander never tired of reminding Stiv about their hot and heavy weekend.

"I think she saw God just before dawn Stiv, she kept yelling for him, that girl was hot! I appreciate you introducing us."

The fact Zander nailed Ariel while Stiv never got close would bother him to the grave. But Zander could do no wrong in Stiv's eyes and was forever forgiven. As obnoxious as he was, he loved him. Zander was a blood-brother from another mother. Stiv admired his benevolent tireless rise to power and sober worldview, ironically wilder than Stiv when they were ferocious kids. Who can explain it? Zander worked hard all his life to get to that office overlooking Central Park, while Stiv goofed off all his life to land where he did. They would never let a piece of ass come between them, no matter how fine, Stiv's jealousy and Ari's good looks notwithstanding.

Even though Zander already told him off, he did not believe it was the end of what Zander could do for him. Why not sue the National Chain Pharmacy? Could he at least get Azar fired? Zander had power and connections. Stiv had to convince him he was not some weak junkie, but a victim of circumstance. A pawn in the great chess game of life and marked for death by stronger powers. He had to make Zander believe...

"*De Nuevo. Que pasa, maricon?*" Zander answered.

"I'm sitting here staring at the Sound. A pod of dolphins were swimming around right out in front of me, about two hundred yards offshore. Absolutely beautiful, sure was nice to see," Stiv said, feeling sad and alone.

"Okay, I'm sitting in my office, busy as hell on a national holiday trying to get out of here. Now I'm wondering, *que pasa, maricon?* Didn't we just have this conversation?"

"Unfortunately, she was new. I know the other pharmacist, she would've helped me out but this new one, what a bitch. Did I mention she was really hot? I'd rather be told off by a hot woman than some fat hairy bitch. How about you?" Stiv asked desperately.

"Look, Stiv, she did you a favor, man, did all of us a favor cutting you off. And for the second time I'm telling you this."

"What?"

"You are a junkie," he said, enunciating each word slowly and carefully. "You know it and I know it, now this pharmacist bitch knows it too. Do you like being a junkie?"

"How am I a junkie, bro, I need those pills for my back pain. I've told you that a hundred times," Stiv weakly protested.

"Why do you treat me like a schmuck, Stiv? You go to your dojo three times a week and get your ass seriously kicked; I've watched you faggots. You run, what, twenty miles a week? Play golf and ride your bicycle all over that beach community of yours and it's all hills. Then you want to take narcotic pain medication for back pain? That's really lame, and frankly you look like a bloody asshole doing that," Zander stated with serious finality.

"Sounds like you and my wife went to the same school of bitching."

"Count your blessings. A lot of junkies have no support, you got plenty. You're one of the lucky junkies, fool. And make no mistake, I'm going easy on you, remember that. You need to quit the drugs, find a new job—again, get serious, Stiv. You're becoming an embarrassment."

"Thanks a lot," Stiv said, hurt now.

"Stiv, I mean to yourself. Not to me, not to those who love you, but think about it."

"I am and thanks for clarifying. I gotta go," Stiv said sadly.

Zander was not finished. "I see insurance fraud liars like you get nailed to the wall all the time, bro, and if you still follow the news, I'm sure you've seen those pain management crooks getting thrown in jail on a regular basis. Do you want to be a part of that?"

"I'm not saying you don't make sense, Zan, but it's a fine line between needing those pills and how badly they might mess a guy up," Stiv said.

"That statement in itself tells me you're wasted. I honestly think that pharmacist is trying to help you. She spotted you out of experience because the country's full of legal junkies walking around like zombies, just like you. Your drug fix was provided by unscrupulous doctors and big pharmaceutical companies who better watch their asses. You legal junkies aren't far from street junkies, only difference is you go to a doctor who prescribes the drugs, you've not broken any laws, but equally as guilty if it's an addiction and not legitimate pain you take the narcotics for."

"Maybe I should've kept watching the dolphins, they aren't so opinionated," Stiv said for levity.

Zander was not having it. "Yup, she saw you for what you are, a well-dressed, well-spoken senior citizen pain med junkie and she cut your bitch ass off, which is her responsibility. You should go back and thank her and knowing you, probably apologize for being a rude asshole too. Are you even looking for a job? What is it with you and getting fired anyway? You've lost more jobs than anybody I know."

"I'm not good with the corporate mentality, Zan, you aren't either, so I know you understand. You do, right? And I wasn't rude to that pharmacist, she said no, and I walked out. Simple."

"You're full of shit, but you're only fooling yourself and no, I don't understand, sorry. You don't work, you don't get no money, and I like money. You're right though, I don't like corporate bullshit and that's why I quit working for someone else opening my own business, my own firm. Only way you'll ever know what you're worth and you get to fire bad employees."

"I've fired people before," Stiv said weakly.

"I think we're having a failure to communicate, bro. It ain't firing people I'm talking about. It's your drug addiction. Have you ever thought your addiction might be causing you all the trouble in your life, like your anger issues?"

"What troubles? What anger issues? What the hell, bro?"

"Stiv, I'm trying to work here and you're watching dolphins in the middle of the day stoned."

"It's a national holiday," Stiv replied defensively.

"Yeah, I know it is, and I'm working. You have no job, just got fired by your doctor, in total denial about your addiction—then you get yourself blacklisted on a national form. Now you can't be prescribed narcotic pain medication legitimate or otherwise, what does that even mean? Who does this happen to, Stiv?"

"Unlucky people like me?"

"Ha! That's a joke, you're one of the luckiest people I know, and for so many reasons. I can't believe you don't understand your so-called bad luck is really a gift, someone's watching out for you, bro, and someone always has. Your marriage says it all, aside from the fact you're still above ground. Believe me, you're lucky. But hey, I don't have time for another free therapy session with you, I gotta go..."

"So that's it? That's your advice? Quit, that simple, huh?"

"That simple because you don't have a choice unless you're gonna buy off the streets. I could see your old ass hanging with the homies on the corner and you're probably stoned right now. Are you stoned right now, Stiv? Of course you are. You've been wasting my time high all day, you probably popped extra pills thinking you'd have a new prescription today. Am I right?"

"Wrong," Stiv lied, wondering how the hell Zander knew that.

"You got balls lying to me, bro. You want me to feel sorry for you? Okay, I feel sorry for you, junkie. Happy Fourth!" Zander hung up.

Stiv sat holding the phone to his ear, hoping for friendly voices from beyond staring out at the Sound. No voices materialized so he put the phone down looking at the jagged city sparkling across the water. His only shocked conclusion after the two nasty conversations was how identical Zander and the wife attacked him. This made him think long and hard about things. Then he nodded out...again.

Chapter 11

The Middle Eight

One Year Before Termination

THE PAWN BUSINESS was a perfect avenue for supplying Stiv's many hobbies, adding to his *regret* of losing the job. Collecting gold coins, gold jewelry, precious metals, handguns, memorabilia, and Rolex watches. Another lifelong hobby: studying theory and training in Japanese karate, which began in 1983 when he first moved to Japan and walked into the dojo his second day on Japanese soil. He worked out hard, karate, bicycling, and running. Zander was right. If any doctor saw his physical activity, they would rip his narcotic prescriptions right out of his hands and tear the paper into confetti. Abundance was his business; if he wanted to take drugs, it was his choice. He could take whatever he wanted, drink whatever he wanted, and so on. Weren't these his choices?

Stiv was also a rabid reader and short story writer although his writing was erratic. He considered himself a storyteller, not an author. Authors got paid for their work, Stiv most certainly did not. He wrote stories based on whatever thoughts cruised through his mind. Then he meticulously edited, proofread, rewrote, and corrected. Then did it all over again. When he was totally satisfied with the finished product, he dragged the Word file into a desktop folder titled *Short Stories* and promptly forgot about it. He never submitted the tales, instead used them for reminiscing about the old days in the dark reaches of his mind. Some he liked, some he loathed. Aside from sex, drumming, traveling, reading, and exercise he could not think of a better way to spend time. His wife asked why he bothered if he had no intention to submit the work. Sometimes she knocked on his door when he was trying to pen an important thought, thus breaking his creative flow. This seemed to happen a lot, reminding him of the writing scene in Stanley Kubrick's rendering of Stephen King's novel *The Shining*.

What was the point of his writing? He didn't know exactly, aside from he enjoyed it. And writing was medicinal, cathartic, regardless of quality or content. As for submitting his work to publishers, he thought about it but did not believe any reader would get his point or humor. More important, he feared absolute rejection due to his literary ignorance, incompetence, and sciolism. Still, anything therapeutic is good in life. He needed therapy. Didn't everyone?

The End.

After his recent termination—again—Stiv was afraid to meet his wife in the condo when he should have been at work like any decent husband. Just one of the many landmines a bloke has to sidestep when his spouse worked out of their home. He did his best to stay out of her way, hiding behind closed doors reading, writing, and listening to music. Not a bad escape.

He had written a short story hours after the recent termination while emotional cyclones spiraled inward, upward, and outward through his mind. As angry as he was, depression overtook him. Not self-destructive, instead he was pissed at himself. Why could he not keep his big mouth shut? Focus on his job, then go home instead of beating the piss out of his co-worker?

Acute elevated self-esteem

Without firm foundation

Bordering on clinical narcissism

A story floated into his brain like a feather in the breeze, innocent and gentle, his first conception of self-pity. He rolled and kneaded the theme in his overheated oven-like brain, having trouble working out the pity aspect. Why should he feel pity for his protagonist? Instead, more like self-loathing. He attempted a singular dark comedy. Another question he asked himself as the writer, why bother with a theme? No one was gonna read the stories anyway.

On that day birds soared lazily; bright green foliage swayed in the summer breeze brilliant against the Sound's colors. A multicolored rufous hummingbird flew past his window like a supersonic missile, returned and hovered directly in front of him watching, spying. Its wings flapped about seventy times per second while the feisty little bird's heart rate beat around 1,260 beats per minute. Talk about a cardio workout. Seconds later, after gathering intel, the mini bird sped off to oblivion, most likely to report on him.

Stiv knew what the bird was doing but could not worry about it. After staring at nothing but space for about the same amount of time the Sound's icy water would take to kill him, he started to write. He called the story "Help Wanted."

Chapter 12

Help Wanted

Help Wanted

A Short Story
By
Steven H. Baker

Anybody who could write worth a damn
Could never write in peace.
-Henry Chinaski

GUILT ASSOCIATED with losing one's job compares to committing a foolish crime, getting busted, found guilty, then sent to the joint looking like a total ass to all friends and family.

It's important in such times to keep busy, keep your mind occupied. Sleep is an escape; unfortunately, it's only short-term relief, and not very lucrative.

Stress-oriented dreams intensify. Technicolor visions,

119

people, faces, stories, scenes from long ago, times to come, shapes and patterns float past like lost phantoms.

The mind, which is a terrible thing to waste, is also the true final frontier. Dreams pretend all night long. Deceitful and mean, until the ferocious urge to pee brings you back to reality. Awake, only to see from the clock that slumber lasted only an hour.

The dead silent night creeps slowly by. Time and tide wait for no man. Distant sounds of traffic, people on their way to work reminding you of guilt and despair. Your personal journey to somewhere, everywhere, nowhere. A lonely faraway train whistle breaks the dark silence, melancholy like a baby whispering in slumber, scared and alone.

After all is explained, the termination story is told and retold...replayed and overplayed. In the end, the story is just played out.

The bathroom mirror shows you where you're at, the reflection of your reality, your situation, life, and times. The only one you really owe answers to is looking into your eyes wanting explanations.

"Tell me why, asshole?" reflection screams using telepathy. "Why are you standing there looking at me? You think you have a right?"

"I'm looking for blackheads and blemishes. Do I need a shave? I really need to pee."

"Shut up and pee! Then go out and find a job, you dork. Who gets fired from a job like that? You, that's who!"

"It's three a.m., and I didn't get fired. Why don't you know that since you're me? You were there, you know what happened. Why are you blaming me?"

"You're so weak. I'm not you, I'm me. Do you think I would've gotten fired from such a place? I hate you!"

"*Like it or not, you got fired. Why do you deny it? It wasn't much of a job anyway, you said so yourself.*"

Face closes its eyes in deep thought. When eyes open, face is smiling, and says, "*What are you gonna do now, pretty boy?*"

"*Well, I suppose I can apply for unemployment insurance, start searching the want ads, beat the pavement, all that crap. But I'd like to take some time off, take it easy, you know?*"

"*Beating your meat would be more like it. Anyway, that's what got you fired in the first place—taking it easy, you idiot! When are you going to hit your head, learn your lesson, stop being so unprofessional and get with the program?*" Reflection speaks in a Southern vowel-breaking drawl the last six words sounding like Hannibal Lector teasing Clarice Starling.

"*Like you've never been fired from a job? Get off your high horse! Stop being so condescending and arrogant!*"

"*You've got some nerve talking to me like that, who do you think you are? Maybe if you could keep a job for more than a few years you could act cocky, but in your case, I wouldn't try. You look like shit, by the way, your nose hairs stick out like party favors and need serious attention!*"

"*Maybe a haircut. My eyes hurt and they're all bloodshot, how old am I again? I feel really old. Please tell me it's the weekend, I feel less guilt on the weekends. No one should have to work on Saturday or Sunday, nor have to think about finding work either, both are days of rest.*"

"*What's the difference? Fired is fired. You are a worthless, good-for-nothing loser. You make me sick!*"

"*Thanks, I am feeling a bit under, as they say. I chalk it up to emotional shock. After all, being betrayed by so-called friends and then a whole company takes a toll on one's nerves and emotions."*

"Ha! Emotions? I got your emotions swinging, buddy, and did you say friends, you wuss? You had no friends there. Look how often your phone rings now that you aren't the boss of that dump. No one liked you anyway. You said so yourself, 'It's lonely at the top,' wherever it is you consider 'the top.' Now you're a lonely, unemployed, phone-never-rings dipshit! You make me want to vomit!" Reflection shouts, grabbing its throat, making gagging sounds.

"You're not helping my depression, you know. Maybe I'll become a drug addict. I hear Valium is good for depression if you can't get heroin."

"Did you say become? And yeah, that's just what you need. Didn't your moron doctor give you Zoloft the last time you were fired? That serotonin inhibitor crap? Remember when you got horny, you couldn't get a woody, even if you were showering with the UCLA girls fast-pitch softball team? You were pissed!"

"So were you, remember? Wow, could you imagine showering with all those college girls? Blondes, brunettes, redheads, steaming hot water, soapy jiggling butt-slapping laughter, breast comparisons, dropping the soap, bikini line shaving advice? Oh boy!"

"Yeah, and you, Mr. I-was-walking-down-the-street-and-got-fired! Yes people, fired! Right, that's you, not me and not a naked girl on the planet wants your unemployed, ain't-got-no-money, how-we-gonna-get-around-on-your-bus-pass? Who's gonna want you?" Reflection sings to a hip-hop beat.

"Very funny, you got any bright ideas?" Face asks.

"Yeah, don't listen to you for starters!" bellows Reflection. "Don't you have any goals, something you want to do on your own with your life? Aren't you tired of making money

for users who throw you to the curb every time something goes a bit astray? Obviously, you can't work for someone else, it's official, you've proven it. But hey, I got an idea for you. How about this? You start a company going around the country doing How-To-Get-Fired-Every-Three-Years seminars. You're a natural with plenty of experience. You could even do TV commercials, 'Get fired in three years, or your money back...guaranteed! We here at GFITY'S are experts in the fine art of losing your employment! Job too hard? Get fired! Job too easy? Get fired! Job too good? Get fired! We don't give a rat's ass why, we'll just show you HOW TO GET FIRED!' What do you think? We got something going here? Huh? Do we?" Reflection asks, reaching down scratching his balls.

Face yawns, ignoring the attempted mirth. "I always thought being a hot dog vendor would be a nice occupation, you know? Pushing one of those weenie wagons around downtown like in New York City. You're your own boss, keep your own hours, just have to meet a sales minimum or quota, I think. Aside from the elements, it might be a fantastic way to meet women. Who doesn't love a hot dog vendor?" Face says.

"Why do I bother talking to you? You don't seem to grasp the seriousness of your situation. Please get serious for both our sakes."

"You got a problem with hot dog vendors? Are you one of those reflections who slanders the reputation of hot dog vendors?" Face asks.

"Yeah!" Reflection yells. "They're a bunch of bums, homeless schmucks spitting in the sauerkraut. It's their only way of getting back at a society who they blame for putting them behind a giant plastic schlong half the day pointing right up their asses! OK, maybe they get paid in the process.

But you can bet there's no medical or dental and you can forget vision!"

"You don't think pushing one of those carts around is an effective way to meet women?" Face asks.

"What about your wife? Did you forget about her, wise guy?" Reflection asks.

"She doesn't think unemployed guys deserve sex. Not deserving doesn't change the need factor, know what I mean?"

"I know what you mean," Reflection sighs. "I could use a good romp myself. She sure does kiss nice and smells so good, I'm getting a woody just thinking about the last time we fooled around. -When was that? Seems like weeks, even months. She keeps it locked tight like a juicy oyster with a priceless pearl stashed inside."

"That's a fact. I wish I could convince her that three minutes of her time would mean a lot to me. She could read a magazine for all I care. Just help me fight off some of this depression crap." Face says sadly.

"Good luck, my friend." Reflection smiles friendly for the first time since entering the bathroom looking in the mirror. "Your chances of getting laid while you're unemployed are about as good as mine. Zilch. Live with it. Hey, since you're in the john, why not spank before going back to bed? That way you don't have to beg for sex you ain't gonna get anyway. Begging for sex from your wife, the pits man, the pits. Nothing makes a man more of a sap than having to beg for sex from his wife." Reflection observes.

"You know what, that's a darn clever idea. I am anxious. Just the thought of her lying there asleep, her luscious firm body all warm and clean, her hands between her thighs, her breasts gently moving with each breath. Maybe she's sleeping with her legs open. Oh boy!"

"*Honey, what are you doing in there? You've been in the bathroom a long time. Come back to bed,*" *wife's muffled voice comes through the bathroom door.*

"*Be right there, sweetie.*"

After a long well-needed pee, hot soapy hand wash, I look in the mirror telepathically communicating, "Okay, you, this shouldn't take long, don't look."

"*I won't," Reflection smiles, "but then it's my turn..."*

-The End

Chapter 13

Going Home, The Point, and Fresh Flowers

3:40 P.M. Tuesday, July 4th, 2017

**Let's just say a charm of hummingbirds
told me.**

THE INTERIOR of his car was hot and stuffy when he woke. His overall condition was rough. He got out with the empty Coke bottle and balled-up chips bag, depositing them in a trash bin a few feet away. His senses were hit with a profound briny sea breeze giving him hope and momentary peace of mind. Walking to a nearby public bathroom, he glided into the Men's hot stinking stalls. Sluggishly he stood in an ammonia stench, vile and suffocating, quashing his hope and peace of mind like cold reeking reality. He washed his hands and dried them on his jeans.

There was not much left for him to do but go home and face whatever Gemini punishment awaited him. Stiv was never faithful to any girl, ever, but for reasons only the heavens knew, his wife's lips were the only he kissed in passion since the first time they stayed together all those years ago. An afternoon of bittersweet passion heightened by a violent, yet magnificent summer storm. Perhaps the most profound melancholy connection he had ever experienced.

As his wife, she was completely satisfying in every way, so he did not need another woman other than friendship and possibly free drugs. Even more mystifying was her love and devotion to him. He doubted even the heavens could explain the phenomenon. These thoughts brought Stiv to a new stoned conclusion. He understood the intensity of being genuinely in love. He also understood the responsibility of being loved. However, there were too many ways of hurting each other. What switch in the human brain-controlled love and why? What flipped the love switch on and off? He had been in love before. Been badly hurt and done some hurting himself. But the intensity he felt all those years ago, the fact he felt the same now, was a gift, hopefully not one-sided.

True love, who can explain the precarious feelings?

Granted, she was tough on him, but he deserved her Gemini wrath...sometimes. She stayed with him, nonetheless. He cherished her level of dedication, and friendship even if she did drive him insane sometimes. She was able to reduce him to a mumbling deranged buffoon at will.

She was relieved and quite proud when Stiv quit drinking, but also stated with brutal irony, "Anyone with a drinking problem can stop for a while. To quit altogether is a lifelong commitment."

In the words of Butthead, "Uh, could you like—shut up?"

Stiv did not have the willpower to be a social drinker, all

or nothing, so she was right— again. He had to stop forever, which he did on May 1, 2014. He committed to her that loadstar day, as long as they lived together, he would not take another drink. There had not been a catalyst, it was just time.

Much to his mortification, she attacked again. "You're quitting because of me, you want *me* to feel guilty like I'm making you quit when you should quit for yourself. I never told you to stop drinking, Stiv Baker, and I never will. I think you should for your health and our marriage but that's my opinion, not my demand. But I want to be clear, I never asked or told you to quit drinking."

"I'm quitting for my health, trust me," he lied. "I know I drink too much and for too long. I wanna be healthy for us and our future together."

Stiv knew as sure as he knew the Catholic Church protected pedophiles, if he and the wife could not make their marriage last forever, he would dash to the nearest booze palace and drink faster than a dehydrated camel at a cool oasis. Nothing could stop him. Nothing.

His attempted reverse psychology failed. Why did he bother trying to deceive her? She was way too smart.

Nevertheless, she stayed and he kept his promise. On the morning of May 1, 2014, three years and a few months prior, Steven Huffam Baker stopped drinking alcohol. His friends could not believe it. Stiv could not believe it either. His daily intake was a minimum of a six-pack or until he finished however many bottles or cans of beer he had, or until he passed out. He purchased whatever beer was on sale plus hard liquor—he would down four or more shots each night—along with his daily ration of Oxycodone and sometimes Valium. There was rarely any beer leftover the next day. It was a deadly combination, but it did not kill him. He often wondered how he did not croak himself, not that he wanted to die but by all realistic biological facts, he should have been dead for many reasons.

I live I die I live I die I live again!

No one was more astonished than Stiv Baker. He consumed liquor in those quantities going on thirty-five years. He was not proud of his distasteful debauchery, simply acknowledged the fact.

His pain medication addiction started in earnest around 2003, but he always mixed drugs and alcohol, had since he was a kid. Sometimes he drank more, sometimes less, but always a large amount by any standard including his anonymous friends at AA. His next drink was always prioritized unless he was sleeping. No matter where he was or what he was doing, he had to get to that next drink. He was a functioning drunken druggie. But no matter how drunkenly wasted he got, no matter how little sleep and regardless of monumental death-march hangovers, he always got up and went to work. Sometimes his nuclear hangovers were so incapacitating he called Uber to take him from his bed to his bathroom. They refused. What kind of crap customer service is that?

Then there were the brilliant Depas and Halcion he used while living in Japan. These narcotics were similar to the drugs he took in America. He really liked pills but always had a problem with them...aside from the fact they were calorie-free.

Looking back at the reasons for his continual loss of

employment, the terminations were obvious and hinged on his lifelong belief he could do no wrong. When his Pops, a functioning alcoholic himself, recognized Stiv was drinking hard at age sixteen, he told him, "I can't stop you from what you're going to do in life, I can only advise you. If you want to drink heavily, you have to eat, and eat a lot—starch and protein are the best to counteract your drinking, but it's your life and hopefully eating will save your stomach and liver."

Stiv took Pops advice and ate to excess, bordering on *living to eat, not eating to live*, which he swore was what saved his life. Also brought his weight up to a super-plus-sized 230 pounds. A bloated wheezing middle-aged man, he looked like walking death and yet she stayed. *Love is blind?*

He turned to Coca-Cola and chocolate when he cold-turkey the booze. Whenever the craving hit, which was often and intense, he'd munch down a fistful of Hershey's Whoppers, the Super-Sweetened Original Malted Milk Balls. He'd follow the chocolate-bombs with an ice-cold Coke. He persevered. Admittedly, having his cigar box pharmacy and a large supply of Oxycodone and Valium helped a lot. He did not consider that cheating. Not exactly.

While living in Japan, Stiv drank to excess, learning soon after touchdown in the Land of the Rising Sun that overindulgence was part of the culture. After work, eat, drink heavily, and chase girls. Before, during, and after band practice or shows, drink heavily and chase girls. After karate practice, eat and drink heavily, chase girls if his body was not too messed up. Hang out with friends, eat and drink heavily, and yes, chase girls. These were social norms, who was Stiv Baker to go against ancient cultural traditions?

Now sober, he craved booze every waking hour and often dreamed of a fat, ice-cold dry martini in a pint glass with an olive or two. But he abstained. Oxycodone was a different story. A very different story.

He stood next to his car and looked out at the city across the Sound. It was just before 4 p.m. He admired the beauty of the blue-green water and the old wooden pilings once part of a majestic amusement park a hundred years before but destroyed by a winter storm. Aside from the sea birds and the gentle, euphonious waves washing ashore, his surroundings were quiet and peaceful. Within a few hours, explosions and all hell would break loose with 4th of July pyrotechnics. There was one last reasonable possibility before scoring pills on 2nd Avenue from the homies and amigo's. His proverbial ace-in-the-hole fail-safe, although expensive and a drastic, disparaging solution.

Back in the driver's seat of his Mustang, he rang the contentious office of Dr. Lapointe. He was introduced to The Point through a questionable but cool pain med addict and pawnshop customer, Carl. Stiv had been to The Point's office three times for boosters and extra meds when he had calamities with Cyclops in the past. The Point was too expensive for a regular gig, the hot girls and drug store menu notwithstanding.

Carl explained that Dr. Lapointe would write any medical narcotic you wanted for five-hundred dollars cash money up front. Meperidine, Codeine, Oxymorphone, Oxycontin, Vicodin, Morphine, Oxycodone, Dilaudid, Methadone, Fentanyl, Demerol, Percocet, or Amphetamines. A doctor like this was a remarkable find. If his old favorite drugs from childhood—quaaludes and Eskatrol—were still available, he would score them from The Point too.

The stupidity of wasted days past.

Of course, you also had to pay the pharmacy for the drugs so The Point was a last-ditch alternative. Cash upfront was mandatory and do not bother asking for a receipt, referral, or recommendation. Future scheduling was acceptable and encouraged. During your visit, The Point expected you to do all the talking with your bullshit anecdote of phony pain. How, when, where, and why you needed your choice of medication was up to you to fabricate. He would write the information down on your phony skewed chart, advise imaginary procedures, then ask what pain medication worked best for you. Then he would ask your desired daily dosage request...your story had to be moderately believable for clinical appearance, but the doctor would not ask for encyclopedic details.

As an added bonus to The Point's pill mill, his salacious receptionists, office girls, and nurses were spectacular delineations of female society and all looked like strippers and overripe porn actresses. The only essential amenity missing was a full bar, although there may have been one, just not at Stiv's level of significance. He loved The Point's office visits all the same.

After four rings, an answering machine picked up and a woman's sultry, silky voice slowly said, "If this is a medical emergency, please hang up and dial 911. Thank you for calling the office of Dr. Lapointe on 12541 S. Ruff Bluff Road. At this time Dr. Lapointe will not be seeing patients until further notice. We apologize for any inconvenience this may cause you. Thank you and have a blessed day."

Stiv hung up, not having a blessed day at all, and still riding slowly on the *Titanic*. So he immediately called his questionable customer from his old job, who answered on the second ring. Calling Carl was always a lesson in patience, chaos, and confusion even though his pain med habit was legitimate.

———

"Hey-low?" came the slow nasal speak of the pain-med junkie. He sounded whacked out of his mind. That was okay so long as he could help.

"Carl, it's me, Stiv. I just called Dr. Lapointe's office. Did he close down or move or something? What the hell, man? I only got an answering machine, I need to see him, I'm hurting," Stiv shouted into his phone.

"Who is this?" came the drawling nasal response.

"Stiv, from the pawnshop. You gave me Lapointe's name a few months ago, remember?"

"Nooo, man, I don't know no Stiv from no pawnshop. Who is this?" Carl asked with an angry slow growl.

"Come on, Carl, I helped you out with your mom's jewelry after you wrecked your Harley last year? I gave you extra money to help you and your mom out and you have a beautiful daughter named Flower, she turned twenty-one in June...Come on, man?"

"Oh shit, dude! What's happening, Stiv? Sorry, bro, I'm all messed up over here. Wow! They upped my pain meds, added some kinda benzo to help me relax and sleep, I can barely speak most of the time, no idea who you were, sorry, bro. Now—what did you ask me?"

Stiv hesitated, took a deep breath trying to stay calm. Carl was an all-right cat, just an ex–heroin addict and now a pain-med junkie due to a motorcycle accident that cost him his left calf muscle and left kneecap; basically his whole left leg was totaled. However, Carl would be a rich cripple in a few months to a year, after his settlement arrived.

Carl used to bring his astonishingly fine daughter into the pawnshop. She would strut around the store in hot pants or a miniskirt drawing every eye in the joint, male and female. Flower possessed one of those elfish faces, narrow and angular, her *kiss me and come back for more* mouth small and sweet with thin perfect lips Stiv associated with sensuality. She wore her long black hair in several different ways and sometimes hid it with different color and style wigs. Her skin was lightly freckled like tiny brown sprinkles, large dark-blue eyes like water-pools of exotic innocence, exciting any man to want to kiss her mouth. She moved with strong sensuousness, tall and feminine in a way only few women can manage without the least conceit. No man nor woman could pass her without looking twice. Most did a double take. Flower was hauntingly beautiful. Also an extraordinary product of humanity conceived by a young couple who were textbook ugly, almost deformed in appearance. Her mother looked like a Caucasian Mike Tyson with a constant grimace like she just ate a large bug. Carl was positively beastly, almost Neanderthal. Fortunately, they were polite and friendly, although difficult to look at. Flower just turned twenty-one in June, another Gemini woman. She modeled during her childhood, through adolescence and to date.

"It doesn't take a genius to stand in front of a camera a few hours a week making two hundred bucks per hour," Carl told Stiv once. "We save every penny for her. Flower could've earned more, but me and the wife refused big money offers after she turned eighteen. No kid of mine is taking her clothes off in front of the camera at any price."

Flower would not converse or even look in Stiv's direction. Instead, she would laugh aloud for no reason causing anyone around her to look in surprise. This intrigued Stiv even more. He went so far as to ask Carl why she disliked him so much but Carl only smiled. Stiv could not help fantasizing about her, the idea of making it with this goddess who hated him so much. It was irresistible, driving him crazy. Flower was over eighteen and hot as planet Venus, and when she did smile, albeit never at him, her lustful appeal was overwhelming. Of course, even if he could convince her to his will, he would never seriously pursue any woman regardless of beauty and desire, including Flower. But just once, one time for the experience, to make it with the likes of a stunning budding Flower who despised him, well, at least he could dream.

Anyone could see similarities in both her parents' deformed faces and Flower's perfect one. Stiv thought of the gruesome chrysalis, then its metamorphosis to a beautiful monarch butterfly. Regardless of Stiv's intense love and worship of the female form, her genitalia was not exactly aesthetically beautiful. Then again, yes, yes it was beautiful, how could he deny this gift of nature to mankind, the tunnel of life we all travel through, beautiful as the possibility of heaven.

"Mother Nature's a mad scientist," Stiv joked to Carl, indirectly talking about his daughter. Carl either did or did not get the irony.

Into his phone Stiv said, "Carl, I asked you about Dr. Lapointe. You introduced me to him last year, I just called his office, the recording said he's not seeing patients. What's up with that?"

"Oh man, you didn't hear? The Point got busted, bro... busted like a motherfucker! They pulled a sting on his lawless ass. The cops was sending undercover narcos there for months. The Point wrote whatever shit they wanted, no questions asked. He's at county jail, bro. Heard his bond is like three hundred fifty grand. Friends of mine who been in the joint with him said he's hating life right around now; yanked his license and everything. Wife is leaving him taking the kids. All of them fine bitches working at his office either got busted too or jumped. Seems some of them hoochies working for The Point was turning tricks right there in unoccupied rooms. Proceeds split with The Point right down the middle. The Point was a scandalous entrepreneur, bro. But dude is ruined, he's gone," Carl spat excitedly into the phone, his voice rising and falling.

"Carl, can you help me out? I'm dry and hurting, I just got blacklisted by this pharmacist. I'm in need, bro," Stiv said. "Hook me up."

"Are you kidding me?" Carl barked into the phone. "I've been hearing more and more about dudes getting jacked by pharmacists. Fuck that noise! No pharmacist is gonna tell me what I can and can't take, I'll lose my shit on some bitch tryin' that crap on me, bro!" Carl threatened in a long tirade.

Stiv patiently waited for him to finish. What else could he do?

"I can offer you some weed, bro, got some benzos if Flower don't snag 'em, but that's all. Everyone is holding tight to their meds right around now, bro, after what happened to The Point, too hard to score. I only get enough drugs to keep me from screaming bloody murder. I showed you pictures of my leg, right?"

Yes, Carl had shown him pictures of his leg. Stiv had

never seen anything like it except when he held Jack in his arms on the way to the ER all those years ago. In Carl's case, he'd been riding down the highway on his Harley when some old woman in a BMW cut him off texting on her cell phone. Carl lost control, hitting the guardrail on his left side at sixty mph, shearing off the kneecap and slicing the calf muscle of his left leg behind the knee. The bike rolled right, then over on the left into the carpool lane, dragging Carl with it. Another car witnessed the crash and just missed running him over. Carl should have been killed, no question, but he was not. They had this fact in common. His kneecap was crushed, shattered—gone. The calf muscle was cut just behind his knee cleanly which could not be explained. The meat hung down to the ground still attached dragging at his ankle through his shredded jeans, exposing his bloody gastrocnemius muscle, tendons, and ripped tissue. The muffler sat atop it, adding third-degree burns to the side of his left leg and exposed flesh. It was gory roadkill, the likes of which the paramedics agreed they had never seen before. A contributor to Carl's future nightmares. The second driver who witnessed the crash lifted the battered bike off his leg while the old woman who caused the crash stood watching, screaming at the carnage she denied causing. Later, doctors were able to reattach the burned calf muscle, but it was useless, the knee destroyed as was his left leg in general. The old woman denied responsibility until witnesses came forward telling the cops the accident was indeed her fault, that she had been on her cell phone. Only then did she admit to everything, taking full responsibility for her negligence.

Carl was looking at eight to twelve million dollars in the settlement since he was debilitated for life, a sixty-forty split with his attorney but he would be set, Flower too. He told

Stiv the most important and greatest relief was neither his wife nor Flower was riding with him the day of the crash. He also said the first thing he would do with the settlement money was buy a bigger, faster Harley. Stiv appreciated his huevos for getting back on the horse that threw and stomped him. Stiv knew he would do the same. Carl snapped selfies and video from inside the ambulance right after the crash while the old woman screamed in horror at the sight of bloody carnage she caused, shrieked in panic and terror at her uncertain future. A policewoman tried to console her before placing her in handcuffs and under arrest. Carl videotaped zooming in and out on the woman's tear- and snot-streaked face, which looked like a Halloween mask. It was deathly comical. The paramedics managed the burned, ruined calf muscle, taking the flesh in gloved hands and placing it back against the leg, wrapping it firmly, all the time Carl shouting in pain and videotaping everything like a scene from a slaughterhouse. Everything was meaty, bloody, and loud.

"Yes, Carl. You showed me pictures of your leg. I wish you'd shown me pictures of Flower instead, she's fine as hell. Are you sure she's your blood?" Stiv asked, unafraid of pissing Carl off since he could not help narcotic-wise and was a crippled fuck.

"Yes, asshole, I'm sure. I already told your punk-ass couldn't afford Flower, so don't hassle me, okay?"

"Yeah, Carl, sure, I appreciate that. But how about getting me a date with her? I'm a big fan and I still can't believe she's your kid. She looks like she could use some adult supervision. Come on and hook me up," Stiv said like Carl was a pimp.

"Nigga, please! Are you stupid or what? I always figured you for a fag anyways. Now what're you gonna do with a girl? Maybe I can introduce you to some of my boys who's fresh outta the joint, they'd like you, Stiv. Pretty boy punkass bitch! And trust me, you really couldn't afford Flower."

"Come on, Carl, let me worry about that, I know some great bedtime stories I'm sure she's gonna like, give me a chance."

"I know you're messing with me, bitch, or I'd reach through the phone and pull your fucking tongue out!"

"Alright, take it easy, Carl."

"It's all good, bro, all my boys try me, seems Flower's popular. Every dude I know hassles me about her, say all kinds of crazy shit, I won't let a nigga go too far disrespecting my kid, but you're okay, bro. By the way, we heard you got yourself fired from the pawnshop, what's wrong with you? Flower and me was asking about you a couple three days ago. Now you ain't got no job so no money, think you're gonna take Flower out? That's a laugh!" Carl croaked.

"It was a thought, bro. Can you blame me? She's fine as hell," Stiv said, trying not to laugh.

"No, fool, it's a joke. Flower would mash you into dog food," Carl growled.

"Sorry, bro, I didn't think you'd mind me taking her out, you know I'm a nice guy."

"It ain't you I'm worried about, son. But I don't mind you teasing me, Stiv."

"Thanks, Carl," Stiv said seriously, wondering what Flower was doing for the 4th of July.

"You looked after me, we appreciate that. But hey, I didn't know you was so violent. What the hell you attacking your boss for? Heard you rocked his bitch ass, bro, fired his shit up," Carl yelled into his phone.

"You know that clown, Carl, always flirting with Flower, talking shit to you trying to impress the girl, that's why I kicked his ass...I won't stand for nobody hitting on my girl like that...fool had it coming. So I lost my job protecting Flower's honor, what can I say," Stiv said.

"Wow, bro, you're her knight in shining fucking armor and I'll tell her you did that. Anyway, I'll call you if I hear of anything narco and I'll tell Flower you said hey. I think she's getting out of the shower right around now," Carl said.

Stiv imagined those long perfect legs going up meeting her midsection and beyond. Drying herself leisurely, meeting him in bed all hot, damp, and ready. What kind of loving would happen?

"Wait," Carl stated. "Yup, there she is, hey, Flower, dude who was fired from the pawnshop for beating up his boss says hi, and put some damn clothes on, girl, you ain't a child no more!"

Stiv heard a young woman's banter, only making out four words, *who*, *daddy,* and *shut up.*

"That girl has a bad attitude and loves to walk around the house naked, answers the damn door naked, sits in the backyard naked. Naked, naked, naked! Doesn't care who's looking seeing her nude ass strutting around, drives me and the missus crazy. She needs to get her own damn place but that ain't happening. We don't seem to get through to the girl and she don't stop neither. She needs her own damn place, I'm telling you," Carl bitched into the phone. "Flower's got her a date with some bigshot tonight, owns that new bar over by the Lake on the Eastside. I'll be showing up too, me and the missus, surprise this bigshot who asked her out, be the last date with my kid I'll tell you that. Happy Fourth of July asshole and peace," Carl hollered into his phone and hung up.

"Carl!" Stiv yelled into the dead phone.

There was no reason to call again except Flower possibly answering. Carl's conversation was always interesting, but Stiv was weakened by that one.

Naked, naked, naked!

That was it though, Stiv's last hope for Oxycodone aside from going down to Second Avenue and scoring from the gangsters, homies, and amigos. He was not afraid to deal with the thugs, they were businessmen, some knew him from the pawnshop anyway. The problem was he refused to pay two dollars per milligram. That was ridiculous crazy bullshit. He was not that desperate yet and still had a few hits left. Stiv sent a vicious mental curse to Azar, wherever the bitch was.

Chapter 14

Money, Sex, and Goblin Barkers

4:15 P.M. Tuesday, July 4th, 2017

Time goes by for better or worse, and love my friend is always in verse.
Glance at the sky, ask who you are, the answers are there, just look to the stars.

HEADING home to face the pre-fireworks explosions of his Gemini wife and her unpredictable personality. He drove the same beach road home but without the same peaceful euphoric feelings of the morning. What plausible story could he tell her? Fear crept around the back of his mind because he never knew which twin was waiting for him. The loving, sweet, understanding soulmate he married and adored. Or the evil, sadistically terrifying twin who tortured him for existing and being a man. Culpability ran deep through his being. He loved her, this beautiful woman who loved him back. Sadly, we hurt the ones we love most. His wife was no exception; fortunately, her tough outer shell still contained a sensitive woman inside.

Arriving back at the condo, he took in the surrounding lush greens; deep emerald, lime, moss, olive, jade, and viridian colors mixed the different foliage encouraged by annual rainfalls. The meaning of these summer colors provided a jolt, a sense of positive energy provided by clean powerful oxygen, thick and good. Momentarily lost in the intoxication of his surroundings, he finally looked up and noticed a young African American man standing by the front door. The closer Stiv got, the more clearly he saw the man's skin was that deep night blue only tasteless eyes called black. He was wearing a messenger's uniform identifying him from The Speedy Talk Messenger Service. He waited at the front door of the building with a shoulder satchel.

A compact car with the same logo on the door as his messenger-shirt further ID'd him. Stiv approached the man, his good looks more apparent the closer he got. Very athletic with broad shoulders and chest, sculpted biceps, and forearm muscles Stiv envied. His cauliflower ear on the left side marked him a fighter. Probably MMA or perhaps collegiate wrestling. Stiv would fight anyone for the right reason but would not want to step in the ring with this guy. As he pulled out the door key he saw his name on the brown envelope the messenger was holding.

"Hi, I think that's for me, I'm Stiv Baker."

Stiv thought for a moment in his narcotic-induced insanity his old company wanted him back so desperately they sent a messenger to request his return with a raise and promotion. Then he mused how absurd his thought was.

"Can I trouble you for your ID, please?" the man asked in a vowel-shading voice with aspects of froideur.

"An envelope, for me? I wonder what's in it?" Stiv asked guardedly but liking and admiring the man's musical soothing tone.

"They don't tell us what we're delivering, sir. We just deliver. Sorry."

"Of course," Stiv said, handing the man his driver's license.

The messenger looked at it, then at Stiv. "Very good, sir, thank you," he said, handing the ID back.

He handed Stiv an iPhone for his signature of receipt. Stiv signed with his finger, the messenger took the phone back, looked at the mark, pressed a button, and dropped the phone back in his satchel. He handed Stiv the envelope, thanked and wished him a happy 4th of July in smooth intonations.

Stiv thought about complimenting the man's beautiful voice as well as his exceptional looks but was not sure it was appropriate. Instead he asked, "Did you ring the bell?"

"No sir, I was just about to when you pulled up. Your timing was perfect."

"Cool, I was just wondering, thanks. Happy Fourth to you too," Stiv said, pulling a ten-dollar bill out of his wallet and handing it to the man.

"That's very kind of you sir, thank you," he said, pocketing the cash and walking to his car.

Stiv watched him drive off, watched his departure until he was long gone, wondering about the young man's world and dreams. Then he looked at the envelope in his hand, turning it over a few times. There was no writing on either side, which seemed strange. After a minute of silent contemplation, he pulled out his switchblade, sprang the bitch to life, and carefully cut the envelope open. There was a typed message and what looked like a cashier's check. He was not expecting a message, much less a check. He was not expecting anything from anyone anytime or anywhere. He believed messengers with messages and telegrams had to be bad news, although he'd never received either before, just something he believed. He pulled the note out first. It was from Zander,

Stiv, my brother, you're a good man and a lifelong friend. You've tried hard in life, I've watched you for over 40 years. I'm not sorry about giving you a hard time today because you deserve it. But you know I love you, as does your wife. We both love you and honestly want the best for you. I'm rough on you when you do stupid shit. I've enclosed a check to help you financially for a while since you got yourself fired again. You need to get off the drugs and start being the better man I know you can be. The money is a gift, do with it as you please, but as your attorney and blood brother, I advise you to use it to clean yourself up. Don't thank me or ever mention it again, these are conditions. Get your shit together, brother. I'm always here for you. Zander

He pulled out the cashier's check. It was a lot of money, close to six months' pay from his old job, and he was well paid in the blue-collar sector. The note and the check stunned him. The terrible day suddenly got better. Money had that power. Money is the gasoline of life. Zander's kindness and generosity inexplicably with lightning-fast speed removed one less worry from Stiv's little cramped confused world. Except for the historical fact receiving money from friend or family, whether borrowed or as a gift, potentially caused immediate problems including guilt.

Standing on the steps of his building, tears in his eyes, he decided that regardless of the horrible, self-induced torture he went through the last time, he was going to quit for real. Stiv was determined. He owed it to his wife, Zander, friends, and family but mostly himself. Of course, he had no idea how he was going to actually quit. Determination was a good start, but it was not enough. Also, losing all the negative thoughts he was having, letting the universe guide his way would help too. He needed a plan plus willpower, but suddenly he felt completely confident, like a new man, a man who just saw over the mountaintop and down into the promised land.

The clouds of confusion and despair

Suddenly parted showing the true-blue sky.

He was going to do it, going to get clean and sober and prove the moronic TV talking heads wrong. First, he had to get his mind straight and consider all possibilities for his future. Perhaps a daily journal to chronicle his new journey to well-being and sobriety. Set specific hours of each day for the most important activities for success, like reading and studying, brushing up on his Japanese. Revamp his resume, even go back to school! The idea of scheduling each hour of each day going forward seemed believable. His excitement at new revelations made him elated to the point he dug into his pocket removing the last blue bullet he brought with him, popped it into his mouth and chewed, swallowing the booster, his fifth pill of the day. He folded the letter and check, placed both into his pocket, and went inside.

His wife was in their living room, dazzling as always, watching a special on America's obesity problem. She ignored him. Stiv walked into the foyer, took off his shoes and went to his room where he deposited the Model 38 and speed loader into the safe. He returned to their living room and walked over, sitting on the couch, his wife on the other end. She was wearing jean shorts and a T-shirt showing off her alluring body.

Long and lean but not too far in between.

She exuded a recently showered woman, freshly shampooed hair, an exotic perfume she wore sometimes. Gardenia by Chanel, Stiv gave her for Valentine's Day several years before after shopping for weeks trying to find the right scent. In his narcotic-induced daze he thought he could smell orange blossom and vanilla. Her aroma immediately turned him on like a hard-rock radio station. The TV show was not Stiv's style or interest, but he never knew where he might gather short story fodder. Silently he watched as an interviewer sat at a round table with six obscenely obese people, talking, bowing their heads in viewer-perceived guilt and humiliation. The sexy Caucasian interviewer with her perfect hair and makeup in her tight skirt, big boobs, and long legs was asking these people, three of each, Black, White, Asian, and Brown, America's current complexion, about their lives.

Azar's annoying but accurate speech screamed through his mind, "Your America is quickly becoming everyone's America, people of color's America."

Was their lifestyle a contributor to their obesity? Did they feel race and or poverty contributed to their health problems? She wanted to know at what point in their lives did they get so darn fat.

"Happy Fourth of July," the wife said, looking over

at him.

"Happy Fourth to you too, sweetheart. Did you sleep well?"

"I did. I saw you spying, I was hoping you'd come into the studio and lie down with me," she said demurely.

"Really?" Stiv asked, surprised. "Wish I knew that, you know I hate waking up and you aren't next to me."

"I know you do, Stiv darling. Are you okay? You look upset."

He decided to tell her everything, almost everything.

So he started with his visit with Dr. Cyclops, how it went, but he did not tell her about Crystal and the gyno chair fantasy. He told her about his argument with Azar the Persian bitch, why she blacklisted him from getting pain medication from the National Chain Pharmacy. He did not tell her about his Azar fantasy or how he seriously considered drawing his Model 38 and blasting her to the other side of fuck all.

He told her about Rep Boy, but not about almost having the cops called on him in the pharmacy. He did not mention his memory of the 4th of July 1976, forty-one years ago. He told her about his conversations with Zander, how his best friend insulted and humiliated him big time. He did not tell her about the cashier's check.

She laughed, clapping her hands. "You're so lucky to have a friend like Zander, I admire him so much. Not everyone has a caring friend like him. I love when he shows you hard love, Stiv. You should be thankful you have a friend who cares enough to tell you like it is. I hoped you thanked him?"

"Of course I thanked him," he lied, thinking about the brutal tell-off session.

At the same time she was protective, not liking even his

best friend giving him a tough time. Her love and compassion took over and she said, "I'm sorry you're having a rough day, Stiv. Was there anything good? Did you hear from any employers?"

"No, not yet," he said, hating the intrusive yet forthright question. "But I have some good leads," he lied, having nothing at all. "I sat in my car down by the water while I called around to different help wanted ads, but nothing solid. There was a pod of dolphins right offshore acting like they were trying to get my attention, like they knew me. They swam around playing and jumping, put me in a really good mood. They didn't stay long but while they were there, I didn't think anything bad. Only happy thoughts," he lied again.

Stiv did not mention putting the bad news end of the Model 38 to the bridge of his nose. He did not mention Carl, Dr. Lapointe, or Carl's fine-ass daughter.

Then Stiv decided to pledge he would quit his narcotic pain medication habit no matter how difficult it was. There was no other way to maintain normality in their lives together. He was determined because he had failed his last attempt, strengthening the talking heads on TV.

You can't quit an addiction on your own.

He was excited, and telling the wife helped. He was going to show her too, although he was pretty sure he didn't mean what he said regardless of the cashier's check or his silent determination. The last blue bullet finally kicked in and it was good—Stiv was floating down a gentle stream of consciousness again. Nothing could hurt him even though on several levels he was terrified. When he was done talking, his wife moved over to his side of the couch and put her arms around him, kissing him long and deep. He was as high as the afternoon clouds and medically speaking, Oxycodone inhibits sexual performance.

What a drag.

Fortunately, this was never the case with Stiv Baker. After a few minutes of fooling around on the couch they moved to their bedroom. Pines by the Sea.

Much later she asked, "Are you okay, darling?"

"No, I'm not, you killed me. Please call an ambulance, I think I'm dead. If I don't move in the next few weeks, sublet the condo, and just ignore me," he whispered.

"Can I bring you anything from the kitchen? I'm gonna get something to drink," she said giggling at his exhaustion.

"How about a triple scotch and water in a tall glass with plenty of diamonds?"

"I don't think we have any scotch —and diamonds Stiv? I can bring you a triple water, want that?" she asked, giggling again.

When he did not reply, she got up and strutted out of the room. Even though he was drained, he still had energy to watch her nude, symmetrically perfect exit out of the door. An awe-inspiring sight to behold. The sumptuous vision lulled him to fast wave sleep floating billions of miles away in the warmth of a narcotic blanket seasoned and spiced with the afterglow fortunate lovers sometimes find. Stiv knew you had to lose yourself sometimes to find anything at all in this world.

He drifted in the expanse of a multitude of endless stars

between deep sleep and semi-consciousness. He watched sea beams, shooting stars race through a distant galaxy, then heard a faraway but familiar voice saying his name in a dark hall so started drifting toward the melodic sound. The voice was very close, whispering his name. A poem he wrote years ago moved slowly through his dreaming mind:

> *Crystal blue waters of the afternoon sea*
> *Cools my mind like the damp towels she lays on me*
>
> *Soothe my heart my body my love*
> *Hold me, touch me, together at dusk*
>
> *Laying as one before the sun sets*
> *She whispers her promises to me*

He drifted around a shrouded corner, only darkness, but soon he saw the light of a distant star now dead fifty thousand years and was only just gracing his eyes as he floated toward the glow. For a moment he was not gliding anymore but floating upside down in a warm, comfortable fluid. He could not see but felt a soft warm wall in front of him. Touching the fleshy tube attached to his belly, his fingertips moved over his face, touched his closed mouth and eyes. He still heard the voice, but it was muffled by the fluid he floated around. An infinity of light and circumstances moved so fast past his thoughts his mind knew all knowledge of creation, he knew God and the endlessness of the trillion galaxies that brought light so bright it penetrated his closed eyelids, then—he woke to his wife's beautiful smiling face close to his whispering his name, her sweet breath of heaven; he smiled back in the deepest levels of love.

Chapter 15

The Truth, Almost

5:15 P.M. Tuesday, July 4th, 2017

SOMETIME LATER, she sat bare legged wearing a loose-fitting black T-shirt. Stiv responded by pulling her close into his clutches. She resisted but he was stronger, forcibly kissing her neck and mouth. She kissed him back then stated, "Okay, that's all you get."

They snuggled in the late afternoon shade, a peaceful warmth permeating the room, the result of their love magical and serene, comfortable, and safe. Stiv was one lucky junkie.

"I love you, darling, but you have to get yourself together," she whispered. "I think that pharmacist did you a favor like Zander said. Someone's watching over you, Stiv, how else could I find your secret hiding place, your drug stash the day Pops died. And how do you explain that pharmacist singling you out as a pain medication addict? Obviously, it's a message. Because the dead can't communicate directly, they use signs and go-betweens to guide us. The dead can help if we let them and if they want to. I still can't believe you lied to me all those years though," she snapped. "You know, I could never understand how suddenly I was pulling that drawer all the way out, it felt like I always knew where to look, but never did, until that day. When I saw your cigar box in that dark space, I felt a mix of relief, fury, sadness, and love. Then I find out Pops died. One of the strangest moments of my life, Stiv, all because you lied to me," she lamented.

Oh, shit. Here it comes.

First, a proper physical screwing, now a long turbulent emotional mind-smack screwing. Maybe he was not such a lucky junkie after all. So now the other Gemini twin was about to make an appearance. Stiv could not tolerate a tell-off session, not after what he'd been through already, good loving notwithstanding. Like the change in seasons, it was coming, deserved and unstoppable. He braced himself, knowing like a looming tsunami, nothing was going to stop her. However, like so many situations with his unpredictable Gemini wife, the tell-off speech never materialized. Instead, she said sweetly, "How can I help you quit the drugs, Stiv?"

As if he was really going to quit. LOL!

"If you're sure you want to help me, sweetie, here's one way. Whenever I get cravings for the narcotics, which will be soon, you can hold me tight and kiss me until the cravings go away. They won't, but that's okay, just keep on kissing."

"Ha, why did I even ask? I should have known. Why can't you be serious? If I believed long kisses would help, I'd do it, but I don't, so I won't," she said, leaning in, kissing him deep.

"Hey, that rhymed," Stiv said.

"Yes, I know that, I planned it that way," she said, looking at her paint-spotted fingernails.

"Well, how about playing SOMF then? The game is easy to learn," Stiv said, leering.

"I'm not falling for that, darling, I'm sure it's something stupid and nasty so I'm not even asking," she whispered, snuggling.

"Fine then, I'm not going to tell you, even if you beg."

"I don't wanna know, Stiv darling, and I never beg."

"Are you sure? It's not nasty, I promise."

"Thank you, no," she said, giggling.

Stiv loved when she giggled in earnest, soft music to his ears.

"Well, your loss, sweetheart, maybe next time. And you shouldn't doubt me. Anyway, it's probably better if you leave me alone while I quit. I'll be going out a lot or staying in my room. If I promise I'm going to stop taking the pills, I will, trust me. But give me a little time to think about it because I have some scheduled job interviews and I don't want to screw those up by actively withdrawing in front of a possible employer. Better if we don't talk about the drugs either, you don't ask and I won't tell until I'm off the skag for a while."

"What's skag?"

"Slang for heroin," he said and yawned.

"Are you taking heroin, Stiv? Oh my god, I had no idea," she blathered out, moving off him.

Stiv stared at her. Then did a big toothy smile and said, "Skag is slang for heroin, heroin is an opiate, Oxycodone is an opiate. I'm not now, nor have I ever, *taken* heroin," he lied. "Sorry I worried you."

"Heroin's the worst, right?" she asked. "I mean like the most dangerous drug?"

"Yes," he said, not wanting to go into the strengths and weaknesses of different recreational drugs. "I might seem really sick, actually, I know I'll be sick, but just leave me alone," Stiv said.

She stared at him in silence and concern.

Like everything else involving her, she studied; rarely, if ever, asking questions without already knowing the correct answer. It could be frustrating. Narcotic addiction and withdrawals were no exception. She wanted to know what was in store for her man. With that, she believed addiction was a human weakness. Stiv agreed. Also, she believed achieving virtually anything was a personal choice. The rule of mind over matter plus energy and the will to get it done, as painful and nauseating as detoxing from narcotics was as a rule.

"We're all products of our choices," she liked to say.

Stiv totally agreed.

They stayed in bed, chatting on and off about her work and his lack of it. He could not tell her he never wanted to work again. That would be a mistake regardless of how he felt. She did not attack him. He was thankful for that. Instead, she explained her *everything is energy* talk. Her main point was how all human bodies are approximately sixty percent water and water is the greatest energy absorber on the planet. Stiv could dig it, relaxing while he listened.

"Everything, Stiv, everything is energy. Not necessarily God but definitely a higher power guiding us. It's pretty simple, everything is energy, period. If you create the energy vibration frequency of the reality you want, then you get that reality. Isn't that crystal clear? It is to me. People think this is a mystical philosophy. It's not. It's simple physics."

"What's simple about physics and how do I obtain the frequency?" Stiv asked, knowing full well, having heard the talk a hundred times. Even though he rarely listened, he wanted to stay close to her warm body.

"Oh my god, Stiv, how many times have I explained this to you? You really don't get it. I'll tell you again and I'll talk slow and use easy words this time, okay?"

"I'm all ears," he said, burying his face against her warm neck and shoulder, her fragrant long hair tickling his nose.

True, she had been communicating her theories for years, also true, he did not listen. After hearing enough and getting his fill of her body heat, Stiv considered shuffling to his cigar box grabbing a blue bullet. Her next statement stopped him.

"Where you focus your energy, it grows, like water to a plant. For example, if you are fixated on not being able to find a job, you won't find a job. You have to feel as if you have that job already. Believe and it will be. Most people want the manifestation first, then the feeling follows. But it's actually quite opposite. Your feeling must be there first and then manifestation matching that feeling unfolds. You can't stop, you have to stay perpetual, over and over. You have to stay focused and you'll gain whatever you're fixated on. Are you listening, darling?"

"I'm always listening and your mouth is on my ear so I don't have a choice."

"If you don't want to listen just say so, I have other things to do, you know," she said.

"No, please continue."

"E equals MC squared, Stiv," she whispered.

"What's that, sweetie?"

"Nothing."

As they reflected together, Stiv was thinking about the very real energy he wanted to utilize making love to her again. Knowing that was not an option he asked, "Where would you like to watch the fireworks tonight?"

"I don't care. But I like that quiet park on the water with the futuristic structures?" she said.

"I love that place. It has a great view and no crowds. Did you know there was an amusement park there a hundred years ago? Destroyed by a storm, I think."

"Of course I knew that. I told you about it," she said.

"I think you're right."

"Of course I'm right," she said matter-of-factly. "I'm always right."

She probably was. What she did not know was the dolphin park was where he spent time making love to his Model 38 earlier in the day.

It was still too early to think about the fireworks, so Stiv went to his computer to write a quick short story and count his drug stash. He decided he was done taking Oxycodone for the day since he took five hits already and was now really running low, with zero refill prospects.

The idea for the story popped into his head while lying in bed, his wife curled up next to him, warm, golden, and half asleep. She smelled so good he considered attacking her again, but decided the rejection would hurt, so he got up to capture the story brewing in his mind.

At his desk, after looking at the late afternoon sky, the multi-shaded colors reflecting off the Sound gave him the name of the story, "Six Black Circles."

Writing was a positive way of bending time. The best way he could think of besides loving his wife. Bending, passing, killing, moving, making, and spending *time* was the secret. Like any illuminating discovery, he flowed proudly, almost giddy with his new realization. Time was an enemy now, a new enemy he needed to move away from, like the rotting corpse of a dead enemy. He needed to move quickly, like a chicken running away from the Colonel. The story was not a new idea, fragments floated around for a while, putting words to paper would be easy. This short story tied to several others he'd toyed with over the years. Sometimes his literary thoughts flowed, sometimes they didn't. He'd give it a bash and see where it took him.

Chapter 16

Six Black Circles

July 4th Tuesday, 2017, 7:40 PM

Six Black Circles

A
Short Story
By
Steven Huffam Baker

GAIL WAS RUNNING LATE. *How could she fetch her daughter at school then Tom at the airport by 4:30? There was no way unless her Land Rover suddenly became a helicopter. Of course the Rover was almost out of gas too. "Almost" meaning so low she could travel perhaps a mile or two, maybe. Why today of all days?*

Gail decided picking up the kid, getting gas, then speeding to the airport was her best plan of attack even though Tom would be furious. She admitted her day's preparation was off. Where did the time go?

Now in motion, she rushed through the house looking for her purse, the kitchen then the living room. No purse. Where

159

the hell did she leave it? Then she remembered throwing it on their bed upstairs that morning after returning from dropping Pam off, shopping, then dashing for the needed bathroom when she got home.

Starting up the stairs she slammed the big toe of her left foot hitting the first carpeted step square and solid, either jamming or breaking the appendage. Pain exploded like an electric shock through her leg, hip, shoulder, then brain where it settled to a dull pulsing agony. Limping up the rest of the stairs, down the hall, she saw her purse on the bed as soon as she turned into the room. Reaching carelessly, grabbing the strap, she turned, accidentally spilling the contents of the large overstuffed dark leather purse all over the bedroom floor. Lipstick, keys, perfume, three old energy bars, assorted receipts, cell phone charger, thick brown wallet, three pairs of sunglasses, assorted business cards, Chapstick, a pair of reading glasses, Mp3, Visine, half a red pack of Dentine, two or three maxi pads, checkbook, assorted change—mostly pennies—a tampon or two, an old toothbrush, half-filled mini bottle of water, tin of Altoids, her gold Cartier watch she'd been wondering about, three packs of tissues, a single gold hoop earring, half roll of Tums, three or four pens different colors, pair of her daughter's mittens, set of headphones and assorted accumulated US currency flew around the bedroom like abstract confetti.

Hands on hips, Gail surveyed the purse inventory and decided she needed every last item spilled. She heard the judging voices of her room saying, "Look at all that crap. Are you going on a trip? She must have subconscious issues."

"I need everything I have in my purse. You never know when you're gonna need something," Gail said out loud to the empty room.

There was no response except the voice of Tom in her

head saying, "You don't need any of that crap. You love clutter."

"Shut up, Tom," Gail said out loud.

On all fours she shoved everything back into the bag, turned, and left the room, limping back downstairs, through the house to the mudroom. Here, family, friends, and visitors left their shoes before entering her home. A little red sign with white lettering on the wall visible to all who entered instructed,

Socks or Bare Feet Only Please

Gail chose loose-fitting clogs because her throbbing big toe was swelling bright red before her eyes. She limped to the garage and waiting Land Rover. The gas station was on the way but she didn't like leaving her daughter waiting in front of school too long. She didn't like Pam out there at all, not these days, not since the abductions. But if she picked Pam up first, then she'd have to come back and away from the airport for gas, making her even later. She didn't mind making Tom wait even if he was going to bitch and moan. At least it wasn't raining.

Dashing through the streets as fast as she dared, Gail pulled into the school's big circle drive, saw her daughter standing with a group of little girls and a teacher Gail recognized. Spotting the teacher reassured and comforted her. Why couldn't she remember her name? She wanted to thank the woman with more familiarity when the teacher walked Pam to the car.

"Thanks so much for staying with Pam, so sorry I'm late. I've had such a crazy day, I can't believe I'm this late! Now I'm off to the airport, I should've been there twenty minutes *ago. My husband's going to be furious!" Gail blurted out in a long breath, sure the teacher didn't care.*

"No problem and my pleasure," said the friendly young African American teacher with a toothy smile. "We were having a nice chat, weren't we, Pam?" she said to the cute ten-year-old blond-haired freckle-faced child, an obvious product of her parents.

Pam smiled at her teacher then at Gail with her blue eyes she got from Tom. Her features were as close to perfect as Gail could hope for or imagine. The little girl was a head turner and Gail sometimes had trepidation about her future. There were consequences when a girl was too pretty or not pretty enough. A sad truth of the world.

Pam was created in passionate lovemaking. An amorous night in San Lucas, Mexico. Gail and Tom lulled and romanced by the sounds of the sea, tequila, and bright green Mexican reefer, a dreamy moon staring down at their nude forms rolling around on a white sandy beach. Pam was the priceless result. Call it intuition, a hunch, but Gail knew she conceived. Not sure what part of the night but sure all the same. Gail leaned toward their first encounter because their dual climax shook them both on the cool damp sand, all hot arms and legs entwined, locked in perpetual motion, his soldiers rushing into battle.

On the plane home she knew she was pregnant. Gail knew her baby would be a girl and they'd name her Pamela. She knew this as sure as she knew Venus is the goddess of love, but never shared her knowledge with Tom. Instead, she told him six weeks later she was indeed pregnant. She didn't bother with "I'm late" or the other foreboding terms women use. She didn't need to see her doctor for verification her baby was a girl. No need to wonder if Pam had blue eyes and blond hair. Gail knew all along.

The pretty teacher held the car door while Pam climbed in and belted herself in the back seat of the forest green Land Rover, a birthday present from Tom the year before.

"All set?" asked the teacher.

Pam, smiling, gave a thumbs up. Gail rushed multiple thanks and a big toothy smile. The teacher closed the door and stepped away from the vehicle as it moved off.

"Pam sweetheart, what's her name, your teacher? I can never remember."

"Ms. Spice, Mom, Ms. Kathrine Spice," Pam said, looking at the cover of the paperback she was holding. "She was in a beauty contest, Mom!" Pam blurted out then back to her book.

That's a pretty name, Gail thought to herself heading to the gas station, the opposite direction of the airport. The little light on the gauge seemed brighter but she knew this was in her head; she also knew she had enough gas to travel one maybe two miles at most. Seeing the blinking light, she shook her head, thinking she should never let her gas tank go under a half.

Pam entertained herself reading the paperback and not talking or asking a bunch of questions like she usually did from her belted position. Gail loved the questions and conversation usually, but not today.

Pulling into the gas station, she picked a pump that cost a little more but offered service from a station attendant. Gail hated pumping gas, getting grease and gasoline stink on her hands impossible to get off. She put the car in park and turned off the engine, impatiently looking around for an attendant. About to honk the horn, she remembered reading that attendants considered honking for service rude and would make a person wait even longer.

163

Turning to Pam she said, "Stay in your seat, sweetheart, I'll be right back. I guess I have to find an attendant."

A little angry, Gail opened the driver's side door and hopped out, forgetting her left big toe until she hit the pavement. She winced as pain shot up her left leg like another electric jolt. She waited for the pain to calm and wondered if she broke the toe. A few moments later she limped to the garage door just as an attendant called from the side of the station, "Can I help you, miss?"

Gail looked at the older gray-haired attendant and said, "Yes, please, would you fill it up on number 6, premium please. Could you check the oil as well?" she asked, smiling.

The old guy saluted, lurching toward the green Land Rover.

Gail continued into the store and grabbed the winning lotto numbers from the drawing the day before, then limped over to the magazines and grabbed a Harper Bizarre. Her best friend from college had an article in the magazine. Gail was tempted to purchase a copy but decided to wait till her subscription arrived. She couldn't wait to read it.

Then she remembered Pam in the back seat. Smashing the magazine back on the rack, she rushed to the car where Pam was quietly reading, the attendant doing his job. Gail hoped her store departure wasn't obvious. She opened the door and painfully got into the driver's seat.

"Why are you limping, Mommy?"

"I'll tell you later, honey, just keep reading and let's go get Daddy, okay?"

"Okay, Mom."

Gail watched the old man and wondered what his deal was. The owner or just some poor old guy who couldn't make ends meet in his later years? A retired millionaire bored with retired life? Or maybe he was an ex-con and grease-monkey work was all he could find. Or maybe he was a killer on the run. She shuddered at the thought, then wondered why she let her mind go in that direction.

When he was done washing the windows, checking the tire pressure, the oil reservoir, and transmission fluid, he presented Gail with the bill. She paid with a credit card. He returned with her receipt and she signed it with his pen then handed it back along with two single dollar bills as a tip. He took the money and thanked her. Gail noticed in the rearview mirror Pam was silently watching all of this.

She eased into traffic, now forty minutes late. She grabbed her purse off the passenger seat and handed it back to her daughter. "Pam honey, please find my cell phone and hand it to me, thanks, baby."

Pam silently took the heavy leather bag, grimacing at the weight, then began rummaging through the purse.

"Wow, Mom, you sure have a lot of junk in here. Why do you need all this stuff?"

"Never mind that, honey, just hand me my phone, please, so I can call Daddy and tell him we are running a little late."

"Sorry, Mom, there's no phone in here, a ton of other junk, but no phone."

"Are you sure, baby?"

"Yup, I'm sure, Mom, no phone, but I found my mittens and some old gum, can I have a piece of gum? I just found an old pack, it has lint on it but I can clean it off."

"Help yourself, honey."

Well, that explained why no furious calls from Tom came through. She visualized her cell phone charging on the kitchen counter back at the house. Oh well, she'd be at the airport soon enough, he could bitch if he wanted. She was sure he'd accuse her of forgetting the phone intentionally. An old argument, although he was right, sometimes.

"Why did you go into the gas station, Mom?" Pam asked in her high-pitched little girl voice.

"I got the winning number results from yesterday's lotto. I bought a bunch of chances on Monday for yesterday's drawing. Hey, in my wallet where I keep cash, you'll find the ticket, you never know, we might be millionaires," Gail shouted with a big smile Pam saw in the rearview mirror.

Pam began rummaging again, quickly finding the wallet and the long ticket with forty sets of six numbers from top to bottom.

"I spent twenty dollars because I was feeling lucky, I never spend more than a dollar on lotto but for some reason, I don't know," Gail said, looking into the rearview mirror at her daughter. "Darn, I forgot to get your father's shirts from the dry cleaners, he's gonna be so mad at me." Gail shook her head. "Here are the winning numbers, baby. Would you check them for me, please," Gail said, handing the little piece of reddish-pink lotto numbers over her shoulder to Pam.

They were on the highway now and with the light traffic they would be in the airport roundabout soon.

"There's so many numbers, Mom," Pam whined. "It's confusing."

"Hey, help me out here, kiddo, the jackpot is twenty-five million dollars. If we win, I'll buy you a horse and a farm to ride her at."

"Really?" Pam shrieked, filling the SUV with ear-shaking sound. "Okay, Mom, you got a deal. Do you have a pen?"

"There should be one in my checkbook. Search around in my purse."

"Searching around in your purse is like going to Mr. Beck's junk store, Mom," Pam said and giggled.

"Very funny. I need everything in there, so just find a pen, please," Gail said, smiling.

A few moments later, Pam stated, "Found one!"

"Good, sweetie, match six numbers from my ticket to the winning numbers and that's it, we're millionaires," Gail said, seeing the airport roundabout just ahead.

"I know how to play lotto, Mom," Pam said matter-of-factly.

Gail smiled to herself, loving her daughter totally, her mini-me.

Following the airport signs to arrivals, Gail saw Tom waiting under the United sign as prearranged. He was returning from a district managers meeting back East for Devil's Lake Breweries Inc. Gail thought about the horrific news the public recently learned. The twelve-year-old daughter and heir, Katie Winslow, abducted and murdered. The story was difficult and intricate, brutal and obscene, like any demise of a child. At least the killer was caught.

Gail looked at Pam in the rearview mirror. She refused to let her mind dwell on such a scenario—No! Chase those thoughts away, even though the Winslow girl had personal security and was still taken. No! Stop! Gail told her brain. She focused on dinner plans: roast chicken, steamed rice, sauteed vegetables, and salad.

Moving slowly with congested traffic, other cars picking up friends and family, she was still a few hundred feet from Tom, who was pointing at his watch.

Then from the back seat Pam said, "Mom, can I show you something?"

"Not now, honey, I'm trying to maneuver in to get your dad. He looks really mad, let's get him into the car first, okay, sweetie?"

"But I want to tell you something Mom, it's important," Pam whined.

"Not now!" Gail barked a little louder than she meant.

A car behind her blared its horn when she unintentionally cut them off but kept moving forward determined. Gail stopped close to the sidewalk. Tom pulled open the passenger door, put his briefcase on the floor, and climbed in, slamming the door hard.

"Did you have a nice trip, darling?" Gail asked quickly, hoping to deescalate Tom's obvious anger.

"No, I didn't have a nice trip and this didn't help. What happened? I've been out here for almost an hour," he said, glaring at his wife.

Gail was silently sorry. She eased back into traffic, looking straight ahead and saying nothing.

"Hi, Daddy," Pam said from the back seat. "We missed you!"

"Hi, sweetheart, how's daddy's little girl?" Tom asked, turning to look at his precious daughter, Pamela. His eyes softened when he gazed at his love, his pride and joy.

"I'm fine, Daddy, welcome back, but look, look at Mommy's lotto ticket, she matched the six winning numbers, here, look." Pam handed the winning numbers ticket to her father, then the ticket with forty rows of six numbers.

Tom saw one row with six black circles neatly drawn around six numbers in ink from the pen Pam found in her mother's purse.

The End

When he finished writing the story, he knew it had zero relevance except killing time. He reread, edited, and changed the draft a few times, finally dragging the file into the folder marked *Short Stories* and promptly forgot about it.

The End.

There were forty or so forgotten stories in the folder. Nobody cared, but writing was good medicine. At 8 p.m., he went into their kitchen to make a quick dinner. He fried thin-sliced calf's liver in butter with bacon, garlic, and onions. Boiled baby potatoes and made spinach salad topped with the liver drippings. A delicious protein-packed blood-based mutual favorite although not exactly conducive to good breath. His wife was in her studio painting. He always knew when she took brush to canvas because she cranked up Holst, listening to and loving *The Planets*.

Fireworks were exploding, blasting off like a distant war zone. After eating, they jumped into Stiv's car and drove to the park where he watched the dolphins earlier that day with his one-eyed Model 38. It was just after 9 p.m. Together they watched the city's pyrotechnics display from across the Sound while holding hands. They hugged and kissed like young lovers. Stiv was jonesing for a hit even though he'd dropped nearly two days' worth of Oxycodone already. As he wrestled with his cravings, they listened to the radio playing the 1812 Overture. A typical cliché piece Stiv was not a fan of so put Mussorgsky's *Night on Bald Mountain* in the CD player, cranking the volume. As the city's main fireworks show was ramping up, she leaned over and kissed his mouth, holding him tight. He looked out at the lights. After each bright cluster of colorful burning fire flowers, the brassy bass report shook the car. They watched the skyrockets, crossettes, dragon busters, thunderclaps, titanium salutes, and goblin-barkers, Stiv's favorite pyrotechnics. *Night on Bald Mountain* was climaxing at the same time in almost perfect sync. When she moved back to her side she whispered, "I love you."

"You're so sweet, thank you, my love, thank you," Stiv said, feeling panicked guilt rising and tears welling. Temporary insanity, then it passed.

"Don't thank me, Stiv darling. Find a new job, quit taking those drugs, we're going to be just fine, I promise."

He was determined to quit the narcotic pain medication now for sure. He owed her that.

Chapter 17

Day One

Tuesday/Wednesday, July 4th - 5th, 2017

THEY GOT HOME after 11 p.m., showered together, and went straight to bed, both sleeping the slumber of satisfied lovers. The blighted day started badly but ended well. Stiv woke with the rising sun. Even though their room was gloomy and cool, he felt strangely at peace with himself, not unlike finishing a well-written book. His wife slept soundly facing him, her pretty face calm in deep dormancy. He was glad she was there; her presence gave him strength and hope. He moved closer to smell her skin, her hair and exhaled breath, all sweet and soothing. She moaned softly, moving away, not waking.

Slowly, the sun began to brighten the new day. Stiv knew this was *the first day of the rest of his life.* He watched her sleep for a long time, understanding nature's genius only seen in the beauty of a sleeping woman. No makeup, no hairdo, nothing but natural radiance like a charm of dancing, multicolored hummingbirds. She was his greatest achievement.

However, he was seriously hurting for his morning fix of Oxycodone. The last hit he had was in front of his condo after receiving the dispatch and good news from Zander. He thought about the money, the love attached from his longtime friend. These thoughts were overwhelming, overshadowing Zander's general sarcasm and obnoxiousness.

Stiv's body suddenly tensed with stomach cramps and intestinal discomfort. The sensation reminded him of the Hollywood scandal of the heartthrob movie star coercing an innocent gerbil into his rectum. Apparently, he used a twelve-inch paper towel core reinforced with duct tape. Then the beast was forced in and up using a cigarette lighter to persuade the critter's forward movement. When the gerbil was in its temporary new home and the cardboard tubing removed, the gerbil blindly moved around back and forth deep inside, scratching its way causing intense sensations. When the game reached its questionable climax, the star was supposed to defecate the suffocated gerbil carcass into a watery toilet grave. But he could not, the vermin was stuck. Nobody wants a dead rodent festering in their butt, nobody Stiv knew anyway.

When news leaked from a local emergency room, this heinous animal brutality was also reported to PETA who wanted the star arrested and charged with animal cruelty, a Class A Misdemeanor. Stiv was sexually open-minded so long as everything was consensual and everyone of legal age. But a gerbil? PETA had a point.

Stiv's guts involuntarily howled for opiates, twisting and screwing down. He calculated how many hours it had been since his last hit; about fourteen.

Courage, man! Strength and honor!

Going forward, he knew he could expect irritability, agitation, depression, insomnia, suicidal thoughts, anxiety, an inability to concentrate, diarrhea, sweating, body aches, runny nose, headaches, high blood pressure, and even an irregular heartbeat. Good times for sure, but he was determined to kick the habit. He owed this to his wife, family, Zander, and himself. Perhaps even society.

He quietly got up and went into the kitchen, then stood at the window looking out at the new day. After making coffee, he sat at his desk counting his drug stash. He had eleven hits of Oxycodone and a whole slew of other medications. He was about to take a hit but did not.

It would have been so easy, *too easy*. The drug had its hooks in him.

"Just wait an hour," he muttered aloud, staring at the bottle containing his rescue. "How bad can it get?" he whispered to the Sound.

He remembered the last time he quit cold turkey. The thought made him nauseous, and he rushed to the kitchen sink and puked up black coffee, some splashing in his face, which sucked. This only served to reiterate how bad it could get. After he cleaned up, he went back to his desk to write another short story.

It took him two hours to write the tale. His fingertips in perfect harmony with his mind, tap dancing over the keyboard sounding like inflected drum rudiments. He decided to focus on composing his stories while he kicked the meds. That seemed the best conceivable way to spend the troubled times to come.

"Corporate Mentality" was an attack on racial stereotypes in America. Stiv based his three characters on situations he knew, as well as many personalities rolled into one. The books he read on the Civil Rights Movement and the sad heroes of that American history. Also, the people who were on the TV show the wife was watching when he got home the day before. Maybe even the good-looking messenger. Stiv never knew where his inspiration came from. He indeed called the story, "Corporate Mentality."

When he finished, he read, then reread the work, not liking the racial slurs but keeping them anyway. He hoped his racially charged reverse irony came across if anyone ever read it, which he doubted.

Stiv believed everyone was cool until they proved themselves otherwise. He believed as he was taught since childhood that every person deserves to be treated with respect, to be given the benefit of the doubt regardless of race, religion, color, creed, shape, size, or ethnicity. Let your fellow man or woman show their true character and then decide if you like them or not. The perfect example was Jane Fonda.

He considered all his writing *creative writing*, whether creative or not. He could not fathom the African American man's plight in America, so he wrote what he felt. After reading Ida B. Wells, the investigative journalist and Civil Rights activist, he thought he might really understand true courage and dedication to a righteous cause. W. E. B. Dubois, historian and Civil Rights activist, also a seriously dedicated man living a life of dismay and sadness because of the color of his skin. A man forced to question God's jealousy. These were two very tough Black people who spoke up and challenged bigotry and racism in White-dominated America in the late 1800s and early 1900s.

Ms. Wells even took on the Klan in her book *Southern Horrors* in 1892. Frederick Douglass called her "Brave Woman" in his letter dated October 25, 1892. Stiv vehemently agreed. A very brave woman who must have been invited to many a Klan bake.

After reading W. E. B. DuBois's *Souls of Black Folks*, Stiv's stigma and fundamentalism on the African American cause changed forever. He read very few Black authors prior and had to question his justifications. DuBois wrote pragmatic responses and observations based on his travels from the tolerant North after the Civil War to the extremely intolerant South, regardless of the Emancipation Proclamation. Seemed to Stiv not much had changed for African Americans in America since *Souls of Black Folks* was published 114 years ago. That was a long time to wait, especially if not much changed.

Hard thing to live haunted by the ghosts of an untrue dream.

Stiv could only hope his writing would not offend anyone, and if it did, whatever. He read "Corporate Mentality," then reread and edited, re-edited, then dragged the story into his desktop file named *Short Stories* and promptly forgot about it...

The end...again.

Chapter 18

A Lesson on War and Peace
11:00 A.M. Wednesday, July 5th, 2017

THEN HE CONSIDERED THROWING up as his body was screaming for narcotics, stomach muscles tightening and twisting, the withdrawals refusing to surrender. It was 11 a.m., Day One, and Stiv was about eighteen hours into the lonely abyss of no narcotics. His palms were sweaty and he felt acute fear about life in general. He unfolded the check Zander sent, looked at it, and seriously considered tearing it up. Money between friends seldom ended well. Stiv took comfort in the knowledge that were the roles reversed, he would be sending Zander a check or go to his aid in his time of need. There was not much he would not do for Zander, legal or otherwise.

Their long-term friendship dictated and justified a journey to the bank, depositing the check, moving forward in a positive direction. Then he would search out an agreeable place to park, make himself as comfortable as possible, and let the pain in. He felt like he was waiting on the edge of a great battle ready to charge. A violent bloody battlefield with guaranteed casualties.

Depression and fear crept soundlessly through the dark

shadows around the condo, stalking, hunting him like an ancient faceless ghoul. The creature had a name, and that name was withdrawals.

Lost and alone even with the Sound and blue morning sky for company, Stiv found no comfort in the fact if he took one of the eleven 15-mg Oxycodone bullets, which were only a few feet away, all would be perfect in the world. Instead, he gritted his teeth and reminded himself why he was so miserable. He pulled on the same jeans, commando-style, the same navy-blue sweater from the day before, forgetting about the dried yellow old-lady gunk, over a clean white T-shirt. Secured the Model 38 in his pants tight against his belt, speed loader in his left pocket and Police Model Spyderco knife in his right hip pocket. Then he left the house, feet again in Sperry's, sockless.

He drove around town for a while, thinking guilty sad thoughts, trying not to see other men his age who should have been at work but were not. Instead, they were doing what he was doing, bending time. Not all of them were unemployed, some had days off or were even playing hooky. Uncertainty washed over him like an icy rain. His thoughts were jumbled but he focused on two important aspects: employment and sobriety. Between the two, sobriety was more important. Also, so he could be the better man Zander knew he could be. Whatever that meant.

⸻

Waiting in line at the bank, Stiv attempted a gangster-lean but was off-balance, sweating and nauseous. Overhead, Muzak was obliterating an old Eagles tune, "Tequila Sunrise," which was not much better in its original form making him want to vomit again. The tune was also a subconscious reminder of the tequila drinking contest he entered back in 1988. Fourteen shots of Cuervo Gold in sixty minutes, one shot every four minutes, twenty seconds. He did not win the contest, or rather, lost very badly.

Stiv waited patiently for the sexy Asian teller he spied when entering the bank, intentionally getting in her line. This was not the first time seeing her but would be their first transaction together. Her good looks eased Stiv's misery some. She was a beautifully manicured young woman looking friendly and professional, her dark eyes and short, layered razor-cut black hair a placard of beauty against the bright white button-down shirt she wore with confidence. Her name tag read *Bian*.

"Is that a Vietnamese name?" Stiv asked with an honest smile, now standing tall before her and already knowing the answer.

Stiv and Zander had both studied Vietnam. The geography, language, food, and the war, each trying to out-knowledge the other. They both felt the Vietnam War was their war because they were growing up while the battles raged. They studied the conflict in-depth. They were fifteen years old when Saigon fell in April 1975.

"Yes, it is," she said professionally with no interest. "Can I help you?"

"I have enormous respect for your country and the Vietnamese people, the war and all. It must have been a horrible time to be there. I'm glad your family made it out. The American dream, right?" Stiv said cheerfully and with enthusiasm.

"*This* is my country, sir. I'm American-born of Asian descent, born in California, the Bay Area. I don't know anything about Vietnam or that war. I've never been to

Vietnam and I have no interest in going. I'm an American. Is there something I can do for you, sir?"

"Call me Stiv. Can you speak Vietnamese?"

"Not a word," she said flatly. "Is there something?"

"I see. I didn't mean to be personal. I have great admiration for the Vietnamese people, their strength and resilience. Are you full-blooded?"

Bian was silent. She looked down at the counter then back up at him, waiting.

"I'm not hitting on you if that's what you think, though you are very pretty. I've been interested in Vietnam since I was a kid. Did you know they used to show combat footage and body counts on the six o'clock news every night? Walter Cronkite, the same news guy that announced both Kennedy brothers had been assassinated, Dr. Martin Luther King, too, I think. When he announced John F. had been shot, he looked like he was gonna cry. Perhaps you've seen the footage? We watched during dinner; it was like a horror movie only real-time."

"Is there business I can help you with today, sir?" Bian asked, ignoring everything he said.

"How old are you anyway, Bian? May I call you Bian? Are you old enough to buy a drink? I'm terrible at guessing women's ages these days. My name is Stiv Baker."

Bian stared at him, her attractive dark features at the very least annoyed.

"Mr. Baker, I honestly don't know what you're talking about. You know more about that country than I do and frankly, I don't care. You're talking about a time and place I honestly know nothing about. Now may I help you with any banking issues?"

"Don't you think it's important to know about your

country of origin? The sacrifices your family made to get out when the South fell to the Communist North?"

"Okay, Mr. Baker, yes, you may call me Bian. Yes, I'm full-blooded. Yes, I can buy liquor but I don't drink. And no, I don't think you're hitting on me, at least I hope you're not," she said with a slight grimace. "I hope that answers all your questions. Now, can I help you? Or would you rather work with the manager?" Bian indirectly threatened in an assertive voice.

Stiv was distraught like he was slapped upside his head. He thought he was being sincere and friendly. He had the gift of gab, an engaging knowledgeable personality, it was his nature like his Pops before him. Wasn't it part of Bian's job to be personable? Her unfriendly attitude sucked. She needed a good thrashing, at the very least verbal. Before he said anything to that effect, he caught himself. Maybe he was being a little intrusive, pushy even. Was he hitting on her? Probably. Regardless, he was nowhere near his usual *Cool Hand Luke* personality as he thought; could it be withdrawals? Agitation was definitely a side effect, as was violence. The Model 38 was hanging tough in his belt under his sweater, in hand's reach. Maybe Bian could benefit from a little real-world experience like the Model 38's one black eye staring her in the face.

Stiv wished Bian could see what life was like in Dak To or Da Nang in 1967 when the VC and NVA were charging South, indiscriminately and in cold blood killing anyone and everyone who got in their way. Men, women, and children. It was a bloodbath meat grinder, people slaughtered in a genocidal insane passion. Bian should know about her country of origin and history. America paid dearly so Bian could work at the bank, live in a nice safe home with her pretty eyes and American passport, rather than some grass hooch next to a rice field in the boonies with a bucket for a toilet. She should know what horrific struggles her grandparents and parents went through to get out when Saigon fell in April of 1975—a real shit storm.

"I'm sorry, Bian. I didn't mean anything, I was just trying to make conversation and compliment your heritage," Stiv said apologetically as he handed her the signed check with his ID. "Vietnam is the only war America's been in that didn't produce a clear victory. One tough group of people you come from. You should be proud."

"Would you please insert your debit card and enter your passcode, Mr. Baker?" she asked, handing back his ID she apparently did not need, her eyes staring into his and again ignoring his observations.

He was so off his usual swagger it was almost comical. Did he *need* narcotics to be himself? High on Oxycodone, he would have her laughing and talking up a storm, flirting with no problem. At least he imagined so. Then he realized she was looking at him like some creepy gnarly old geezer. She was correct, of course, but that did not make her right. Her rudeness was neither acceptable nor excusable.

"Please fill out this deposit slip and Form 8300 for the IRS, Mr. Baker."

"What's this form for? I've never seen one before," Stiv asked guardedly.

"Any deposit or withdrawal over $9,999.99 has to be accompanied by this form. It's a federal law, Mr. Baker, for the IRS?" Bian stated, looking excruciatingly bored at his ignorance.

When he was done with the paperwork, he slowly pushed the papers back to her, very slowly with negative intent. She took the form from his slightly tanned wrinkled hand with her unblemished, manicured candlestick-

181

fingered hand without reaction and started entering information into her computer. Stiv could not decide how angry he should be. He thought about Azar and how enraged she made him but that was different. Apparently, it was Azar's job to be judgmental, not this bitch, good-looking or not. Stiv decided she was too rude and there was no acceptable reason for it. She needed training. Plus he hated rude people, including himself.

Bian handed him his receipt with cold efficiency. Stiv lingered, continued staring into her eyes, then said, "You should be a little prouder of your heritage, young lady. People died so you could be working at a bank here in America with a crap attitude, did you know people died so you could be here?"

"I do know that, Mr. Baker. Thank you. Is there anything else I can do for you?"

"Yes, there is. You can try practicing good customer service so in the future you can avoid upsetting your customers, intentionally or not. You never know who you're dealing with or what kind of personal tragedy they might be experiencing, or what your bad attitude might tempt them to do. Also, when you have a chance, please look up the terms *Double Veteran*, the *Phoenix Project,* and the *Hanoi Hilton.* Then perhaps you'll understand how lucky you are and want to thank me and *my* country for helping you to have a better life. Thanks for your help," Stiv said authoritatively.

And with all those words ringing grandly in the bank's air-conditioned ambience for all to hear, he turned, walking tall and proud to the exit, neither waiting for nor expecting a response. He was oblivious to the people around him or what kind of personal tragedy Bian might be experiencing that day. Then he realized he forgot his driver's license at

Bian's window so he turned proudly and strutted back. Bian was holding up his ID in her pretty fingers, waiting for him with an unreadable look on her face. She did not react or move to return his property. At the window she made no attempt to hand the ID over, instead making Stiv pluck it from her fingers, which he did. Then he turned and walked out for good.

Back in his car, still in the bank parking lot, his mind screamed!

What the hell is wrong with you

Mr. Steven H. Baker, you stupid old junkie!

He aimlessly drove around town, feeling worse. There was nowhere he wanted to go except perhaps back to the bank, walk in and open fire. Or maybe just tell Bian off again—or, get on his hands and knees, forehead to dirty floor, to beg her forgiveness.

Instead, he went back to the beach and sat in the parking lot with cell phone in hand. He realized there was no one he wanted to talk to. It was 12:30 p.m., about twenty hours into his disgusting cold turkey meal.

There was no one.

Stiv knew how dangerous it was to stop a long-term narcotic addiction all at once. Halting could mean serious issues like his central nervous system doing flip-flops, even shut down altogether. Feet and hands could swell up, he could experience seizures, perhaps even death, but he did not care. Throughout his life, Stiv tolerated mental and physical pain by imagining worse scenarios; sometimes this worked, sometimes it failed miserably.

He thought about pain and suffering people experienced through war, starvation, loss of loved ones, terminal illness, and prison.

If given the chance, he would explain to Bian what he knew about Vietnam. Not sure why except perhaps the exceptional history of the country. His knowledge was more about the war but history all the same.

For example, the conflict is America's longest war. Didn't she care as an American, 58,318 were killed in action? No one could bring those dead soldiers back, but the military still carried 1,589 missing in action. These are America's sons and daughters. Wasn't she at all interested in the Tet Offensive, the turning point in the war? In January 1968 when approximately 85,000 NVA Regulars and Viet Cong Guerrillas surprise attacked multiple American and allied positions, towns, hamlets, and villages during *Tet*, the Lunar New Year. The enemy breaking a signed treaty as only a sieged, occupied determined people can. Their battle cry,

Crack the sky! Shake the Earth!

Stiv considered this directive pretty darn profound. The American embassy was attacked and overrun. Forgive and forget? Stiv thought not.

He thought about the true events made into the movie, *Come and See*, about World War II Nazi Storm Troopers attacking a Belarusian town inhabited by old men, women, and children. The frenzied ecstasy of indiscriminate rape, torture, and mass murder without repercussions portrayed by compassionate men, fathers, and husbands themselves who loved their own families, their own children wanting the best for them. But were able to participate in slaughter of innocent people in the name of war. Arbitrary bloodshed an acceptable force of nature. Perhaps this proved God hates the weak but loves violence.

Wait, what?

With these thoughts floating through his mind, Stiv humbled himself, bordering on embarrassment because how could he let some bullshit—granted painful—withdrawals mess with him so badly? Things could be a whole lot worse.

Stiv hated weakness in people, especially in himself. He quit drinking by substituting alcohol with chocolate and super-sweetened soft drinks, which was okay, right? Of course, he had Oxycodone and his cigar box full of substitute drugs making the transition from alcohol that much simpler, which was not okay. Switching one addiction for another, a dangerous one, was one of those weaknesses. At least he quit drinking.

Kicking his alcohol habit helped him lose a ton of weight. He did not need the high blood pressure, gout, and rosacea medications anymore—all booze-related issues, obesity included.

Until sobriety, from alcohol at least, he could not remember a time liquor was not a part of his sex life, as if the two nouns were made for each other. From drunken sexual violence, impotence, and exceptionally bad choices. Drunken sexual secrets he would take to his cold dark grave. The stupidity of drunken ghosts past.

Chapter 19

Still Day One and the Duggie
1:45 P.M. Wednesday, July 5th, 2017

THE BRIGHT SUNNY day depressed him more; he had to kick the drugs. His body sent out distress signals. There were two ways of reacting: pop a blue bullet or shut up and take the pain. To calm himself after the bank he listened to Samantha James and David Sylvian CDs, sitting at the beach and contemplating life and pain in general. He did not call anyone, and no one called him. He felt desperately alone but understood this was part of his journey.

He decided to drive home, go for a run through the park on the Sound. This was on a short mental list of the last activities he wanted to do but he knew it was necessary. His stomach cramped but he was not hungry. Still, he stopped at the market anyway to buy a six-pack of icy Coke in cans and ten boxes of Hershey's Whoppers. Ten boxes for ten bucks, best deal in town. Sitting in the parking lot, he poured chocolate malt balls into his mouth, blissfully chewing the super-sweetened poison, savoring the sugar like a *dead man walking's* last meal. He chased the mud with ice-cold cola, unable to remember a better flavor combination.

Back home, his wife's studio door was still closed. Stiv was seriously hurting so stayed away. He did not want to see her anyway and doubted she wanted to see him. Instead, he changed into running clothes, strapped his fanny pack on containing his wallet, cell phone, headphones, and keys. He clipped his Spyderco knife to the belt as he always did when he ran.

He heard his wife on the phone speaking to someone about a recent design project. His lightning-fast thoughts were fleeting like the hummingbird's because he did not care about anything, mind and body fixated with anxious, apprehensive dependency.

Walking several hundred yards down to the park entrance, he stopped, got his headphones out, attached them to his cell phone, and pressed PLAY. A little Herbie Hancock for his head needing the mellow jazz. The colors of the Sound with contrasting green summer foliage to his left made for a dazzling sight. The scenery so vivid for an instant he forgot his misery. His run began slowly at first, then he upped the pace, noticing an older couple far off walking toward him, the only other people in sight. Their unleashed, mangy dog chased down the beach then back to the couple. Ignorance of the law is never an excuse and the leash laws in the park were strictly enforced. The large, boundless energy mutt was running up and down the beach like a furry torpedo, back to the couple, then breaking wild in free canine euphoria.

Watching the shepherd-mix reminded Stiv of the nickname he called dogs since he was about twelve. He took the name from a book on Jack the Ripper. Apparently, English coppers tracking the killer used bloodhounds, unfortunately never catching the fiend. They called their dogs duggies.

After three minutes of low-speed labored jogging, Stiv's

stomach rebelled. First twitching, then rocking and rolling. The choking, gagging sensation was foreign, but obvious. He stopped, turned left away from the water and barfed up a super-sweetened mix onto the green foliage side of the trail. He wheezed and choked, heaving his guts, and worrying he might rupture something the pressure so strong. Moments past before the wrenching, convulsing onslaught subsided. Slowly he straightened, hands on hips, chest heaving, eyes looking up toward heaven. Super sweet vomit dripped from his mouth and chin onto his shirt. Turning back toward the mellowing Sound, Stiv was just in time to see the savage beast bounding toward him. There was no time to react.

Muddy paws hit Stiv gut-center. Sixty pounds or more hit his knotted mid-section at about twenty miles an hour almost knocking him off his feet. Stiv swung Bruce Lee fast, hips first, a perfect pivoted powerful well-aimed back-handed fist snapping the duggie's cheekbone square. All Stiv's body energy exploded on the duggie's head with his top two knuckles connecting squarely. The swing was flaw-less, a perfect shot causing the duggie to cry out in pain as it backed away yelping, tongue lapping. Stiv had trained for the last thirty-four years, a long hard road of pain to throw that perfect backhanded fist on that stupid duggie's head. And it was good. The surprised beast's eyes were guilty innocence watching Stiv in shocked surprise while he prepared to blast the mutt again. The old man came shuf-fling over, yelling at Stiv as he came, "Hey!? Hey you! Did you just strike my dog? What's the matter with you!"

Slowly turning from the duggie to face the old man, eyes narrowing in lunatic rage, his mouth dripping brown vomit, he must have looked like a deranged maniac. His running shorts and lower part of his shirt were now muddy.

Two perfect paw prints, the same color as his puke, were stamped on his shirt, belly high.

"There are leash laws in this park, sir," Stiv began in a slow snarl. "There's a sign right there," he pointed. "Or can't you read? I suggest you get a leash for your wife too. And make no mistake, friend, your stupid mutt got off easy today. Remember that, asshole," Stiv spoke in a malevolent, threatening growl.

"You are very rude, sir. Very rude! My dog is just a puppy, and a harmless one at that. You shouldn't have hit him and you should not insult my wife!"

The duggie, now playfully and haphazardly chasing seagulls on the sand, came bounding back up to the trail, stopping next to the old couple and panting, tail wagging. The old woman grabbed its collar.

"I'm rude, huh? You break the law, you let some unpredictable mongrel run free to attack innocent park-goers, the damn thing jumps on me and I'm rude? Be glad your damn dog isn't dead on the ground. That mutt is a menace and so are you," Stiv bellowed into the briny Sound air, slowly walking away while eyeballing the old man, the duggie too.

As he passed, Stiv made a threatening move toward the duggie, fist raised, causing the mutt to cower. The old woman holding its collar was almost pulled off her feet as she mumbled something unintelligible.

She let the beast go, it immediately bounded over to the puddle of barf and started lapping it up.

Stiv began to run again, slowly, painfully.

"I'm going to report you!" the old man yelled after him. "And...and my wife doesn't need a leash!" the old man screamed.

"Go ahead and report me, you dip-shit! Your wife needs

a leash and a muzzle!" Stiv shouted to the blue sky and the light breeze of the summer day.

He felt physically terrible. Yes, he felt emotionally terrible as well. He didn't want to smack the damn dog, he loved dogs, even considered himself one most of the time. Belting the law-breaking stupid old man would have been far more satisfying. The duggie was doing what duggies do. It was completely the old man's fault and Stiv was pretty sure the geezer knew it too. Leash laws in the park were strictly enforced. The old couple risked a beefy $500 fine as was clearly warned on the signs everywhere in the park. None of this knowledge helped, his joints screamed in pain, even after throwing up, his guts were knotting and cramping like those angry snakes were fighting in his intestines again.

Fear crept in his heart, he kept telling himself the negatives were caused by his nemesis ex-friend, and new enemy Oxycodone. Faithful friends should not hurt one another. He held to this resolve, had to keep reminding himself of the damage the drugs caused him. Bending time, that was the answer if he was going to make it through this hellish experience not only successfully, but alive.

As he tried picking up speed, the briny summer air nursing him along, he thought about NA, Narcotics Anonymous. He did not need AA, Alcoholics Anonymous. Then again when he kicked alcohol, he had his cigar box. Yes, it was true his cigar box waited for him like a naked lover, demurely waiting to calm his nerves and pain. Now, the only drug he considered using was Valium and only at night if he could not find sleep.

He was not looking forward to the night when the deathly silence, ghouls, and creatures of temptation come out looking for victims weakening victims. But if he made it without popping an Oxy by midnight, that was one day, twenty-four hours bent and spent. His reward, a new day to fight through.

At the end of the park, the woodland trail turned sharply up a steep tree-lined hill leading through a vista to the main parking area. Suddenly like a match to gasoline, the explosive memory of the hellish car crash that killed Jack back in 1977, forty years before, flashed in his mind. What conscious moment sparked the PTSD memory was forever a mystery. Since he could not keep the memory away, he decided years ago to let the decaying recollection run its painful course. What else could he do aside from hoping the memory passed quickly.

The ancient, massive red oak tree, a living breathing monster, waited centuries for their arrival that night, the subsequent head-on crash. It waited for human blood, perhaps getting revenge for human treatment of the Quercus Rubra's kin and millions of other trees throughout history.

As the four friends sped up that dark old road, ominously listening to The Grateful Dead's "Help on the Way," forever an ode to Jack in Stiv's heart. The boy was dead, that was true. Fagin was driving, that was true too. But any one of them might have been driving that night. That was also true, they all drove Fagin's car. Fate decided who sat in the death seat. Stiv believed then as he believed now they were all guilty. The judge agreed, ordering Stiv and Dean to AA meetings twice a week for six months.

They abstained the entire six months. Instead, they discovered and consumed quaaludes, which were far less fattening.

The Alcoholics Anonymous meetings they were assigned to in the late 1970s consisted of wayward lascivious teenage boys and girls with serious alcohol problems. Party-crazy, booze-loving females who would walk a mile for a drink. Stiv and Dean were well versed in the natural act of young courtship and introduced the lovelies to the magic and wonders of quaaludes. There was nothing funny or ironic about this history, it simply is. Many years later, when the realities of youthful mistakes come back to haunt you, glorification is the last intention. However, they knew Jack well. He would not want them to stop their partying ways as he was a wolfpup wildchild himself. He knew the score. They all did, living dangerously fast together. And not just them either. All their friends, all the other groups who shared the North Shore. It was the way of the times and never would be repeated again.

With quaaludes, a sedative of the quinazolinone family of hypnotics, alcohol was not necessary. The boys refrained from drinking, but their new female friends wanted booze desperately, so the boys provided the girls as much liquor as they wanted. Jack would have wanted it that way. Their debauchery and freelance womanizing was an ode to Jack, their dear departed friend gone way too young.

Stiv's post-traumatic stress disorder hypermnesia never lasted long. But he could not curtail the emotion. The images had to run their agonizing course through his mind, like an out-of-control brushfire. Then it was gone. No cure, no medicine, only time. He lived with the condition and made friends with the trauma so he would not be haunted by guilty blood on his hands. Unfortunately, the stains ran deep.

Turning up the hill, he pushed himself away from the sublime Sound. He was on the opposite side of the park. He decided to run through the lush evergreen woods back to his condo and bottle of Oxycodone twenty more minutes away. As he entered the woods high over the Sound, he looked off at the islands in the distance. The cool, damp air was invigorating and forgiving. Fresh oxygen emitted from endless evergreens, soaking and soothing his damaged body and mind. The PTSD had thankfully run its course.

Everything hurt, joints, stomach, and lungs. He had a wicked headache and maybe even a pulsing toothache or two. Stiv had to push himself, he always had to push himself, no pain no gain. The route led to a maintenance vehicle lane becoming gray pavement strangely out of place in all the green. Surrounded by the judging trees was the old couple and their stupid duggie just ahead, now leashed. A dark blue uniform was writing in what looked like a citation book. This scene also looked out of place under the green canopy. As Stiv got closer he saw the dizzy geezer eyeballing him, so he altered course for straight-on impact, accelerating to ramming speed. The ranger had his back turned but the old couple and duggie saw Stiv clear as virgin's blood on a white sheet. Just before the collision he veered left, causing the duggie to retreat, again nearly pulling the old woman off her feet. He heard her shout in surprise and perhaps pain followed by a weak reprimand of the mutt.

"You should arrest both those lawbreakers and lock them up! The stupid dog, too!" Stiv shouted over his shoulder.

He received no reply. Turning to look as he exited the park, he saw the old couple staring daggers at him from a distance, surrounded by green. The park ranger was oblivious, completely absorbed in performing his sworn duty.

Stiv smiled to himself but was not proud of what he'd done. Taking his pain out on someone else was evil. It was not his style. If he had been stoned on Oxycodone when the duggie jumped he probably would have played with the canine and complimented its good looks and temperament, screw the muddy paw prints. Stiv simply would not have cared. Oxycodone offered enlightened heightened forgiveness.

Wait, what?

Back in the condo where the elevator waited, Stiv had a sudden crippling panic attack. For a moment he wondered why he even continued living, though the thought quickly passed as did the attack. Rather than glide up the four flights to his unpredictable wife, he decided to go out back of the building to the hidden, tree-enclosed courtyard. An outdoor concrete walkway led to a patio shaded by huge maple and pine trees. The walkway had bright green ivy running up the sloping back property. Stiv loved this part of the complex. The foliage, clean air, and positive energy rejuvenated him. Often he brought a book to read or music to listen to on the breezy sunny patio, high up over the lower basin trees offering a superb view of the Sound. A secret, wonderfully lonely place for reflection.

He followed the walkway, hoping he would be alone. To his right were the lofty maples that offered a perfect canopy; the sky barely showed through its thick leafy cover. Stiv looked at the floor of ivy and large ferns sprouting here and there. The color combination and growth were surreal and sparked a wistful memory of a photograph from his youth, found in the photobook, *The Family of Man.* The image, *Child in Forest,* had been captured in 1951 by Wynn Bullock. A young girl pale and nude is lying face-down on a forest floor of green ivy. Stiv spent a great deal of time staring at the image trying to see through a faint misty dawn. The book was on the Baker living room coffee table from the beginning of time, a family favorite. He was mesmerized by the girl in ivy. She captivated him in ways he could not understand or explain, whispered questions and forbidden secrets to his young ears. Stiv was nine when *Child in Forest* asked him about desperation, loneliness, sadness, want, innocence, love, fear, guilt, and lust. Although he did not know these human emotion terms yet, he certainly felt them and wondered what it would be like to lie next to her in all that tickling, emerald hedera. He longed to touch her bare skin, be secret friends and whisper softly and maybe kiss. It was a long-ago dreamy memory of adolescent love, desperation, and confusion he never forgot. Stiv knew even then we cannot run from who we are. He sat on an old cast-iron weather-worn patio chair, a veteran of countless storms and wind, thinking about Ari's dream she shared with him on that tripped out 4th of July 1976, forty-one years and one day ago. He was sweating from his run and in pain, pissed about the old man and his mangy duggie.

It's the withdrawals, man. It's the withdrawals. Don't let them fool you.

He looked out at the green islands and contrasting sapphire sea. Massive cargo ships moved slowly over the water to unknown destinations from unknown ports with unknown cargo, crews, and stories. Memories of his own sea adventures sailed through his mind when suddenly a male Anna's hummingbird darted in, twittered, hovered, its bright red neck and gray body shimmering against the blue sky. Then two more. They chirped and chased each other, not a game but territorial behavior Trochilidae perform to protect their feeding grounds. Suddenly a charm of the tiny hummingbirds darted around like raiders from another world. They moved too fast to count but Stiv thought there were at least ten of the rocket-like creatures looking like multicolored sparks noisily squeaking, chirping, communicating. He wished he could join them as he wished he could have joined the dolphins the day before. Different worlds the two forms of nature inhabited, although in a sense they lived as Stiv did. In search of food, shelter, and a mate to reproduce the species.

If the three species could trade a natural trait or ability, Stiv wondered what they might want. He wanted to fly, although swimming under the world's oceans had appeal too. Flying forty-five miles per hour would rock.

A difficult choice.

The hummingbirds were gone as suddenly as they appeared. He knew the hummingbirds were spying on him, knew his wife spoke to the tiny endothermic vertebrates and that they told her things. Secrets about him mostly.

Mostly.

His reverie was interrupted by his iPhone's ringtone...an alien sound from outer space as he had the ringtone set to Black Sabbath's "N.I.B." Caller ID showed it was his friend Sam, another alien creature from outer space. Stiv did not want to talk to him or anybody else. They had known each other going on five decades, having played Little League on different teams at the beginning of the 1970s. They ran with different crowds in later years, but in 1983 they ended up in the same town in Japan and became fast friends. They trained karate at the same dojo in Osaka, and now at the same dojo in Northend. They had taken a few memorable drunken road trips together as well. Sam was the first of their Osaka group to own a car. It was one of life's ironic twists of fate they lived in the same city yet again. Destiny chooses us sometimes. But he had no interest in talking to him, he could be aggravating and Stiv was in no mood to get hassled. He picked up anyway.

Big mistake.

"Yo," Stiv answered in a low, tired voice.

"Yo, whaaaat'sss up, loser?" Sam yelled into his phone from the other side of town sounding like McLovin.

Stiv sat staring out at the Sound with the phone to his ear wondering why the hell he answered. Sam knew about Stiv's Oxycodone prescription and addiction. He liked the drug himself and would take an occasional pill whenever Stiv offered, which was often and usually after karate practice. They had trained together for almost thirty-five years. What are friends for?

"You going to the dojo tonight? I'm going. I need a good workout," Sam yelled.

Even in Stiv's rough condition, he found Sam's statement hilarious as well as ridiculous because Sam taught hot yoga five days a week. He also went to the dojo more than Stiv. How good a workout did he need?

Stiv was silent and fearing, looking into the void. Why did he answer the damn phone? He was just about to hang up when Sam yelled, "Hey! Moshi moshi!"

"Yeah, I'm here, could you please stop yelling in my ear?"

"Sure!" Sam yelled.

"Damn, bro, give me just a little break, please? I just finished running five miles, I got attacked by a vicious hellhound in the park, damn mutt tried to bite my leg off, probably has rabies, plus I'm trying to kick Oxycodone. I'm about twenty-three hours in. I think I'll just kill myself instead."

"You shouldn't talk like that, man. But hey if you do it, can I have your car and cigar box?"

"Yes."

"Please put that in writing before you're dead. How will you do it anyway?"

"Fuck you."

"I don't think that can kill you."

"Eat shit then," Stiv barked.

"That might do it. Come to the dojo. A good workout will make you feel better. Do you have any extra pills since you're quitting?" Sam asked.

"You're joking, right? I'm miserable, bro, and you're making stupid jokes. I'm a mess," Stiv said.

"What else is new? You've been a mess for years, I tease

you out of love, Stiv. You know that, but I'm serious about working out, best thing for you."

"Best thing for me is thirty milligrams of Oxycodone and a triple fat glass of good scotch. That would put me straight and back to normal again."

"You aren't gonna start drinking again, right? That's the last thing you need, the last thing anyone needs, the last thing the world needs is for you to start drinking again."

"Very funny, and no, I'm not. But I'm sick, my whole-body hurts, my nose is dripping, and there're wild animals trying to rip their way out of my stomach."

"Look, Stiv, all bullshit aside. Sorry for busting your balls but you're one of the strongest people I've ever known. You've overcome some serious issues, you almost went to prison for Christ's sake," Sam yelled into the phone again.

"Thanks for reminding me and please—stop yelling," Stiv said miserably.

"No problem," Sam yelled. "But we both know you can take the suffering and it's not forever; you know this. It ain't terminal, bro, and you quit drinking for Christ's sake!"

"I had narcotics to get me through kicking the booze," Stiv reminded him.

"No matter, you stopped being a pain-in-the-ass drunk, you aren't too bad as a junkie."

"Thanks."

"Welcome, but you did it, crutch or no crutch, you can quit the Oxycodone too. But give me whatever you have leftover, will ya?" Sam asked.

This cracked Stiv up, he laughed the sad laugh of the condemned man. He looked at his phone, it was 4 p.m. He would have to leave his house by 5 to get to the dojo by 5:30. He had no interest in going, less than zero. It was fight night. He enjoyed fighting when he was younger but could not take the punishment anymore. At his age he preferred kata training. There was less chance of getting hurt; he did not heal as quickly as he used to.

"I guess I'll be there but I'm in crap condition. I'm a cripple. I might puke all over whoever I work out with. Hopefully, it's you, asshole. But I guess training's better than sitting in my room feeling sorry for myself."

"Don't worry, you won't be training with me, why would I want to train with a vomiting cripple? I'd like to see you vomit on one of those IT millennial dickheads in there. Notice Sensei never lines us up with those guys? And I agree, feeling sorry for yourself is lame, bro. I'm leaving here now and coming from a long way. You better show up."

"Yeah, same here. See you later, I'll try not to spew on you."

"Eat a big bowl of spicy chili and a glass of grape juice before you leave the house!" Sam shouted and hung up.

Why did he answer the goddamn phone?

Stiv had to get moving if he was going to Northend. He was not worried about canceling, the easiest decision in the world. But he knew, much like running through the park, this was another way of bending, spending, and using time. The journey to the dojo, warmups, workout, and hopefully kicking the shit out of one of his adult *kohais*, Japanese for "underling." Driving back home would bend more time away from the mean and angry cravings that were alive and whispering. The voices started making terrifying sense.

Bending time was the secret to kicking the Oxycodone. At least he hoped so. Stiv was about to jet when his favorite neighbor, Beta, a five-foot, 165-pound bull-dyke prison guard, sat down in the chair next to him. When she was not wearing her dark blue guard uniform, she wore the same outfit every day: baggy faded jeans, a white cotton button-down shirt, and biker boots on her small feet. Her overall impression was masculine.

She wore her hair bleached blond and cropped short. Beta had pretty sky-blue eyes that sparkled, complementing her squared pit-bull face. She was actually quite attractive for a man-hater. Stiv liked Beta, she was one tough woman. He admired any person who had the guts to face humanity's worst for a living. A serious weightlifter and collegiate wrestler in the 55 kg class, a no-nonsense woman who spoke her mind adding her own ironies, often hilarious. Four years in the Navy taught her a sense of humor, she liked to say. Her voice was constantly hoarse from yelling at confrontational inmates. And even though Beta hated men, and made this fact clear, Stiv's wife was insanely jealous of her. Maybe the wife saw something Stiv did not. Beta considered his wife a *very trainable talent*, she told him after he introduced the two. He could not deny the intel intrigued him although he would never share his wife with anyone regardless of his fantasies.

"What are you doing down here, bro? You look like shit."

"Thanks, Beta, and you look like Britney Spears," Stiv retorted.

"Oh my, I'd love to get my hands on that saucy bitch. I'd keep her tied up for weeks, take care of all her personal needs, yum," Beta said in a raspy, horny voice dreamily staring at the Sound.

Stiv looked over at her frowning. "Um, me too, I suppose. What are you doing down here?"

"I like to get the afternoon sun, I thought you knew that.

201

Anyway, I heard you on the phone. So, you're kicking Oxycodone, huh? How long you been taking them?"

"About fourteen, no fifteen years, eighty to a hundred milligrams a day plus alcohol when I was drinking. I'm twenty-something hours in, it's like having the flu and food poisoning at the same time. I just finished running through the park, got attacked by a wild fucking dog, damn mutt was running loose. I'm thinking of going back and putting a bullet in the rabid beast's head. Now I'm going up to my dojo to get my face kicked in."

"Don't make jokes about hurting dogs, Stiv, not to me. You know better than that."

"Who's joking? You'd rather me get attacked? Fuck that mangy mutt," he exclaimed.

"Calm down, bro, and no, not exactly but I don't believe you about a dog attack so let's just not make jokes about hurting dogs, or any other animals. Clear?" Beta said in her trained, anti-violence convict-soothing voice.

"Fine," Stiv said, shaking his head, unable to get a break.

He was not about to mention scoring that perfect backhand shot upside the mutt's head. Mentioning his momentary animal cruelty to Beta might be suicidal.

"At least you have the right frame of mind, right mindset, Stiv. You have to keep busy. The pills will call you, talk to you. Your addiction is tangible and will lie, tell you it's okay, just one more pill to quell the pain. You can't listen, you have to be strong and hate the pills like you hate the clap," Beta stated, her voice raised. "You don't have any pills left, do you?"

"I have eleven 15-mg pills upstairs...just in case."

"In case what? That's junkie talk, Stiv. What're you, stupid?"

"No, Beta. That's survival talk, I'm dying here and yes, I am stupid."

"Then die, bro, vaya con Dios, amigo! I mean, either you want to stop or you don't, right? If you want to stop, that's it. Done...end of story. You're gonna feel like bloody roadkill for a few days but too bad and so fucking sad. Or go upstairs and pop a pill like a bitch so you can stop whining. But if you do, I'm gonna lose respect for you, I've never thought of you as a bitch, Stiv."

"Thanks for the compliment, I think."

"I remember when you quit drinking, man could you pound it, I couldn't believe how much beer you drank. I only saw you down here barbecuing in the spring and summer, you'd drink four or five beers in the short time we were hanging out. I know that wasn't all you drank. I'd see you coming home from shopping. You always had a twelve-pack. Like every day, bro."

"Stalking me, huh, Beta?"

"Hardly, you ain't exactly my type."

"That's a shame," Stiv said, smiling to the Sound.

"Bro," she continued. "You always had buttloads of liquor, you were hard to miss, plus the recycle bin was always full. You were fat as a hog, a regular Jenny Craig reject. You didn't seem to have much trouble when you stopped drinking and lost all that weight. You look much better thin, Stiv. You aren't bad looking for a man."

"Thanks, and I'm honored you spied on me, Beta, I didn't know you cared," Stiv joked. "Yup, booze was easy to quit since I had my Oxycodone to help me, the pills are far less fattening too." Stiv smiled.

"I'll make you a deal, *Alice*," she countered. "You have your cock and balls amputated and I'll spy on you for real.

You'd make a good punk and I'll teach you the ropes, literally."

"Okay, Beta, I take it back, you weren't spying on me."

"Good boy, Stiv. Don't be a wise-ass, clear? Either way, just take the pain, it ain't forever, maybe a week to ten days, you can handle that, right? A lot of the cons in the joint were pill heads, then they turned to smack. Don't do that, Stiv, you'd be in a world of hurt, and I'm sure you and your wife will get along better when you're sober. If I were you, I'd do everything and anything to have a good relationship with that woman of yours. You need to keep her happy. You ain't never gonna find another woman like her, you can believe that."

"What's that supposed to mean?" Stiv asked, turning to look at her.

"You know *exactly* what I mean, Stiv. Don't be a *skel*."

"Beta, what the hell is a skel?" Stiv asked, incredulously.

He was tired, hurting, and annoyed with the conversation.

"Look it up, but it ain't good. Just don't be one, and for the record, I never spied on you. Anyone could see you stumbling around drunk all the time. You were never exactly discreet."

"Okay, I won't be a skel, whatever that means," Stiv said, shaking his head, not enjoying the conversation at all.

"Stiv. Your wife's a gem, one in a million. A real angel and you better be careful. I'm sure she's got admirers besides me. Just because she stayed with your ass all these years, you better not take it for granted, don't push your luck," Beta said, looking at him. "I've heard you two fighting, everyone in the building has. This condominium's like a vortex the way it's built. All the entrances on the one side with the back-property trees and hills. Sounds swirl and travel real easy, especially when windows are open, you know that, right?"

Stiv stared at the Sound staying silent.

"You both go for the throat, but I'll commend you for not putting your hands on her. We couldn't be friends anymore if you did. I won't tolerate a man hitting a woman, I don't give a crap what she did." Beta turned to look at Stiv again dead-eyed.

The trees whispered secrets to the ivy for a few minutes while Stiv and Beta pondered their own thoughts. Hummingbirds darted around squeaking, twittering in the afternoon sun.

Then Beta said, "Well, that's enough sun for me and enough advice for you. I don't want to ruin my pale complexion. Time to go back upstairs, get ready for work. I can't wait to get there, I might get to bust some heads tonight if I'm lucky." She leered at Stiv with professionally trained, terrifying, sparkling blue eyes. "Good luck, brother. I'll see you around. You can do it, bro. I have faith in you," Beta said as she got up to leave.

"Yeah, thanks, nice talking to you. I'll look up *skel*," Stiv said, thinking Beta's ironies not so hilarious this time.

She extended her hand, Stiv accepted her muscular appendage and viselike grip, shook, released. She smiled warmly, her blue eyes sparkling in the afternoon sun. She really was quite beautiful.

"You know I care, bro; I wouldn't shit you because you're my favorite turd," she said, giggling. She turned and disappeared down the long corridor.

"Favorite turd," Stiv mumbled miserably.

At 4:30 p.m. when Stiv reached the condo on the fourth floor. His wife's studio door was still closed, but now there was a colorful, surrealistically drawn sign of asymmetric architectural cliffs in the distance. Large post-like forms with strange faces stood in the center, invoking *danger* secured to the door with a unicorn Band-Aid on each corner. In the center of the work, she had written in blood-red gothic print, *DO NOT DISTURB*, so he did not knock or go in although he noticed the sign was hung crooked. He had no interest in seeing her anyway. Guilt compounded with pain and nausea was not conducive to good conversations. It was like having a pitiful dream from which he could not wake.

Beta was right though, keep busy bending time and get past the bullshit, take the withdrawals and do not be a bitch. Stripping off his sweaty running clothes, he rinsed in the shower, the water stinging his body like the death of a thousand knife cuts. His stomach growled and twisted ominously, threatening to heave, but it was empty so he only convulsed and dry-heaved. Realizing he had not eaten anything but Hershey's Whoppers, he wondered if that stupid dog enjoyed eating his sweet brown vomit.

Dressed in his dogi, he fastened his old faded black belt while his flesh popped with goosebumps. Leg muscles were cramping, torso joints aching and nose running. His heart raced and pounded like tom-tom distress signals. Could he even make the thirty-minute drive to the aged village of Mawguwa in Northend? He pulled his fleece jacket over the dogi, the black belt's two ends hanging low around his groin like protective vigilant snakes. He liked the look. It gave him enhanced confidence and swagger. Both important components of Japanese karate.

Stiv packed a clean change of clothes in case his friends

were going out for drinks. He thought they were and did not anticipate going but wanted to be prepared. He was justly paranoid, feeling dense dread forcing himself to the front door.

Standing there before exiting, he heard the faraway voice of the other man who lived inside him, who only appeared when *he* wanted,

This is a huge mistake, one 15-mg blue bullet won't kill you. It's a long ride. Pop a pill, then go, you'll thank me later.

Stiv marched back to his desk and decided to cut a 15-mg Oxycodone in half. Seven and a half milligrams to ease his weighted blues. What did that smug dyke Beta know anyway? He grabbed the bright green bottle and shook it next to his ear. Its rattle was the sweetest, most passionate melodic music. Popping the top, he poured a single tiny pill into his palm. Looking at the devious blue bullet, Stiv decided to take the whole blue bomber.

Chapter 20

Over The Hills and Far Away

4:50 P.M. Wednesday, July 5th, 2017

HE STARED at the tiny blue enemy in his palm like the shadow of death, a high-velocity bullet for his head. The happiness, desire of relief stared back at him, understanding that his discomfort could be controlled in minutes. Why not take half or even a quarter? At least he would not be dope-sick for the ride to Northend.

Beta's prophetic words echoed through his mind. Maybe she did know, maybe he was not giving her high-powered lezbo perception enough credit. He dropped the pill back into its secure bottle and said quietly, "I'll wait till I get home, pop a pill then. I'll need it more later."

"Who are you talking to and where are you going, Stiv?" his wife's soft voice called from the doorway of her studio. She wore a long-sleeved navy blue unitard, long black hair pulled back, feet sockless and exposed, all body parts pronounced and beautiful as any summer sunset. His heart skipped beats, his mouth salivated.

"I was talking to myself and where does it look like I'm going, sweetie pie?"

"Well, be careful. I'll see you when you get home. Drive

safe and be careful at the dojo. Tell Sam and Sensei I say hi," she said before turning back into her artistic sanctuary, closing the door behind her.

Stiv crept over. For a moment he considered trying to get her into bed. That unitard was so sexy. He would be happy to trade lovemaking for a dojo beating anytime. Her outfit lingered like a bloody kill in front of a hungry jackal. Yes, sex was the best excuse for any cancellation, no man would deny this. A man will always give up responsibility for intercourse and sex in general. Neither Sam nor Sensei could or would challenge his decision if lovemaking were on the bargaining table.

He listened, ear pressed to the door. He could hear her softly sobbing. Her tears of sadness all caused by him. She would never let him see her like that, too proud but still a woman with deep-rooted female emotions. Her tough exterior could only hide her inner feelings for so long. A crash was inevitable. Why did love have to be so agonizingly sad?

Stiv was no spring chicken, more like a crippled rooster not worthy of the cookpot. Also unemployed in a tough competitive marketplace for his particular skills and past. He was proud of himself for not taking the pill. It would've been so easy, like taking Hershey's Whoppers from a baby.

Stiv promised himself a treat when he got home, perhaps a quarter hit, just the slightest taste of the narcotic to quell the terrible anxiety invading his being. Maybe he'd get some loving compassion from his wife, although that was a lot to hope for.

Then, like a phantom-gorilla slap to Stiv's head, Beta's not too funny ironies washed over like a cement truck unloading on him. Suffocating with absolute crystal clarity, he understood exactly what Beta meant. The knowledge crushed him, mummified his spirit, and worse, Stiv knew Beta was absolutely right.

He would never find another exceptional woman to love him as his wife did. Never.

Instead of the narcotic, he dropped three ibuprofen 800s from his cigar box then walked to the sink, filled cool water in a glass, and washed the pills down. He needed the pain relief but was not sure how the strong medicine was going to affect his empty sensitive stomach...and a possible broken heart.

Stiv left the condo at five o'clock. Thirty-one minutes to Northend. He drove over the hill high above his condo through town where Crystal the nurse was probably just finishing work at Cyclops's office. He listened to Jimpster's song, "State of Mind," telling his story.

He took the bridge to the viaduct, looking out over the Sound from the opposite side of his dolphin beach. Traffic was as light as Stiv's head. He tried to focus only on driving, moving forward and away.

You can only put your foot in a river once.

He turned off the viaduct onto First Avenue where high-rise office buildings looked out over the Sound. Stiv admired anyone working in the hundred-year-old offices, admired anyone who had a job. Admired anyone who was not a narcotics addict and was not withdrawing from a self-induced dependency. Such thoughts made him sad—also angry at himself and at the world for making his tiny existence meaningless. Damn, he should have dropped that Oxycodone.

Soft mellow jazz was not helping anything, so he switched the CD out with an Insane Clown Posse disc,

"Chicken Huntin'" (slaughterhouse mix), and cranked the volume. There was nothing mellow about ICP, the intro raw, meaty, and excellent.

> *Well, I'm heading down a southern trail*
> *I'm going chicken huntin'*

> *Boomshaka Boomshaka hair jumps in the sky...!*

After the first and second verse, then a chorus, the music's grinding intensity convinced Stiv to drive off the Mawguwa Bridge about a mile ahead. The span was old and steep. It traversed up into the village of Mawguwa at the top, the location of his dojo. The imminent feeling of his premeditated crash was so strong and climactic he began to plan the design in his mind:

He'd pick up speed at the entrance of the flyover, stay in the left lane, accelerating to at least eighty mph. At the center, he'd pull the steering wheel hard to the right, forcing the Mustang up and over the raised sidewalk, wall, and guardrail. His car would fall about two hundred feet before hitting the ground below—a storage parking lot for military vehicles. The flight down might be a Dutch roll. Perhaps he'd even unfasten his seat belt. Hopefully, he'd be killed on impact, but if not, his extensive injuries would finish him off. And if not his injuries, then certainly the explosion and subsequent fire would waste him.

Stiv wondered how his sudden death would impact his wife, family, and friends. If Zander knew it was intentional he would probably curse his soul and perhaps even his memory. People would mourn, social media would react, anyone who remembered him would have a word to say, some good, some not so good. Whatever was left of his mangled, twisted body would be donated to science, the rest cremated, unless the car fire-roasted him to ash.

His car passed the *gambling with death* center span on his way up and into the pretentious, wealthy village of Mawguwa. He parked in front of the dojo feeling hopeless. He never should have answered his damn phone. What was he thinking?

It was 5:27 when he got out of his car, wanting to fall to the grease-stained pavement and stay there. Instead, he walked unsteadily to the open door of the dojo.

The children's class ended at 5:15, and twenty or so eight-to-ten-year-olds were running around like crazies, whooping annoyingly, playing tag, or leaving with a parent. Many of the waifs remained on the mat horsing around and playing noisy games.

They all knew Stiv. When they saw him, they stopped immediately and bowed out of trained respect for elders, invoking the standard traditional dojo greeting of *OSU Sensei!*

Stiv nodded with little enthusiasm. He did not need to bow to anybody below his rank or stature. He bowed to most adults out of respect for Sensei and his dojo culture. Stiv was treated with earnest respect because he was old-school. He trained in Japan at the Yagyu Dojo with Sensei and Sam in the red-light district of downtown Osaka. He was a sempai, an O.G. or senior member. Stiv paid his dues and *made his bones* while having some dislocated and broken in the process.

Sensei was talking to some parents on the mat as Stiv walked by. He stopped, bowed deeply with a loud, *"OSU!"*

Sensei ignored him and continued his conversation. Stiv was required to bow to Sensei, Sensei was not required to bow to anyone. A gentle giant at six foot, three inches and

220 pounds, they had trained together since 1985, the crazy old days living in Osaka and training full-time.

The Japanese karate practitioners held a strict military seriousness. Traditional and violent. The Japanese guys never said it, but their silent disdain expressed, *Okay, white boy, you wanna learn our sport? Get on the mat...we'll teach you...*And they did.

He walked through the room smelling of sweat and pride to the doorway in the back leading to changing rooms. Stiv turned back into the dojo, faced the front where high on the wall the American flag's stars and stripes and the Japanese flag's rising sun proudly hailed side by side. Above the two flags, framed in deep mahogany-brown, was a picture of Grandmaster Arashiyama with his eternal locked-jawed frown of disapproval scowling down at the students. Because of his immense stature in the karate world, he was known as Arashiyama-Soke, *Soke* meaning *the head of the family, grandmaster.* A serious badass even at eighty years old.

No one paid attention to Stiv, but his action was mandatory dojo etiquette. The training room was a large, sparse room with wall-to-wall rubber mats and mirrored walls decorated with pictures of Sensei competing and fighting in the old days. Fields of golden trophies with red, white, and blue ribbons, medals bunched up in different corners. Bouquets of glory decorated the room in testimony of Sensei's many tournament wins and championships.

He turned down the hall to the changing room, pushing the door open to find Sam sitting there. The room reeked of reefer, or more accurately Sam did. The smell stuck to everything like skunk spray mixing with old sweat and strong cleaning solutions. Stiv liked the smell of marijuana except then; anything foreign or out of place was offensive to his senses. The normal stench of the room combined with weed was worse than usual, further aggravating his existence. The two old friends nodded to each other.

Stiv sat down and said, "I can't believe I answered your call. I should've locked myself in my room, listen to music all night. Instead I'm here in this stench."

"You're welcome and stop your whining, you pussy, and sitting in your room is really going to help you get through this. What you need is a good workout and sweat, fool," Sam said, not looking up from peeling dead skin from his hobbit-like gnarled feet.

Years of karate, yoga, and the ever-present dojo fungus had rotted his freaks-of-nature appendages into deformed slabs of veins, skin, and bone with toes. Amazingly, they still functioned as feet. Having one connect to your gut or upside your head sucked. Sam could deliver man-dropping kicks at will. He was tall and sleek, a bit older than Stiv but with a ripped body, every muscle in a state of perpetual flex, which Stiv both envied and found annoying. He was a gentleman and a tough competitor, like Sensei.

Thirty-five years before, he took a kick to the balls during a tournament, crushing his right testicle, forcing him to stay down on the mat for twenty agonizing minutes until he was carried off. He won the fight due to illegal contact. Everyone believed Kyoufu Sensei, a known racist American hater, kicked him in the groin intentionally. Sam should have been rushed to the nearest hospital ER but he refused medical attention. Instead, he waited forty minutes for his next fight even though he could barely walk. He stepped onto the mat and fought the best he could...and lost. One tough son of a bitch. After, they all went out drinking, getting hammered until the last train. Sam drank right along with the party complaining of nausea and stomach pain. No one paid attention. The next morning, his scrotum was the size of an overripe cantaloupe. Finally he was taken to the hospital where blood was drawn from his split testicle three times a day for five days without anesthesia. The long-needled syringe used for this procedure looked like a harpoon. He ended up losing the split testicle and was told he would never father children. As was often the case with modern medicine and doctors in general, they were wrong. He fathered five kids.

When they were suited up and ready to train, Stiv and Sam silently walked out of the changing room onto the unforgiving mat, bowing before setting foot. They were just in time to start the bow-in tradition. They lined up according to rank and seniority. Sam was first in line, an older *sempai*, or senior student, between Stiv and Sam, then eight students to Stiv's left and ten in the backline, all junior ranks, adults, and a few teens. Stiv stared straight ahead, not wanting to meet Sensei's judging eye nor see his own down-cast reflection in the front mirrors.

Sensei knew Stiv was hurting but was not sympathetic. Stiv expected no sympathy because no matter the circumstances, dojo rules were the same. If you could not give the training one hundred percent, then stay home. If you choose to stay home, you better have a damn good reason why. This was a traditional Japanese dojo in America.

They practiced *Shitoryu Karate*, founded in 1934 by Kenwa Mabuni in Okinawa, Japan. The style was an offshoot of the original Okinawan karate styles started in and around the thirteenth century. For the most part, all four of the major Japanese karate styles were the same, aside from stances and kata theory. Stiv considered karate glorified, highly polished street fighting, which was okay because he liked committing assault without getting thrown in jail.

The students were instructed to kneel in *seiza*, a traditional Japanese sitting style with one's lower legs and knees under the body. Until a practitioner got used to the position it was uncomfortable. Stiv used to painfully practice *seiza* for hours as a discipline.

Early in Stiv's karate career and first frigid Osaka winter in 1984, the dojo students were sitting in *seiza* for two painful hours on a freezing-cold ancient shrine stone floor. Arashiyama-Soke used this shrine annually for speeches. Arashiyama-Soke gave an incomprehensible speech after New Year's, droning on and on sitting in *seiza* himself the entire time chain-smoking cigarettes and extinguishing them into an ashtray on his right. As soon as he finished a smoke, Soke removed another from the pack next to the ashtray. The same sempai kneeling closest would jump up and light Soke's fresh smoke. He never missed a beat.

Stiv's legs froze to complete dead numbness. When the speech was finally over, he could not get up. Fortunately for his delicate pride, he was not alone. The torture of sitting like that for so long on the frozen stone floor was an endurance test, preparing him for the coming years of punishing training and annual shrine New Year's speeches. It took his legs forty pin-stinging minutes to straighten before he could make the painful, laborious walk out of the shrine toward the nearest bar for hot sake and cold beer. Arashiyama-Soke always paid the expensive bill.

Now, sitting in *seiza*, Stiv remembered that night because the pain in his legs screamed through his hips, ankles, and feet. A burning sensation just like the newbie pain back in 1984.

Withdrawals.

If he popped that pill, Stiv could sit in *seiza* for a week pain free. He was about twenty-six hours in. Peak physical discomfort time would hit at thirty to thirty-five hours. The emotional discomfort could last for months. He was nauseous and wanted to go home.

Sensei called the students to stand. They began warmups. Two hundred jumping jacks, stretching, two hundred sit-ups, each student counting ten. Over onto bellies for one hundred push-ups and back to a standing position. The sudden motion was making Stiv ill. He stared straight ahead, avoiding his reflection. Standing basics were next, consisting of punching in place and blocking practice. Each thrust of his arms sent nausea to his stomach like half-inflated balloons coming up his esophagus. He made the mistake of looking over at Sam, who was watching him, shaking his head in disapproval. There was no break between these exercises. Kicking practice was next with gut-wrenching repetition. They started with front kicks, one hundred with each leg. Then roundhouse and sidekicks ending with three different kinds of back kicks all in reps of one hundred. Afterwards, all members went to one side of the mat for moving basics, repeating all punches, blocks, and kicks but this time moving up and down the mat with full speed and power. Stiv's heart pounded like the intro to Gene Krupa's "Sing, Sing, Sing" drum solo.

"Move faster, stronger! Hit 'em!" Sensei yelled at everyone to smoke their imaginary opponent.

At 6 p.m., the class broke for a five-minute water break

before they started on katas. *Shitoryu* has more than sixty katas. Stiv knew the moves to about thirty, and was competent in none, at least at a level anyone above his rank would commend. But he loved the ancient forms of unarmed combat and practiced them hard and often. In the more advanced kata, eye-gouging, nose ripping, ear shredding, scrotum slapping, and throat crushing were all incorporated as well as the standard kicking, head butting, and punching. Glorified street fighting.

During the break, Stiv sat miserably alone waiting for the second half of the class to begin and with the will of King Neptune, end quickly. A ridiculous hope. He could hear Sam and Sensei talking and laughing but did not give a shit what they were saying.

Sensei called class to order. Everyone got back in line, waiting in *musubi dachi*, or ready stance.

"*Mokuso! Heian Shodan!*" Sensei called.

The room erupted with, "*OUUUSSUU! Heian Shodan!*" repeating the command to perform Heian kata number one of five, on count.

Sensei yelled, "*Yoi, ichi!*" The class responded by moving into the first block and waiting for the second command. The first move was turning left and center blocking. Stiv almost fell over and was sure he would vomit. He was clammy, nauseous, and unbalanced. They went through all five Heian katas twice. The first round was slow but with power, so Sensei could go around the class correcting everyone. While he adjusted each student everyone else had to hold their stance. Excruciating pain. When Stiv could get away with it, he dropped his stance to relieve the pressure in his legs, only to be caught by Sam's further disapproving eyes.

Stiv gave Sam his *why did I answer your phone call* look. Sam gave Stiv the finger.

At 6:20, kata training was finally over. Sensei shouted for everyone to put on fighting gloves, which were more for protecting knuckles than an opponent's face. There was no break except to put the gloves on. Sensei yelled for lines to form again. Once formed, he shouted for the front line to turn and face the back line. Stiv turned facing a cocky eighteen-year-old high school football player who wanted to be Bruce Lee. At 6'1" and 210 pounds, he was big, strong, and capable. He could take a punch as well as throw one. Two years of training earned him a green belt; next he would earn his brown followed by black if he continued another few years. Green and brown belts were most dangerous if they were powerful. They have something to prove without the skill to practice full force without making dangerous contact. Stiv considered grabbing another workout partner, which he could do if he wanted but did not want to tempt the ever-watching eye of Sensei.

He beat the piss out of this jock a few times but never intentionally hurt him. Stiv respected the jock's drive. It was all in the name of training anyway. The sparring was not supposed to be fighting, rather an opportunity to try new techniques, although the two aspects often overlapped. Full contact to face and head were forbidden with fists—but it happened constantly. Kicks could be as hard as the practitioner could throw to the head, face, and body. The groin was off-limits but painful contact happened there often. Stiv was in no mood to practice new techniques or even continue training. He wanted to lie down on the mat, curl into a ball, and die. Instead, he pushed himself, tit for tat with the jock. Even though Stiv was a geezer, the dojo knew he was fast, crafty, and could fight with long-term practiced skill. Sensei yelled *Hajime*, the command to begin sparring. The jock attacked with a quick one-two combo. Stiv was driven back, then a front kick scored hard just below his belt, buckling, and smashing him against the dojo wall with an attention-grabbing thud.

"What the hell was that, Stiv! Are you serious right now? Block and counter! Are you kidding me! What're you doing out there? Hit 'em!" Sensei yelled from across the room.

"OSU Sensei!" Stiv replied weakly, staring at his young opponent who had a smirk on his face, knowing he just scored a perfect kick on his sempai in front of Sensei.

Stiv moved back to center mat, sizing the jock up and anticipating his own response to the slight, albeit solid technique. The jock attacked again using the same move, an amateur mistake. Stiv was ready and blocked the one-two, side-stepping, catching the kick with his left arm, pulling tight against his side, right foot stepping in fast landing behind his opponent's left leg. Grabbing the front of the jock's dogi for control he pushed hard, upending him, slowly lowering him to the mat.

He could have let him fall hard. In a street fight, Stiv would grab the man's esophagus, nostrils, eye sockets—all power focused for maximum damage—then push him hard to the pavement like a rock.

Stiv put the surprised helpless jock down gently but authoritatively, holding tight to his dogi. Once flattened, Stiv did a mock kill shot, one-two! Left-right to the jock's head with his favorite fist style, snakehead, or *hebi te* in Japanese, his middle phalanx of each index finger reinforced with phalanx of each thumb. This strike was designed for eye sockets, pressure points, and solar plexus. He struck with an explosive *kiai* but did not make contact.

Only his point.

The jock, stunned at the speed and effectiveness of the technique, was on his ass. Stiv was shocked himself but showed only arrogance and swagger, both important parts of the karate mentality. Sensei saw the whole thing, then turned away when Stiv looked over for approval. Stiv gave the jock a hand up.

"Stiv Sensei," the jock asked excitedly. "Could you please teach me that move after class? It was killer."

As a fourth-degree black belt, Stiv was instructor-grade, taught often, and enjoyed coaching. He looked at the jock a moment, sizing him up. Suddenly a blind panic struck him out of nowhere in the region of his lower intestines. The snakes in his belly viciously fought to get out. He dashed to the back doorway, bowed out, then turned to the men's bathroom.

Kneeling on the disgusting piss-wet tile, no doubt the remnants of the eight-to-ten-year-olds' watery urine, he gripped the fetid, yellow-stained toilet bowl and vomited violently for the second time that day. White bile and pinkish lines of blood screamed from his guts, twisting and turning the liquid trying to fight through his *rectus sheath* and not happy about the recent kick it received. Equally as suddenly he felt another distressing and uncontrollable sensation, extreme pressure ready to explode. He stood, quickly dropping his dogi pants, pulled the top up, belt tips flapping around his face like two black butterflies dancing in the wind. He spun around and sat on the seat-up toilet, almost falling through, and shit out a long stream of vile intestinal funk that filled the small bathroom with an odor so noxious and foul Stiv could not believe the stench came out of his body. When he was done releasing, eyes shut tight, head down and arms wrapped around his knees like pre-plane-crash position, Stiv got himself together, cleaned what needed to be cleaned. Back to the floor, knees and elbows piss damp and nostrils assaulted. Sensei looked at him but said nothing verbally. He did not need to; his frown spoke volumes. Stiv lined up across from the jock, and they started fighting again.

An important aspect of karate was quick recovery from whatever the practitioner encountered. Tough it out. You had to be able to train and fight in any physical as well as mental condition, ready to rumble at any time. The redundancy of training a metaphor for life as well as self-defense on the street.

Like a good Boy Scout, always be prepared.

Stiv glanced at the clock on the wall, 6:33, finish time. He knew the jock backed off a bit so Stiv decided to go in hard, get some payback and administer a little painful reminder not to mess with Stiv Sensei in the future.

Stiv's idea was to inflict a bruise or two by feinting with a jab and shuffling in with a right, then a straight-arm punch with the left, driving the jock back against the wall. This would give him room to wallop him with a roundhouse kick upside his head. It did not work.

Stiv began his forward motion, firing a stretched-out right cross. The jock anticipated and planted his right foot back, left foot forward, throwing his own right cross hitting Stiv dead center chin, the crack sounding like a goblin-barker firecracker report dropping him like a sack of rocks. He was out cold.

Chapter 21

The Ride Home, The Man & The Other Man Who Lives Inside Me

7:00 P.M. Wednesday, July 5th, 2017

THE FEATHERLESS PTERODACTYL looked rust colored against the horizon and screamed its predator warning as it soared toward him. Waves were so big they washed the flat tops of the three stone platforms in the strange harbor Stiv was gazing out at. Cetacean blue ocean water sprayed in his face as he jumped for cover. The flying dinosaur's tail hit Stiv on his ribcage with a crack. He was hit with an actual wave that came over the cliff, drenching him. The seawater brought him slowly back from that scary place. He woke to uproarious, almost uncontrollable laughter.

From the dojo floor, Stiv looked sideways at Sam,

Sensei, and the rest of the dojo population. Sam and Sensei were laughing so hard they were almost crying, slapping their knees and holding their guts. Stiv's face was soaking wet from the water Sam threw on him. The front of his dogi was drenched. He felt like a deer might feel when hit by a car, not killed, but mangled and rolled by the undercarriage a few hundred feet and left for dead. His jaw hurt and liquid was pouring out his ear canal. He looked around the room and spotted the green belt jock staring at him. Stiv wanted to fade into silent oblivion.

"Do you need a hand?" Sam finally stopped laughing and asked.

"Not from you I don't, and what's so funny? Haven't you ever seen a guy get knocked out? How long was I out anyway? Lucky punch," Stiv said to no one.

"Hey, kid, I'll get you for this. You know that, right?"

"*OUUUSSUU*, Sensei!" the green belt shouted and bowed.

"So, what's so funny? Me being knocked out?" Stiv asked Sensei directly.

"No, it was the way you attacked *then* got KO'd. You got clocked! You dropped like a dead man and we were watching at the perfect time, saw it clearly. Almost as funny as when your ex-wife knocked you out that time in Osaka," he said, laughing again. "I can't believe I didn't have my camera rolling!" Sensei roared.

Stiv was nauseous and in pain. His body hurt like hell. A lot of the pain was withdrawal related. He would deal with that mentally, accordingly, and in time. He wished so badly that he had two 15-mg Oxycodone pills. Since he did not, Stiv decided to get up and try to walk tall, even though he just got his ass kicked by a green-belted jock.

He was dazed, but on his feet when Sensei called for

line-up. The class kneeled and bowed out. Stiv bowed to Sensei and Sam, got to his feet, and slowly walked to the doorway. He turned and bowed to the room. He did not say a word or look directly at anyone. In the change room, he grabbed his bag without changing and left. Sensei and Sam were talking in the middle of the mat. Students were working on kata with others hovering as Stiv passed them. He was oblivious to their existence and in a trance of tragic absurdity brought on by narcotic withdrawals and a solid knockout punch.

"*OOOSSSSUU*, Stiv!" Sensei shouted, directly demanding a formal farewell without saying it. He was deadly serious.

Stiv stopped and turned. Sensei was always serious in the dojo. Polite greetings and farewells to sempais, especially Sensei, were important formalities. You better bow to those above you in rank, especially Sensei. Stiv almost spaced this extremely mandatory dojo etiquette. Inner circle friends or not, disrespect in the dojo was inexcusable and met with disciplinary punishment in the form of pain. Even though they laughed their asses off when Stiv got KO'd and made that nasty remark about his ex-wife knocking him out, a true story, it was a bad idea to disrespect.

Stiv bowed deeply, not meeting any set of eyes. He turned to the edge of the mat and faced the front wall with the scowling photo of Arashiyama-Soke and bowed out. He could only think of going home, grabbing his bottle of Oxycodone, and getting normal again.

He knew Sensei, Sam, and Zander had his back one hundred percent in almost any situation except drug addiction. Weakness was not a part of the karate mentality or culture, not in the Osaka dojo or in Sensei's Mawguwa dojo. Forget about it.

His three lifelong friends would accept Stiv for just about whatever, but they would not agree or condone him being a pain med junkie. Stiv could expect no compassion or mercy from these three inner-circle friends. He also knew none of the three or all three at the same time had a problem kicking the shit out of him if necessary. Intervention karate style.

Stiv wondered if they knew how long he had been hooked on the pain meds. What was he thinking ... of course they knew.

They cautioned him about the long-term negative effects years ago. So Stiv gave them a few hits and they shut up. Zander never partook. Neither ever asked for the drug, nor did they try to score their own prescriptions even though both men lived their lives in daily pain. Stiv did not listen to anyone anyway. Moderation was the key, but like alcohol, he could not do the narcotics in moderation. All or nothing.

Stiv drove past the spot where earlier he visualized killing himself by driving off the Mawguwa Bridge.

Five years before in March 2014, months before he quit drinking, the dojo had a wild celebration after a promotion or something. Stiv could not remember the reason as the dojo never needed a proper reason to party and drink. They were at a local pub that employed scandalous free-pouring barmaids. Stiv had taken his daily ration of Oxycodone as well as some aspirin. Sensei, Sam, and Stiv shared a joint and were already pretty high before they sat down. He gave each a 15-mg blue bullet, adding to the volcanic buzz. None of them drank water after the sweaty workouts, which was not very smart. They preferred the extraordinarily refreshing qualities of ice-cold beer instead which was approximately 90% water anyway.

On that particular evening, they toasted with pints of Devil's Lake Lager. After the toast, Stiv switched to pint glasses of double Grey Goose and tonic. The good looking free-pouring blonde did an eight-count for his cocktails, 80/20, making for a fat Goose at five or six shots per glass. Before he stumbled to his car at 10:30 p.m., Stiv had consumed eight pints at eighteen dollars each. He was death-march wasted, felony DUI intoxicated, and also walked out on his tab.

He told the group he was going to the bathroom, a drunken white lie he had to tell since they would never let him drive in his wasted condition. He chewed a blue bullet in the driver's seat and dry swallowed before bolting out of the parking lot, heading back toward the West Side and home by the waiting Sound.

He gangster cruised through Mawguwa low in his seat, feeling like a jet fighter pilot, down the steep bridge onto the road that would take him back. A waxing gibbous moon bright in the cloudless sky motivated him to howl like the wolfman on a hunt. Pantera's "Cowboys from Hell" blared in the dim cockpit. It was a straight ride on the coastal road although he paid no attention, focusing more on keeping one eye closed to stop his vodka-generated double-vision.

He took the rundown entrance to the viaduct from 1st Avenue slated to collapse in the next big earthquake, which was not a question of if, but when. Once he was out from under the overhead he felt better, which lasted only a heartbeat because in his rearview mirror he saw the bright sparkling red and blue berries of the Highway Patrol's Police Interceptor. A deep-freeze harsh reality lit him up like bright prison spotlights during an escape.

This traffic stop was vastly worse than an 8.0-magnitude shaker. He might survive that. Stiv was finished, his life was over. He finally did it, decades of buzzed and drunk driving finally manifested against him and he was looking at a felony DUI charge. For added penalties a $10,000 fine, license suspension, and possibly an all-expense-paid vacation at the notorious county jail for an unspecified length of time.

He was screwed and had no choice but to drunkenly pull over onto the gravel litter-strewn shoulder. Stiv activated all circuits searching his Grey Goose-soaked brain for possible escape, something, anything. He had no intention of going to jail, again. He was almost too drunk to think or even panic but managed to roll the windows down. *Sober* was a distant planet a million miles away but he had to move the liquor-reeking air.

Suddenly, like a gift from the god Dionysus, he had a monumental revelation, a universal concept so grand and ingenious he felt on a level with Einstein, Newton, Elon Musk, and Steve Jobs. In his rearview mirror, he could see the police officer doing something in his cruiser, no doubt running Stiv's tags, which were clean. He took the opportunity to reach behind the passenger seat and grab a large bottle of hand sanitizer, his genius idea materializing. Also, on the floor tucked under the passenger's seat was his Model 38, locked and loaded, ready to join the party.

Possibly a horrendous surprise party with a fresh new note of terror.

With hand sanitizer bottle in his lap, other dark explosive frightening muzzle-flash images passed through his inebriated mind of another escape alternative. The Model 38's report providing Stiv's guiding light of freedom. A bloody surprise ending for the copper's evening tour and command, a violent murderous option facilitated by Stiv's trusty but apathetic .38 revolver and the opportunistic indifferent *other man who lived deep inside him.*

Stiv shook his head fiercely to separate himself from that *other man's* lunatic diabolical conclusion to the situation Stiv created. Wrenching anxiety overtook him but he was able to make the thoughts float away like blackish-gray smoke from a crematorium chimney.

He opened the hand sanitizer bottle and squirted a large amount of the smelly antiseptic on his pants and shirt, took a piece of gum from his console and put it in his mouth, then put the hand sanitizer bottle on the passenger seat. The fuzz was standing warily near the back of Stiv's car, not next to his window for security reasons, yet close enough. His right hand gripped the butt of his sidearm, in his left hand pointing at Stiv's red bloated face, a Maglite illuminating the scene. Cars screamed by like hypervelocity comets leaving light trails heading points south.

"Sir," the police officer shouted over the traffic noise. "Do you have any weapons in the car or on your person?"

"No, Officer, I do not," he shouted back, with lying desperation.

"Thank you. May I see your license, registration, and your proof of insurance," the police officer shouted again.

Stiv's hands were on the steering wheel together at the

metaphorical strike of midnight position for the copper to see.

"I have to go into my glove box and get my wallet out of my back pocket. Is that okay, Officer?" Stiv slurred.

"Yes. Just go slowly, sir."

Stiv got the requested documents and handed them to the copper, who was still slightly behind the driver's side window.

"Please wait in your car, sir."

"Yes, I'll do that, please be careful Officer, lots of crazy drivers out there," Stiv slur-shouted with the straightest of straight-man faces.

This was deadly serious business. Stiv watched the cop through his rearview mirror sitting in his cruiser performing some police duties. Stiv put his hands back on the steering wheel at the twelve o'clock position and waited for the second cruiser to show up, a sure sign his drunken dumb ass was going to the slammer. When the cop returned to Stiv's driver's side window he held his documents but did not offer them back. Instead, he leaned close to the open window and said, "Mr. Baker, have you been drinking tonight?"

Stiv hesitated. His inebriated brain sent out panicked distress signals like a sinking ship in a nor'easter. He knew he deserved to get busted down hard for drinking and driving. Driving while under the influence of narcotic pain medication as well, also illegal. A danger to himself and any innocent people barreling down the highway. Also, a loaded handgun under the passenger's seat waiting to be invited to the party. He was toast. However, self-preservation took over as it always did in Stiv's egotistical habitual mind.

"Why no, Officer, I have not. Actually I don't drink, sir,"

Stiv slurred, breathing Gray Goose-laced spearmint breath into the air.

"The reason I pulled you over, Mr. Baker, is because I witnessed you make three lane changes without using your indicator. Each time is considered a moving violation. Then when I asked for your information, I smelled a strong scent of liquor. So I ask you again, sir, have you had any liquor to drink tonight?"

Stiv knew he had nothing to lose, nothing at all. If he could dig his way out of the quicksand he stumbled into, he would try.

"Officer, I've already told you *no*. And I don't drink liquor. I think what you're smelling is this," Stiv slurred as he snatched the bottle of hand sanitizer from the passenger's seat handing it to the blue-fuzz through the opened window. "I spilled this crap all over myself at a red light before I got on the viaduct. I'm sorry about the lane changes without my indicator. Thank you for bringing it to my attention. I understand if you have to write me a ticket, sir."

The cop examined the bottle, smelled it, then removed the top and smelled it again. He replaced the top, squirting some in his hand smelling the liquid yet again. Finally, he returned the bottle to Stiv, who put it back on the passenger's seat. Then the second police car pulled up behind the first and Stiv's heart stopped beating.

A memory passed through Stiv's numb brain like an ice pick through his temple. In 1987, driving home from a gig with his guitar player Rik the mick, Stiv decked a Japanese highway patrolman on the Skyway heading south. He was pulled over for speeding. Of course, he was drunk beyond reason, Rik passed out in the passenger's seat. Stiv almost died that night going home from downtown Osaka, but he didn't. He also walked away after bitch-slapping the Japanese copper. Second time in his life but in different countries. The first time back in 1978 on his birthday.

"Okay, Mr. Baker. This is what I smelled. I'm sorry for any inconvenience."

Stiv's heart started beating again. The cop looked over at the newly arrived police car and held up four fingers to the heavens for the newly arrived cop to see, did a slash motion across his chest and the second car eased back into traffic, putting pedal to the metal and disappearing into the night like a space rocket.

"Thank you for your cooperation, Mr. Baker, and drive safely. Please be conscious of using your indicators in the future. Good night, sir," the cop said, handing him back his paperwork and license.

Stiv watched the officer walk back to his cruiser and get in. After a moment and with siren and lights blazing, he took off into the waiting night. Stiv sat on the side of the dark highway, hand sanitizer fumes invading his nostrils. Cars screaming by heading south. Before charging back into traffic and home, he hit the play button, Deep Purple's "Highway Star" filling the car and his head. A song he associated with Mitch all those years ago driving to the Planting Fields.

Digging into his pocket, he removed and popped the blue bullet and chewed, dry swallowing. Then he tried to remember if he had any cold beer at home or did he need to stop at the store?

Yes, Hedone, goddess of debauchery, was looking out for him that lucky night three years before and Stiv was glad he quit drinking altogether. He could not believe he drove away unscathed from that life-destroying traffic stop back in his personal days of wine and roses. But he did.

His jaw pulsated, sharp pain radiated with every racing heartbeat, about 240 beats per minute, and even though he was harshly sober, driving was a challenge. He was sweating heavily with the AC on high. Maybe he would pick up some Jack Daniel's to ease his pains and emotions. He could quit drinking anytime, he proved that. Alcohol was an excellent anesthetic and he really needed a drink. He drove past the market, his willpower winning that battle. Now close to home, he thought about the day's painful events.

Day One of his narcotic withdrawal adventure was a state of panicked, apprehensive shock. Day Two was approaching faster than a speeding blue bullet with all the fun of a group of condemned spirits contracting the plague. Day Three was waiting around the corner with days four and five, fuck! His mind screamed like an angry banshee chasing terrified children through midnight mist.

Stiv considered food. He had not eaten anything since the chocolate Whoppers the stupid duggie was probably digesting at that very moment. The thought made him gag. He was not hungry, but he was thirstier than ever before. Stiv could not wait to wash down those pills with an ice-cold Coke. Then he would drink another and perhaps another. He might eat some Hershey's Whoppers for dinner too. It would be a sweet pain-free night.

Chapter 22

Interpretation of Dreams, Night One

7:45 P.M. Wednesday, July 5th, 2017

FINALLY, in front of the condominium, Stiv was so stiff he could barely get out of his car. There was a knot on his chin and his spinal column would not turn as if he were wearing an invisible brace. He thought his neck muscles might be sprained while his ankle joints were cramping, as was his stomach. Oxycodone was willing and waiting to perform its magic on his head, take away all his blue torture. When he got up to the fourth floor, he leaned his forehead against the solid wood door of the condo whispering to himself, "This really sucks. I'm getting too old for this shit."

The realization of his life, his pain and misery, came flooding into his brain like a bullet train through the center of his head, loud and echoing. Everything was his fault, his and only his. Every negative reality. He wondered if this was a moment of clarity they talked about in AA. Perhaps the shot to his jaw rattled some badly needed good sense into his head. The pain and nausea, the trouble at the pharmacy, the fight with Azar, all the fights with his wife, his addictions, and the loss of jobs. They were all his creations, dreadfully expensive investments that failed. This fact slapped him across his face so hard he thought it would knock his eyeballs out. Then without warning the condo door swung open. Stiv lost his balance and fell into the foyer in a painful sweaty heap. He stayed down like a weighted corpse. His wife jumped out of the way just in time. She was equally surprised by him falling into the doorway like a cadaver in an old, haunted house movie.

"What were you doing in the hall, Stiv? How long have you been out there? You scared me and haven't changed your clothes, you're all sweaty. Are you all right?" she demanded.

She stood towering over him like a triumphant gladiator waiting for a thumbs-down from the spectators. Then she would finish his bitch-ass off with a dull longsword through his heart.

"I'm fine, sweetie pie," Stiv lied from the floor, his voice muffled. He landed arms first so his face was buried in his sweaty dogi sleeves. "Don't I look alright?" he asked the floor, his voice barely audible.

"No, you don't. Can you please get up so I can close the door? Go take a shower, you stink, but first wipe up all that sweat," his wife stated.

She walked away, not waiting for him to rise from the dead. He glanced up to see her fine ass switching in blue pajama bottoms. She did not see the painful purple-green goose egg pulsating on his chin.

Stiv did as he was told and got up and closed the door. He wondered if he should have even bothered. There was a sweaty imprint of his body on the floor like a chalked homicide crime scene. He kicked off his shoes before walking into the carpeted living room. The wife had retreated to her studio where he heard her madly rearranging, water running and the sound of paintbrushes clinking against glass jars sounding almost musical. He was glad she had her own sink for cleaning the art supplies. He went directly to his desk and grabbed his bottle of lifesaving Oxycodone and tipped out three magic pills into his moist palm. The sweat imprint on the foyer floor could wait. Next, he dashed to the refrigerator and snatched an ice-cold can of Coke, popped the top, and drank deeply, finishing the carbonated water, sugar, caffeine, phosphoric acid, natural caramel flavor, and secret ingredients in a mega-guzzle. The drink was shockingly delicious and he thoughtfully considered this.

Only two people on the planet knew the secret ingredients that John Pemberton invented over 130 years ago out of coca leaf and kola nuts, a fruit native to Africa. The original recipe is locked in a vault in Atlanta. The company still used coca leaf extract and was only slightly different from the ingredients in crack cocaine. Pemberton's delicious invention was introduced to the public in 1886. Stiv wondered if Pemberton ever imagined how successful his product would be. He also wondered how the hell he knew so much about Pemberton and Coca-Cola.

He crushed the can and emitted an earth-shaking belch that rattled the kitchen fixtures and utensils but fortunately did not summon his wife. He opened the fridge and craned another can and went back to his desk, still holding the three blue bullets in his left hand when he sat down.

Looking out at the night, at the Sound with shimmering lights dotting the expanse like stars in an endless universe, he lowered his gaze to the three alluring hypnotic pills in his palm. They represented three-quarters of his daily prescribed dosage. Just the knowledge of having the tablets and being able to consume them had gotten him home. The drugs had been his driving force for the long painful ride, the embarrassment at the dojo, all his grief and despair. Like a donkey pulling the cart by following the carrot on a stick out of reach. The tablets were blue hope in pill form. Stiv's junkie hope. He continued staring at the meds while his mind screamed garbled disjointed intel. Although these pills were his salvation, his happiness and relief from pain, the clinking and chaotic reverberations from his wife's studio brought him back to reality. The drugs were, in fact, his enemy. He could hear the pills calling him, promising soothing relief, trying to convince him to use their magic elixir to quench his misery, just as Beta the dyke said they would. In his mind each tablet had a different flim-flam voice, a comforting friendly speech that he wanted to trust. They were definitely his friends. They would not lie to him...but whispered encouragement in his mind:

Pill One: *"Come on, Stiv, you don't have to be afraid of us. We're here to help you. Don't worry, we'll figure out how to get more of us. Forget that foreign pharmacist bitch. She doesn't have your best interests at heart, we do. Trust us."*

That sounded like infallible logic. Why should he be fearful of something that had made him so exuberant for so long? They should know how to procure more of themselves, right? Ha! No way the Persian witch wanted to support him, no way. But then again, why was he sitting here feeling like bitter-cold death?

Pill Two: *"We're on your side, bro. We want you to get back to normal. You haven't had a hug and kiss from us for almost thirty-five hours. Aren't you feeling like shit? You look like shit, I can tell you that. But we can help, we're your best friends. And that's some wallop you took on the chin, must hurt like hell. You don't have to look or feel this way, you know? Your solution is in your hands. Just take us already, Stiv."*

"Just take us, huh?" Stiv whispered. "Hmm, there's something frighteningly wrong here."

Pill Three: *"Yeah, Stiv, are you worried about your wife? Look, if she hasn't left you yet with all the bullshit you've already put her through she ain't never gonna leave you. Of course she doesn't want you to be pain-free, she's your wife, man! And she's a Gemini, born to torture your ass. Just take us already. Give us twenty minutes and you'll feel like a brand-new man, all happy and healthy. Then you can go take a shower, talk sweet to your wife, and maybe get some loving. Wouldn't that be nice?"*

Well yes, that would be nice. And he was worried about her. Just because she had not left him yet didn't mean she wouldn't leave him if he didn't get his life together. Then in what nightmarish dimension would he find himself? Stiv would never believe she did not want him pain-free, that was bullshit and he did not appreciate false intel from so-called friends. She was undeniably a Gemini woman, that much was true. The pills did not sound like friends on his side though. And what the hell is normal anyway? Yes, he felt like shit, but that was because he'd trusted these blue pills for so long, allowed them to invade his world like creatures from a dark and evil planet. He did not need to be reminded how much crap he put the wife through. And Stiv never liked sexual references towards her by anyone but himself and maybe Zander. He was getting pissed, friends or not. Stiv could take the pain on his chin and body but he was starting to believe he could not take the emotional pain inflicted by these narcotic enemies. They were not his friends, Beta the dyke was right, fuck these pills!

He closed his hand around the drugs, squeezing, silencing the deceitful voices in his head. He brought his fist to his heated forehead, the side of his thumb and index finger touching his feverish flesh. He gripped the pills as hard as he could but they would not crush. He did not just want to pulverize them, he wanted to kill them.

He got up, stomped to the kitchen, and held his hand over the sink letting the pills free-fall like lemmings off a cliff into a churning sea. They landed on the cold dry metal basin of the inner sink, clinking, bouncing around like wild pinballs on the clear-coated Game of Life's playfield. Stiv abruptly junkie-panicked and straight away plucked all three pills out, death-saving the bullets before one or all fell down the black-forever gobble-hole drain, lost and drowned forever. His face was red with both anger and fear, his chin swollen, painful, and purple. He was suddenly very hot in the cool kitchen. His usual sparkling green eyes were tired and bloodshot red, looking as if in the tight grip of a bad allergy attack. His damp dogi stuck to him with fresh sweat, then he was cold, but drips of perspiration formed, running down his forehead into his eyes, adding to his newly secreted psychic tears of sadness. Was he having a panic attack because he tried to kill his friends? He held the innocent pills close, cradled them to his heart like lost scared puppies, reassuring them, calming them, and in his mind he thought— *my precious*. He wanted the pills to forgive him. How could he have doubted their intentions? Back at his desk he replaced the drugs into their safe bottle and placed the bottle into his safe cigar box, the cigar box Woodrow Clemons gave him forty-nine years ago when the battered wounded hero returned from the Vietnam War all fucked up.

Head down alone at his desk, Stiv slowly looked up hoping to get a glimpse of the Sound, perhaps see the moon's reflection. Instead, he saw himself in the sliding glass door. Or was it him? A strange man stared back, moving when Stiv moved, stooped and disheveled, wearing a dogi like Stiv's. Suddenly the stranger began to laugh a deep sardonic laugh of the deranged. Stiv tried to stand like the man in his reflection stood. His sweet wife appeared next to him; if he could see her in the reflection, so could the other. Then her arms were around him and she whispered, whispered promises of love.

He woke alone in his damp cold dogi feeling deep despair. He was an entirely different animal. Still sitting at his desk, the lights were out and only he was in the reflection. No one else.

In the dead hush of midnight, Steven Huffam Baker knew the troublesome hallucinations were due to his withdrawals. He also knew, like a hopelessly frightened lunatic in an asylum, he was completely and soundly losing his mind.

It was 1:35 a.m., Day Two. After getting up from his desk and coming to terms with his distorted narcotic personality traits, he took 20 mg of Valium from his impressive V supply. Ironically, the Valium was blue as well and he put them aside.

Yes, he knew Valium was a narcotic. Yes, he knew Valium was addictive. Yes, he knew he was substituting one narcotic for another, but he was not addicted to Valium, not yet anyway. He needed help from somewhere, anywhere, everywhere, and nowhere. Time was running out like the dismal death row inmate with no more last-hour appeals.

In the bedroom he took off his funky dogi, put it in the laundry basket, and took a long hot shower, standing under the spray and leaning against the wall, softly head-butting the moldy tile. After washing away the negatives of the day he put on clean boxers and a bleached white T-shirt. From his medicine cabinet, he took out an unopened bottle of Nyquil Nighttime Extreme Flu Relief, cherry-flavored: 10% alcohol, 30% Dextromethorphan, or *Dex*, if you are street-cool.

This would be his nightcap. The pills were calling from the other room from their green bottle confinement. He was trying to ignore their generous offers, determined to quit. He hoped Valium, Dex, and sleep would get him through that first appalling darkness. Of course, he had the rest of Day Two to deal with. He got the two V's from his desk and popped them, chasing them down with a double shot of Nyquil. The blood-red syrup tasted wonderful but the medicine did not relieve his violent attack of narcotic hunger. He got into bed and turned off the lights, hoping his wife would not bother him, not even for sex, which was as out of character for Stiv as the night sky being made of puffy white marshmallows. As soon as his head hit the soft pillow, deep sleep directed him down like a dead man in a cold morgue. Dextromethorphan and diazepam were perfectly lethal sleep inducers to reach subterranean REMs.

Stiv stood in front of the dream-world factory where he was the general manager. He'd been happy working here even

241

though it was in the most dangerous part of the Middle District. The night air was warm and silent.

He walked into the building where he could see many changes. His assistant manager greeted him, explaining a new wing had been added to the older building, although the new construction was not a new wing or addition, but rather another part of the building they didn't know about. She suggested Stiv inspect the new area because she was too busy. She said a trusted employee had died in the new wing recently. A violent death. Her mouth moved, no words came out, but Stiv heard her clearly.

He walked through his office to a wall with a hallway cutaway off on the left. As soon as he turned into the hall he saw everything was covered in crimson blood. He started up the staircase that appeared before him. On the blood-soaked first landing were severed human heads cleanly lopped off, their faces in eternal screams. Arms, legs, and feet were strewn about. There were naked male and female torsos, armless and legless, severed faces grimacing. Stiv started up the next flight and heard a woman screaming. He kept walking. The second landing was covered with human noses, breasts, ears, eyes. The human meat looked like it had been cut with razor-sharp instruments. The walls dripped with human blood. Stiv continued up.

At the next bloody landing, a large room with wires hanging from the ceiling, and old dead fixtures waited in frightening silence. The metallic iron smell was as thick as an invisible veil stifling his breathing. There were no lights, but the room illuminated a scene of bloody carnage that left a wide swath of sticky pools. Stiv heard screaming then, very loud and very near. A large nude woman ran past, ignoring Stiv. She had deep slash marks all over her body and face, blood spurting freely. A huge Pacific Islander ran past Stiv in pursuit of the terrified woman, bare-chested and wearing a grass skirt that made whooshing sounds as he moved. He waved a gleaming machete at the air, shouting in an indigenous tongue.

Just past Stiv the huge man stopped, turned to look at him. Stiv tried to run but his feet were stuck in the fresh steaming coagulating blood that gave off an iron smell he'd not smelled before. With all his will, Stiv finally got his legs moving, running, running for his life, down bloody halls, through rooms scattered with body parts as the huge man chased him screaming his native oaths. Stiv knew this savage meant to cut him up. No begging, no reasoning, and no pleading. He meant to kill Stiv slowly with savage complacency.

He turned a corner to find the bloody nude woman on her knees, the huge man standing above her holding her hair, his blade sideways in her closed mouth, terror in her eyes. The massive man smiled a lecherous smile then looked down at the woman, whose eyes were on Stiv. The man slowly pulled the blade across her mouth, slicing through her cheeks all the way to the end of her throat. Her eyes bulged. He removed the blade as her hands came up to her mouth, blood pouring down. The man ran at Stiv so fast there was no time to react. The blade came down, slicing his skull wide open, running through his neck stopping at his shoulder bones. Stiv saw all this as his head parted in two perfect slices.

He watched from each side as the woman fell face first onto the bloody floor.

Stiv woke at 5:31 a.m., according to the digital clock on his bedside table. His dream was traumatic, and Stiv was glad he *was awake. He could see his wife's sleeping form in the full moonlight shining through the opened curtains. Her presence was reassuring. He thought of waking her for a hug. He needed compassion and warmth after that nightmare. As Stiv's brain forced the shadowy blood-soaked dream away, he realized the moon should've traveled to another hemisphere by then. He looked around the room again more closely. The bedroom was different. The mysterious shrouded veil of shimmering moonlight was making the room strobe in abstract illumination.*

He turned back to his wife. Her innocence in sleep, the soft sound of her breathing, made him long to hold her. Stiv put his hand on her shoulder, ever so gently shaking her sleeping form. She moaned softly in protest, not a protest that said, leave me alone. It was her "I'm sleeping but I'll wake for you, darling" moan. He loved her so much. She moved, positioning herself to sit up, slowly turning toward him. Stiv was met with the nude slit-faced woman from his night terror. The woman began to scream, a ghastly obscene echoing wail that resonated through his head. Her mouth sliced ear-to-ear gave her the most obscene grin. His bed, walls, and floor were bright crimson in the moonlight. He tried to escape out the door but the huge bare-chested man in the grass skirt ran at him from the doorway screaming savagely with his blood-soaked machete overhead, prepared to slash!

Stiv awoke covered in sweat, his heart pounding a mile a minute. He took a deep breath and looked at the clock; it was only 2:30 a.m. and his wife was not sleeping next to him. He was in a tangled spider web of blankets and sheets, his sweat-drenched clothes stuck to him like a second skin.

He rubbed his eyes and took another deep breath. As he woke, the pain started, then nausea. The depression was close behind, so he got up and went to his wife's studio door. He needed to know she was safe. She was on the phone and laughing with one of her girlfriends in Japan. Stiv loved hearing her laugh. He listened for a moment; they were talking about an upcoming show where she would be showing some of her paintings—but not his favorites, he would greedily see to that.

Painfully he made his way to his desk, got 30 mg of Valium, stumbled slowly back to his bathroom, where he poured another shot of Nighttime Extreme Flu Relief into the plastic-provided cup to chase the pills down. In the kitchen, he got a cold bottle of water out of the fridge and drank some. He shuffled back to his room with the plastic bottle in hand, got back in bed, and put the cold-water bottle on his bruised chin. He slowly drifted back into pitch-black oblivion.

Chapter 23

Sometimes Better Not to Know
3:00 A.M. Thursday, July 6th, 2017

HIS DREAMS WERE GENERALLY fragmented reproductions of memories and possibly past lives. But you don't know you were dreaming until you wake up, so who really knows for sure.

Stiv and his wife went down south to stay with Pops, who was living with yet another wife. She was a nice generous woman who loved his father, which had to draw questions and raise red flags. Nevertheless, Stiv and his wife liked her. Pops new wife was also a pill-junkie like Stiv, although her ailments were real. She readily shared her excellent meds and kept the house stocked with excellent scotch, vodka, and gin, securing a place in Stiv's heart.

The large horseshoe-shaped house was surrounded by alligator-infested ponds. Its master bedroom was in one wing and guest rooms were in the other. In the center was the living room with kitchen behind that and offices on either side of the front door. A well-planned well-situated luxury home Stiv and his wife enjoyed very much.

Both Civil War armies marched through the land 150 years before. Marching through sweltering mosquito-rich swamplands had to be only a step above traveling through incomprehensible hell.

Arriving late the first evening, they went to bed just after the dead hush of midnight, giving the witches, ghouls, goblins, and ghosts time to awake and haunt. Stiv woke rough with moonbeams on his face, his tummy quaking, mouth dry. As usual, he needed a few moments to clear his head from the narcotic-booze-fueled state of confusion he generally woke in. When his eyes focused in the dimly moonlit room he saw a tall pale man in the open doorway clad in a black suit and white shirt. The man's face was pale as death. He stood staring at Stiv and his sleeping wife for a minute that felt like hours. Then he slowly floated backward. Stiv went back to sleep, immediately forgetting the nightmare, which didn't scare him so long as he could wake up...

The next day they toured the old southern town, enjoying southern cooking, southern liquor, and ingesting both Oxycodone and Oxycontin. They were back at the horseshoe and in bed by 11 p.m. Stiv had the exact same dream, and then the next night, and the night after that. Always the same statuesque man, same death mask face, standing, looking at them then floating away. On the fifth night, Stiv told his wife about the possible manifestation and she freaked out.

"Why did you wait four nights to tell me?" she wanted to know. "Does he talk and make facial movements or just stand there?"

"No, he just stands there looking at us but his eyes don't move. I think he wants to speak but I don't know. It's only a dream, you know? I'm not seeing ghosts in my Pops house."

"I'm not so sure. I'm staying awake tonight, I wanna see," she said excitedly.

Stiv wasn't so sure how this would play out. He woke to see the tall black-clad ghastly pale-faced man standing in the doorway again. His wife had dozed off and was sleeping peacefully. He turned back to the doorway to find the man already gone. He went back to sleep and when he woke his wife wasn't there. Stiv got up and walked to the kitchen, where his wife and stepmother were chatting. A table full of food was prepared and waiting in the breakfast nook drenched by morning sun.

"I thought you were going to stay up last night to see the man in the doorway?" *Stiv asked after sitting.*

"I did stay up and I saw him, Stiv. You were sleeping, and—I know who he is," *she said, looking from him to his stepmom.*

"That's right, Stiv," *his stepmother continued, picking up where his wife dropped off.* "The man you're seeing or dreaming about comes in different forms, sometimes in dreams, sometimes in this dimension. I don't know why he manifests when he does. But don't be frightened, he's just curious."

"Curious about what? And who is he?" *Stiv asked, anxious for answers.*

"Is this him?" *his wife asked, handing Stiv a faded black-and-white Polaroid.*

It was him.

Same suit and same deathly pale complexion, but in the Polaroid the man was lying in an elaborate coffin, eyes closed, arms crossed over his chest. As Stiv studied the picture, the man's eyes snapped open. Stiv blinked and the man's eyes were closed again. Because he wasn't sure if he'd just seen the dead man's eyes open, he handed the picture back to the wife, saying, "Yup, that's him. Who is he?"

They all looked at each other a moment, then the step-

mother said, "Why don't you two come with me, I want to show you something. I've already explained this to your wife, Stiv, but we were waiting for you to get up so I could share this family secret. Ready?"

"I am," Stiv's wife said. "Are you ready, Stiv darling?"

"Sure, let's see this family secret."

"We're going back to the room you sleep in. You haven't seen the man anywhere else in the house, right?" the step-mother asked Stiv.

"No, just in the doorway. Who is he?"

"My last husband. He died three years ago," she said. She got up without another word.

Stiv and the wife got up and followed her. The step-mother ambled back through the hall to their room and went in. At the closet she pushed the sliding wooden door aside and half-stepped in, reaching high on a shelf and taking down an ornate sealed vase.

"These are his ashes. We've always kept them here and I think he wants to be sure they're safe. He comes to look almost every night. I'm sorry I didn't tell you about his urn being stored in this closet, but he was always comfortable here. He died in this room, in that very bed you sleep in," she said.

Lovingly, she stared at the urn she held in her wrinkled claw-like hands. Her face began to contort and change to a hideous monster so vile Stiv and his wife were unable to move.

"I overdosed the bastard before he finished that ridiculous will he wrote me out of. You and your wife are next you snotty brats!" She shrieked, then lunged for them.

Stiv slept until 9 a.m., waking hungover and ill. The bottle of water at his side was warm. He drank it anyway and saw he was still alone. That was fine. Stiv did not want to think about anything, do anything, say anything, hear anything, see anyone. Too, dreams are often deceitful, an important fact to remember.

The two dreams lamented through his mind like sad secret whispers. There was no reason to get up. He thought of staying in bed all day or until death, whichever came first. He needed to pee badly and thought about the power the narcotic pain medication had over him. He was their slave, their bitch. He did not mind being a slave to his wife, but these stupid pills. Really? Seriously?

Stiv was getting closer to the tragic absurdity of his addiction as he reached thirty-nine hours without Oxycodone. He studied his dread and dreams, his pain and anxiety, leading to real unhappiness. How could he do this to himself? Did God hate him this much or was the universe testing him? These were thoughts that immediately came to mind, but they were not the right ones. As always, his mind shifted to his wife and he saw her hair and clouds and stars in his mind. Her beauty and love was a force of nature he needed to absorb, channel for his own strength, but where the hell was she? He could use a hug or two, perhaps some energizing compliments. He would not wait too long because the moment might become eternal and he did not have that long. Stiv went to the bathroom, then back to bed alone, pulling the covers up to his bruised chin like a scared child after seeing a phantom in the mist.

His thoughts shifted again. He forcefully moved the overflow of thoughts away from the dazed state he woke. The asinine TV commercials on every channel flooded his brain, causing his central nervous system to beg for narcotics. As a mental workout he attacked the nauseating rehab commercials. The talking-heads in Stiv's mind spoke in a Brooklyn gangster accent to whoever was watching, and listening:

You can never quit your pain medication addiction alone, ever! Forget about it. If you try, you'll fail. Forget about that too. And without the proper medical care and supervision you might die or run the risk of long-term addiction and life-threatening withdrawals, or worse, you might become a politician. Addiction is a disease and you can't quit a disease! No one can quit a disease alone. You need our help. Call now, loser! Have bank statements, social security number, and credit cards ready!

When the talking-heads in his mind were finished, one of those micro-machine speed-talkers stated:

Have bank statements, social security number, and credit cards ready! We take money orders, cashier's checks, and all insurances! Car titles and home deeds! We'll also consider wampum! Available in every state with no exceptions! We do not guarantee recovery from narcotic pain medication or anything else! We only guarantee you will pay and pay big time, you sap!

Stiv was pissed at the scenario his brain created. Plus, he knew he might not quit his own addiction for the second time. He failed the first time due to defections in the ranks of his willpower, but that did not make the smiling moronic talking-head shysters right.

Stiv quit drinking alcohol, dammit, and that was something. Unless you counted the ten percent alcohol in the Nyquil Nighttime Extreme Flu Relief, cherry flavored. As for the two dreams that slithered through his subconscious, Stiv blamed the Valium and Dextromethorphan. Talk about a pharmaceutical hypnagogic hallucination... At least he slept and woke from the negative dimension. Anyway, he was positive he would quit his narcotic addiction next time if defeat overtook him on his current long and winding road.

So due to extreme overconfidence, he decided to pop a blue bullet.

He got up slowly and painfully like his bones were grinding together suffering through the retribution his body meted on him and went to the kitchen then to his desk. He took one tiny, insignificant 15-mg Oxycodone pill out of the bottle and touched his tongue to the bitter blue bullet.

Eat me, eat me, eat me, you bitch! The pill shrieked its deceitful, malicious seductions. He tasted its acrimonious flavor of hopelessness.

Codeine methyl enol ether offered a comfortable oblivion but at what price? The chemical taste was in realty mean and stubborn and like biting into a sheet of burnt tinfoil. The flavor didn't used to bother him, what was happening?

He let the blue bullet rest on his moist tongue. This caused his mesolimbic reward circuits to immediately activate releasing a minuscule amount of dopamine he did not feel or acknowledge.

"The hell with you," he whispered to the pill. "What kind of friend are you? I don't have friends who treat me like this, hurt and lie to me, die," he whispered sternly, dropping the damp pill back into its secure green bottle.

"Alright for you, Stiv Baker!" The pill screamed in his head.

He had not eaten anything except chocolate which he vomited up, and knew he needed something more substantial. He was dying for anything sweet. He made coffee, added three heaping teaspoons of sugar and whipping cream to a large mug, making liquid coffee candy. He toasted whole-wheat bread to crispy brown and slathered sweet cream butter, then spread Acacia honey made from Black Locust blossoms. The sweetest honey the store sold. Supposedly the bees cried when they gave up their regurgitated monosaccharides. Stiv hated bees, but he loved their honey...

He ate two slices and then prepared and ate two more. Drank his coffee and took his vitamin-aspirin cocktail, no Oxycodone. His stomach was knotted, his chin was sore, and he hurt all over, but the life-sustaining food seemed to help slightly. The knot on his chin pissed him off more than the pain. Pride had more nerve endings than his mandibular prominence apparently.

He showered off the unpleasant smell of the nightmares that accompanied his Dex and Valium night terrors, got dressed, and grabbed his gear for the unpredictable day to come. As usual, he collected his wallet, the Model 38, and speed loader with five extra rounds. He put the switchblade in his pocket and Rolex Submariner on his left wrist. Topping off his fashion for the day, he pushed his skull ring on his right ring finger. In a small ice chest he put a couple of boxes of Whoppers and a six-pack of Coke from the fridge. Then added ice. He had no idea where he was going or for what. He did not want to expose his wife to his misery, he was sure of that. She would be compassionate, but deep down she would see him as lame and weak. Which was true because junkies are lame and weak.

As far as she was concerned, drugs, liquor and porn, or

any other addiction controlling someone's life was a foolish way to live, plain and simple. She admittedly had a chocolate and ice cream addiction she did not like to talk about, but her sweet indulgence was forgivable.

Her studio door was closed, although the cool sign had been removed. Stiv left the condo and went down to his car, packed the gear, and drove off down the beach road. There was a wide berth on the right-side people used for U-turns or to park and walk across the street to the beach. Stiv slowed to a stop and put the Mustang in neutral. His head hung in deep contemplation. It was 10:31 a.m. He was looking out at the Sound, his emotions singing and lulled to dolomite-blues, when his cell phone rang. He figured it was the wife but he was wrong. The digits were local though unrecognizable, probably a wrong number or a douche-bag telemarketer.

"Hellloo?" Stiv moaned miserably into the phone, sounding like Carl the pain pill junkie.

"Hello, is this Mr. Steven Baker? This is Dee Rett calling from Ocean Blues Jewelry," a confident, rhythmic voice said. "Do you have a moment to chat?"

Stiv was caught off guard and dead silent. He momentarily forgot he had no job, no income, no insurance. He emailed out a bunch of resumes the week before, one of which was to Ocean Blues Jewelry, a store associated with the biggest jewelry company in the world.

He could only think about his drugs. Waiting for him to return from a violent and bloody war, his sad and lonely lost lover in waiting.

"Ye... Yes. This is Stiv—Steven Baker," he forced out, trying not to sound as bad as he felt.

"I am the district vice president for Ocean Blues Jewelry and I received your resume. I was wondering if you would be available to meet me for an interview today?" she asked with genuine interest.

"Oh, I'm so sorry," he said, drooling a little. "I'm booked solid today," he lied, wiping the saliva from his lips and chin with his free hand.

"Well, I have time slots available tomorrow or even the following day. Are you interested in working with us, Mr. Baker? According to your resume, you have extensive jewelry sales and retail management experience. You might be a perfect fit for our fast-track store manager or multi-store manager training program," she stated. "Would you be interested in meeting with me?"

Stiv was momentarily lost in Zombieland with no sign of Emma Stone. And for a few moments also lost in translation watching the local murder of crows chasing a flock of dizzy seagulls through the blue summer sky out over the Sound. There may have been the corpse of a fish they were fighting over but Stiv was not sure.

"Mr. Baker?"

"Yes—yes, I'm very interested and thank you for calling me. I'm so sorry, I've been having trouble with my phone. It seems to cut in and out. I can meet tomorrow late in the afternoon if that works?" Stiv hoped by the morrow's late afternoon he'd be over the mountaintop and closer to the plains of normality, rather than the current gates of delirium that encased and surrounded him.

"Great, how about we meet at 4:30 p.m. at the Rivers Mall, the Perfect Bean coffee shop on the second floor?"

"That will be fine," Stiv said, knowing the place but wanting to vomit from the gut-twisting withdrawals. The idea of work made him want to puke even more. "Thank you again. Do you need me to bring anything?" Stiv asked, totally miserable when he should have been happy with a potential job offer on the table.

"No, sir. Just bring an open mind and those sales skills you listed. See you tomorrow then, Mr. Baker."

"Yes, see you tomorrow...and thank you, Ms. Rett."

Stiv hung up, feeling wasted and wounded knowing perfectly well it wasn't what the moon did. Was he getting what he asked for?

Fatigued, and paranoid, the line *double-secret probation* kept going through his head, over and over like a dry paint-brush painting a wall. No idea why. And he wanted a hit of Oxy like a condemned man clings to life and begging instant sympathies. But he would receive no reprieve. Slowly he drove out of the stopping spot and headed down the beach road, up the tree-lined hill to his favorite market very close to his ex-doctor's office, Crystal, and the Persian witch, Azar.

He decided to buy a small bottle of booze to get through the long dismal day. He figured he would do his nightmare-inducing Valium and Dex cocktail again to sleep that night, forget the night-terrors so long as he woke up. Whiskey was a great time killer, he knew this from previous death-march benders from his drinking days. He thought his old friend Jack Daniel's would patiently listen to his problems and help him get through future desperate moments in time, a radical calculation. JD always listened in the past, always understood without any rejection. That is what old friends did, with compassion and without judgment.

Stiv parked across two well-marked parking spaces for no other reason than he did not notice nor care. He went into the market and was immediately assaulted by the rotting stink of the many kinds of cheese the market sold and merchandised at the front of the store. It was delicious torture; the ripe vomit smell made him want to barf again. Rotting coagulating milk proteins produced a thick invisible stench-curtain, blocking life-sustaining oxygen and making him gag as he walked through the polluted air. His gagging did not dissuade him from striding over to the liquor section and grabbing a pint of Jack Daniel's Old No. 7 off the shelf.

Together, JD and Stiv walked past the offending cheese section.

"Good morning, ladies," Stiv mumbled to the smelly displays, causing Jack Daniel's Old No. 7 to laugh out loud at the old and timeless blind man's joke. They continued snickering together with insane bursts of laughter as close friends often do, unable to control the outbursts. At the checkout counter they were deathly silent and straight-faced. The checker and bagger eyeballed Stiv suspiciously. It was 10:50.

Back in his car with the engine running, AC on, Stiv sat staring at the unopened square-shaped bottle he held in his right hand. Then thirty minutes later the bottle remained untouched, unbroken, and still a virgin. He remembered the paper he wrote on Jack Daniel's Old No. 7, for Ms. Howling's English class in high school. The paper received an A. He thought the work deserved an A-plus, but whatever. During his research, he found an original advertisement in the school library for the sour mash spirit from the 1920s. The typeface was Century Old Style and very cool. The ad announced in what Stiv imagined a white-bearded Southern gentlemen's deep vowel-breaking drawl sounding like Looney Tunes, Foghorn Leghorn,

"Not a blend, I say, but a pure straight Whiskey, the kind

your father, and your grandfather and your great grandfather drank. An old-time Sour Mash Whiskey honestly made and properly aged. Has the endorsement of the medical profession, I say."

Stiv liked the medical profession endorsement; it was ironic, archaic, and uniformly absurd. Like Coca-Cola of old being made with cocaine for that extra *pick me up*...those were the days.

The memory dissipated so he hit the play button on the CD player. David Sylvian sang about nostalgia, played like dark ominous blues of a regal time and realm. It was one of his favorite tunes, dreamy melancholy trip-hop sounds that invoked memories of profoundly happier days of personal loves and triumphs.

He was morose and would not deny it, the withdrawals wounding his consciousness. But oddly, he felt a depth of buoyancy in his heart, his mind translucent, resolved to bend time, get past the suffering. Then suddenly like a strong earthquake, the vicious urge to pop a pill rammed and shook his body. The comfortable momentary normality erased by the need for narcotics. His body tensed, muscles spasmed in his legs and stomach. He grimaced wanting to scream, but fought the pain and discomfort which slowly, obstinately moved away like fumes of spent mustard gas over trenches of dead bloated bodies. The Oxycodone demanded dominance, wanted to control him through physical and emotional addiction. Much like the unscrupulous pharmaceutical companies scandalously controlling him too. Stiv imagined a conversation between executives at the company who manufactured narcotic pain medication.

· · ·

Hey, let's give the doctor a commission every time they write a prescription for our product. So what if the medication is dangerous and highly addictive, we aren't babysitters, we're a business. We'll make billions. The doctors too! Make Stiv pay, make everyone pay!

So legitimate pain sufferers who are prescribed narcotic pain medication by doctors for a pain free better quality of life, using as directed, become slaves to the needle, so to speak. An endless hypocrisy and money stream preying on the desperate, creating an international epidemic of misery and death. Who is responsible, who should be held liable?

Stiv knew a lot of people. And everyone he knew had someone in their life addicted to or profoundly troubled by Opiates, including accidental death. Of course, the *personal choice* argument loomed heavily although rage by the public was understandable. If you can't trust your doctor, it seems all could be lost.

Sweat creased his brow, dripped down his armpits, T-shirt sticking to his back. If he could just get past the next hour, sixty minutes, thirty-six hundred seconds, he would painstakingly work on the same measure of time after that.

"One minute at a time, son," Jack Daniel's Old No. 7 whispered in his Southern vowel-breaking drawl.

"Thanks, Jack," Stiv mumbled.

He closed his eyes, letting David's lyrics into his head to soothe him. He felt strong and confident with Jack...there would be no surrender with Jack, who always had his best interests at heart. Jack would know and would always watch his back.

"Better than your front, that's for sure," Jack Daniel's Old No. 7 yelled.

Then Jack burst into a throaty laugh.

Stiv stared hard at the bottle of whiskey and thought of all the damage booze caused him. He ignored Jack's weak, but good-intentioned joke. Jack obviously wanted to lighten Stiv's mood any way he could, even dumb jokes. That is what friends are for.

Thoughts of drunken days past flooded his memory like a tidal wave swamps a helpless town by the sea; beautiful but deadly. Some of his memories were profoundly painful, drunken foolish acts he committed that would not be forgiven. He kept those dark secrets buried deep like a secret murder, lying in wait to rear lizard-like Hydra heads in violent reflections. Some of his recollections were like the Hand of Glory opening locked reminiscences no buffer could quell. Tattooed on his conscience, memories of grief on his being, escape and forgiveness impossible. He could not turn away from the dreaded flashbacks but had to accept the shocking deeds as a sad monopoly of *drunken ghosts past*.

Stiv clearly understood, accepting the fact that sitting in a grocery store parking lot, in that car on a late summer morning was due to his choices. As his companions, a loaded revolver in his belt and bottle of whiskey as his friend, confidant, and passenger was a tragic absurdity. No job, no prospects, and all at his age was like going under for the third time, not a lifejacket in sight. This realization was as serious as walking on rusted razor wire barefoot. He did not blame Jack Daniel's Old No. 7 for the cheap sarcastic joke, *"Better than your front."*

Ha-ha! Very fucking funny, Jack.

Fortunately, JD was an old and trusted friend. Always had been, always would be. Stiv needed a friend, someone who would listen, someone not judgmental or hostile like the Oxycodone.

A conversation resonated in his mind. A conversation with Jack because he knew Jack would listen. Stiv had plenty to say to a friend who would listen without prejudice —he desperately needed someone to listen.

This concept has always bothered me. All the warnings from the dark universe, like there's someone or something out there, out there in the distant void, the endless lacuna and infinite timeless space. Such a curious mystery, don't you think, Jack ol' boy? I imagine a benevolent creature from the shadows, watching, guiding us in some sort of triumphant belligerence, and this scares me, frightens me beyond my ability to describe, until I consider and accept the chilling even more troublesome knowledge that we're all hopelessly alone right where we are. Completely and totally alone. Can you help me understand this, Jack, please?

Jack was silent, keeping his own counsel. He only listened, not judging, prejudiced, or hostile. That was good enough.

———

Stiv decided at that precise moment his silent one-sided conversation with Jack ended, to stop blaming anyone but himself for his Opiate addiction. Stop blaming anyone for any of his other faults, malfunctions, and problems. Realistically, how could he? How could he blame anyone for any of his misfortunes?

His wrath for Azar was on several levels but how could he blame her? She was probably sincerely doing her job. Was it possible she intentionally, yet subconsciously helped him? And how could he blame the pharmaceutical companies? Stiv recently read pain med junkies were suing big pharma companies and winning, winning large, how could he get in on that he wondered. Did the big pharms intentionally get him hooked? Maybe. But no one put a gun to his, well, except himself but for different reasons.

In turn, should his wife blame the ice cream and chocolate industries for her inability to kick her sweets habit? Maybe. But no one put a gun to her head either, he was sure of that. These were personal choices. Was all this strangely manifested bad fortune a gift or sign from the universe, the gods, or his better angels? A final warning perhaps, a preverbal message in a bottle?

He decided not to blame the *khoshgel* pharmacist anymore, even though Azar started the domino effect of his blighted suffering. Perhaps she had some evil intent, but it didn't matter. Stiv was the guilty party in the tragicomedy of his life. Time to stop blaming others and take responsibility for his own actions, stop hiding behind his lifelong weaknesses.

Steven Huffam Baker would now accept the fact that:

Sitting in his car at that exact time in history, Model 38 in his belt, bottle of whiskey on the seat next to him, miserably withdrawing from narcotic pain medication was the long-manifested conclusion of his decisions and subsequent status. And there it is—! The facts of the case, as Zander might annoyingly say. The current existence he occupied was a carefully manufactured and orchestrated product of his personal life choices. He was not the result of his environ-ment, but his thoughts, plans, and actions brought disap-pointingly on himself by himself.

Of course, not everything was bad. Stiv considered himself the most fantastically lucky junky ever. Luck, unfortunately, was not always the conqueror of misery and depression, but it was a darn good comrade and starting point.

———

Thoughts of all the people he had hurt as a drunk and pain-med junkie was masochistic and could cause him to become unhinged. It was difficult keeping his ferocious conscience under control without a whip, chair, and starter pistol. A lot of his self-medicating came from his inner fears and regrets, challenges, and mistakes. He also knew making friends with the feelings helped keep the emotions from haunting him. It was high time to accept responsibility for his actions and the wrongs he committed. This thought reminded him of AA's step #8:

"Make a list of all persons I have harmed and become willing to make amends to them all."

"How sweet and tender," he mumbled into the interior of his British Racing Green Ford Mustang coffin. "But fuck that noise!" he shouted, echoing in the vacuum of the car's interior.

———

At least he felt total completeness with the love of his life. His wife quenched his fascination with the female form, fulfilled on every level, his needs and desires rewarded for his love, and dedication. His fidelity had to be counted as well. Of course his continual fear of her savage retribution played a significant role in his loyalty. Her absolute ability to perpetrate male genital mutilation was a serious deterrent. Stiv contemplated the immense power she unknowingly had over him, but she must know. Beta's words flooded his mind, or was she warning him too? Angels do that.

Stiv was lucky he was able to maintain the long-term friendships he had. He wasn't sure how he managed, but that was unimportant, he would take the extra perks. Junkies do that.

———

Stiv pulled the Model 38 with his right hand and placed the 98.6-degree barrel against his right temple, pulled the twelve-pound double-action trigger. He didn't hear the revolver's report because the 127-grain hollow-point entered his skull and then his brain at 1,100 feet per second. The slightly disfigured bullet broke through the driver's side window of the Mustang, shattering glass, all senses off, the crushed bullet landing twenty feet away on the pavement. Bloody pieces of skull, hair, brain matter, and gore, were sprayed in the interior and stuck to the projectile. He didn't hear anything, feel anything, see anything. No one waited, nothing was waiting for him, no angels nor demons, only silence, Stiv was all alone.

But there was nothing peaceful about it.

———

Stiv indeed pulled the pocket-rocket Model 38 from his belt and placed it next to his pal Jack, who was resting on the passenger's seat, waiting. Looking at the two room-tempera-ture life-terminating objects, Stiv wondered which of the apathetic killers he should put in his mouth. He grabbed the bottle of Jack Daniel's and twisted the cap off, then smelled the wonderful sour mash whiskey with its hints of dry spice and oily nuts, its smokiness reassuring and honest, reminding Stiv life was good. He brought the neck of the bottle to his lips, anticipating the fiery spirit's wonderful burn, when his iPhone rang. The brown liquid touched his lips but he lowered the bottle without drinking. His tongue involuntarily licked the mist of brown liquor. He replaced the cap and put the bottle on the passenger's seat, where it made a clinking sound hitting the Model 38's steel barrel. Stiv answered his phone out of desperation, hoping the call was from God or some social worker. Whoever it was he hoped they could talk him down off the skyscrapers roof of withdrawal hell-in-the-sky, the freezing wind blowing through his hair, cars on the street like ants.

"Hello?"

"How's the chin, loser?" Sam's throaty giggle yelled into the phone.

"The chin's fine, you ass. I'm not. You and Sensei suck, you know that? And could you please not yell?"

"I'll tell him you said that," Sam yelled into his phone, scrambling Stiv's brain.

"Thanks, and I'll tell him myself, don't worry. I'm sick, really sick, and your yelling doesn't help. I can pop an Oxy and be fine or continue suffering like this. I don't think anything will help anyway. Nothing."

"You're a whining bitch, you know that, what the hell, Stiv? You're stronger than this and you know it. Stop whin-ing!" Sam demanded.

"The pressure I'm feeling is a mix of emotional, psychological fear and physical pain. It's really bad. I don't know how long I have to feel this way or how much longer I can stand the pain. I've never felt anything like it."

"I didn't ask bro, and it sucks to be you apparently," Sam said with indifference. "And stop complaining, will you? If it were terminal then okay, but it ain't."

"Thanks. I can't wait for the next time you're crying over some fat bitch who dumps you. I'll get even, just wait. Drug-sick and lovesick withdrawals are very similar. And since you fall in love and get dumped all the time you'll see. I'll get even."

"Oh yeah, like how?"

"Like next time you get dumped by one of the hairy bitches you date, calling me to whine because she won't answer your pathetic phone calls, I'll say, 'Well, it ain't easy answering the phone with some guy's bone in your mouth...!'"

Sam was silent. Then in a humorless monotone voice asked, "What movie did you steal that line from?"

"*Ruthless People*," Stiv admitted. "Danny DeVito and Bette Midler. Pretty funny but the humor might be too advanced for you."

"That's an old one."

"So are you, fucker, and I'm sure you hear that a lot from those senior citizen women you help into bed," Stiv said, laughing best he could.

"Look, asshole, I'm sorry you're not feeling well. I've never been a junkie before and I was thinking you could write a book about your withdrawal journey. Your journey to sobriety," Sam said with annoying irony.

"Believe me, if I make it out of this pit I will write a book even though you dis my writing. I feel anxious like time is standing still, like time is crushing the life out of me.

I'm feverish with bugs crawling all over my body, my heart-beat is like a drum solo. I feel like puking and I'm gonna shit my pants, at least that's how I feel. I need the strength to wait for time to pass and the mental energy from the universe to bend this moment into the next, to a moment when I'm not so totally jonesing," Stiv said in a slow dialogue. "Who is this again?" he asked Sam.

"Your writing does suck. Have you considered yoga? At least you won't get knocked out—again," Sam said, then howled with laughter.

"Considered yoga for what, picking up men?" Stiv asked when Sam was done laughing. "I'll leave that to you maricon since you're at least half a fag, and I think I'll drink this pint of Jack Daniel's before I blow my brains out."

"There you go again, Baker, that's a stupid thing to say!" Sam said, suddenly serious. "Even for you. One of the stupidest things you've said in a long line of stupid shit you blather out. Wait a minute, you said something about doing yourself yesterday, just stop, okay? I don't want to hear that crap," Sam said evenly with no humor. "Whatever you're feeling ain't terminal bro, get over it."

"How do you know? People die from kicking narcotic pain meds every day. I almost took a drink before you called. I'm daydreaming bloody thoughts and want air. I know where I am, but I'm lost. Who is this again?" Stiv asked.

"Hey, Forrest Gump! You're seriously messed up and that statement made less sense than usual, and your writing does blow but you're not a bad storyteller. You should write about that time we drove to Aoi Beach in 1984. Remember that? What a party."

"Yeah, I remember. That was a damn good trip," Stiv said of the positive memory. "And my writing might be crap, but at least I write. Not wasting an English Lit degree on scribbling sappy poems to your latest cheesy flavor of the month. Do you recycle that rubbish?"

"No, but that's not a bad idea."

"It's a great idea," Stiv said. "Too bad you can't come up with one on your own. Seems like all the lanky bushy unshaved women you hook up with love your sappy poetry. It might be a yoga thing, or perhaps your verses, if you can call them that, attract women who used to be Bigfoots. And everyone knows you love it hairy and ripe, Sam."

"Whatever, dude, and maybe you should start drinking and taking those pills again," Sam replied, coldly annoyed. "I think I like you better as a drunken druggie."

Chapter 24

Put Up or Shut Up

10:55 A.M. July 6th, 2017

I fear my death as much as I feared my birth.

"DID I HURT YOUR FEELINGS, Sammy you fruit?" Stiv said in baby speak, feeling better at Sam's expense.

"You sound like your usual obnoxious self. How'd that happen? I was hoping for a new Stiv. Everybody was hoping for a new Stiv."

"Sam, you like sweaty neanderthal women, how's that working out for you?"

"Not too bad, I just hold my nose like I'm jumping into a stagnant pond," he replied.

"Nice, bro, a great description!" Stiv shouted, feeling temporarily better again. "And Aoi Beach was a great trip. I don't remember ever thanking you. So thank you."

Stiv was tranquil in the memory of the deep, transparent blue Sea of Japan and the cloudless, luminous night where the endless infinity of stars dotted the sky like trillions of watching eyes. And the wild but fleeting one-night love affair with Noriko and Megumi, two eighteen-year-old girls, cousins in fact, showed their true feelings for the boys

269

after Stiv poured some powder out of his straw hat he wore for sun protection. The girls loved them mutually slow, easy, and perfect, sharing them for hours.

"You never need to thank me in this lifetime, Stiv. Your friendship and constant source of moronic infantile entertainment is thanks enough."

"You're welcome," Stiv said, exhausted. "Strange how time and fate bring people together. I remember the first time I met you. It was Little League, spring 1972. A sunny summer day at the downtown ballpark. I was pitching for Smith's and you were playing for the Animal Shelter team. I was twelve and you were thirteen. You sucked, the worst on your team. You couldn't hit a parked car with the bat, while I was homerun king."

"Bullshit!" Sam countered.

"I beaned you with my famous fourteen-mile-per-hour slider-curve-change-up fastball, like being hit with a Nerf ball but you cried like a bitch at home plate, snot dripping outta your nose," Stiv said, laughing the best he could. "The ball hit you on your helmet, remember? You cried and cried, rubbing your eyes. Both dugouts were screaming and throwing mitts and shit at you, but you kept on bawling like a bitch."

"No! You beaned me and I charged the mound kicking your monkey ass up and down the field," Sam yelled.

"Um, no. You stood there crying like a scared girl. Your parents and coach ran to the plate to give you a big hug and wipe your nose because you were scared."

"That's bullshit and you know it."

"Cried like a bitch," Stiv mocked, feeling okay even though his guts were folding in on themselves. Insulting Sam was good medicine.

"Whatever, dude. So, are you gonna take a drink or

what? I'm inviting you and your wife to the house this weekend but if you're gonna be drunk, forget about it," Sam said, putting his New York accent on the last three words. "I'm inviting that pious group from my church. You all hate each other, but you love picking fights with them. What's up with that? I already told them you weren't coming so they'll be here for sure. That manhating-twat Big Bird's coming too, friend of my sister's and all, figured you'd wanna be here, do you know if your wife is free?"

"If I see her I'll ask, and if I don't grease myself, I'll be like the walking dead by the weekend anyway. I can't see a difference, dead above ground or below. And I'll be way too sober to deal with those zealots anyway, although puking on Big Bird has serious appeal."

"Bro, I asked you not to talk about suicide, okay? It's stupid. I don't want to hear it again, it ain't cool. Remember Ivan? Look what his death did to us. He should've talked to us before he did himself. Broke my heart. I don't wanna hear that shit again, okay?"

"I'm talking to you now, aren't I? And I think if a person wants to call it quits, take the last exit off the highway, it should be their right, their choice, don't you agree? I mean, it's my life, right?"

"I guess so, but we both know it ain't that bad, so just man up and stop acting like a pussy. Put up or shut up, Stiv," Sam said, deadly serious. "Put up or shut up."

"Keep your panties on. I'm not gonna do it, I'm not gonna drink either. I have to make it through today. It's Day Two without any Oxycodone and my reward at the end of all this is fatigue, depression, and sadness. Plus, my bowels are likely to explode like they did last night at the dojo. I had a bowel attack after that mutt nailed me in the gut. I was gonna knock his ass out but I lost my balance. He scored that lucky shot. I could've been badly hurt. I had that same dream I've told you about, it's all so weird."

"The dream about the Pterodactyl, the roaring sea, that one?"

"Yup, that's the one."

"How nice for you, and your reward, asshole, will be a better life and health. Maybe you can stop being such a dickhead. But that's your natural personality so who knows."

"Thanks."

"Welcome. And even completely sober you still might be a total douchebag," Sam continued.

"Are you gonna tell me why you two blades were laughing at me or not?" Stiv yelled, feeling feverish.

"Chill, Stiv, chill. Do withdrawals make you an impatient prick or you just being Stiv?"

"Would you tell me, please? Then again maybe I don't want to know," Stiv said.

"Sensei explained last night, or don't you remember?" Sam asked.

"Yeah, I remember and don't ask me why but I wanna hear your version," Stiv said.

"No you don't, so listen," Sam began. "Sensei and I looked over at you at the same time. You were prancing around the mat fighting like a crippled ballerina," Sam laughed. "You got both our attention you were so lame, I've never seen anything like it, you looked ridiculous, Stiv, pathetic! I mean your *kumite* always sucked, your karate in general sucks, but the way you were dancing around was comical, off center and moving like a drunken mime," Sam said, his laughter intensifying.

"Well, thanks for explaining, really appreciate the talk. I gotta go."

"Then you lunged in like some leaping fairy with both hands waving in front of your chest, like slapping away a baby bumblebee. We couldn't believe it; you telegraphed exactly how you were gonna attack. You pranced right in, smashing his fist with your jaw. Is that some new technique I've not heard of? He caught you with that right cross and dropped you like a sack of shit, sounded like a Goblin Barker going off. Can't believe I didn't have my phone videotaping you. Second time I've seen you knocked out, second time, you could've won *America's Funniest Home Videos*. We both started laughing and couldn't stop, the whole dojo was laughing at your dumb ass!"

"Glad I have such caring friends."

"Stiv, we knew you weren't hurt, you dork, I mean, you've been knocked out before, right? Sensei and I were there for that too, like thirty years ago when you were living in that second-floor apartment. I'm not sure which was funnier. We were laughing because we've both seen you knocked out twice, both times ridiculous. We'll probably be laughing into the next century, you dope!" Sam howled with laughter.

"Hey, Sam?"

"Yeah?"

"See if you recognize this sound?" Stiv waited...then hung up his phone, wishing he could have slammed it down making the disconnect louder in Sam's ear. He tossed the phone onto the passenger's seat, next to the bottle of Jack Daniel's and the Model 38, not expecting Sam to call back. He did not.

Stiv's eyes were transfixed on the dashboard clock. The second hand made its forever indifferent circle around the face, representing another lost unit of time he could never get back. No one could. The hands moved forward with each innocent second, minute, and hour, subtracting time from mankind's ultimate destiny and fate. There was no stopping or reasoning with the irrevocable forward progress, advancing and taking all things, living or dead, with it. Time, the most destructive of all energies.

For over an hour Stiv sat staring, wondering, thinking thoughts that made little or no sense. His mind was hypnotized watching the clock.

Tick, tick, tick.

No man knows the moment nor the hour, not even the angels,

The Grim Reaper waits patiently to claim human eternal souls, perhaps the only energy time cannot conquer, or perhaps the two nouns are synonymous. Stiv did not know but cared a lot, contemplating the fact that time always moves at the same speed no matter one's perception.

For whom the bell tolls.

He wondered if there was help outside his group of friends, family, or brighter light, his wife. He was surprised he hadn't heard from her, glad, but surprised. The conversation with Sam pissed him off and his pride was a bit shredded, but he would not feel that way for long. Sam was a mate, a member of the *Stiv Baker Inner Circle Club* along with Zander, Sensei, Ribso, Po, and few others. So Sam could get away with such impertinence perhaps once in a super blue moon, and always be forgiven, his relentless ball-breaking notwithstanding. Stiv would get even with him later; he always showed Sam the errors of his ways.

Put up or shut up—god damn right. Just as right as when you order a Lemmy at the bar, you better get a Jack Daniel's and Coke or the barkeep ain't worth a spit and obviously has his head stuck up his *culo*.

"Ain't that right, JD!" Stiv shouted in the car, looking at his waiting friend Jack Daniel's, Old No. 7 on his passenger seat, silent, keeping his own counsel.

Sam was dead right about *put up or shut up*. If a man wants to talk shit about anything, including taking the last exit, he better act on his words. Because his word is all he really has even though that finality is cold and dark.

Seppuku, the ancient Japanese honorable way to croak yourself. *Put up or shut up*. The Hemingway Out too. *Put up or shut up*. Chewing on the end of the Model 38 as well. *Put up or shut up*. Take the pain life has brought or not, yes or no, in or out.

Put up or shut the fuck up!

Stiv should not talk about the *last exit* unless he was ready to *put up,* and he was not. Loss by one's hand only leads to dark places for the survivors and loved ones. So he needed to *shut up*. He would refuse the suicide thoughts moving forward with time. He had no fear of death due to the inevitable obvious and permanent reality.

No one gets out of this alive

Trying to count how many times he should have died simply was not possible. He had been so close to all biological functions ceasing so many times he smelled and tasted the bright red blood on the beast's claws and fangs. Each time, they circled and snarled at each other, dancing the ghost dance face to face, the face of death. Fortunately for Stiv, each instance ended the same, they turned and walked away. He knew he would lose in the end unless he somehow became a blood sucking *Nosferatu*.

Now he simply wondered *when* and perhaps *how*. *Where* was an afterthought. But the *how* ultimately didn't make a difference. For that matter, neither did the *when*...

The feelings were short-lived and faded quickly after the call with Sam. His withdrawals became an entirely different animal, strengthening to a Cat 5 hurricane. The tempest drove life-ending winds with dangerous chaotic whitecaps in the sea of his emotions. Stiv grabbed his cell phone and googled, *Narcotics Anonymous near me*, hoping they could lend him a lifejacket, or at least some positive advise.

Chapter 25

Angels and Prisoners

12:30 P.M. Thursday, July 6th, 2017

THE FIRST LINE that populated was:

The Narcotics Anonymous Hotline.
Help For All With an Addiction Problem,
Real People with Real Solutions.
Please Call 24/7, We are Here To Help and Listen
to You.
Call Right Now.

Speaking with a trained professional should help, he hoped. This was not an admission in any way that Stiv needed what the smiling morons on TV offered. However, he understood other people addicted to Opioids needed outside involvement, which was cool—for them, but not for him.

Speaking with someone who understood cold turkey and the painful misery, the fear and loathing should be able to help. It couldn't hurt. Stiv was ready to bravely fight the shrieking, clawing, biting monkey on his back, then kicking the beasts hairy ass out the door for the last time. Like cracking that stupid duggie upside his drooling head.

He dialed the 800 number and waited. A distinctive pressure gripped him, extending down to his withering life-force. His enthusiasm level was slowly fading to black. His skin crawled and he felt the crippling effects of absolute panic and terror. Where did all this come from? Were his pains and discomfort getting worse? Was that even possible?

The conflicts in his heart, both rational and irrational, were tearing him apart. He was leaning toward the negative flaws of the dark side. The almost forty hours of suffering would be meaningless if he popped a blue bullet, like days on a starvation diet then gorging at an all-day dessert buffet. However, taking an Oxy would bring him back to normality, but would also be a questionable expedition backward to his personal addiction bondage. His mind, body, and soul all suggested with firmness to take a blue bullet to his head and be done with it. Then Beta the dyke's words echoed again. His addiction was calling him, whispering promises of warm painless orgasmic freedom from the discomfort, pain, and iron maiden effects of withdrawals.

He waited. Waited for help from the other side of *tomorrow is nowhere*. The phone rang and rang, he waited and waited. Junkies hate to wait, they really hate to wait.

The ringing became a fixture with each passing second, the reverberation sounding like it belonged to the moment, was owned by the moment. Finally, a pleasant-sounding woman answered from the other side of nowhere. Her voice was reassuring, almost motherly. Stiv saw light at the end of his endurance-testing tunnel of pain.

"Thank you for calling the Narcotics Anonymous Hotline. If this is a medical emergency, please hang up and call 911. If this is not a medical emergency, how may I help you?"

"No, this is not a medical emergency, well, not exactly. But I am very sick and withdrawing from about a hundred milligrams of Oxycodone a day. I've been taking this amount for about fifteen years. I used to drink a lot of liquor on top of the narcotics. I stopped drinking a couple of years ago and I took the last narcotic pain medication about forty-five hours ago. I'm having some very dark thoughts. I'm so sick. I was hoping we could talk. I need your help. I really need to talk to someone who understands. I don't want to go to the ER," Stiv spewed out in a long hurting junkie whine.

"Oh my goodness," said the pleasant-sounding woman. "I'm so sorry for you. I wish I could help but I'm just a switchboard operator. I take the calls and then transfer them to our relay stations, who then route the calls to one of our trained professional volunteers. Would you like me to transfer you?"

Stiv did not answer but opened his eyes wide glaring at the dashboard clock like Charlie "the punk-ass bitch" Manson. He was trying to telepathically make the second hand move faster. He could not. Time moved even slower.

Wait, what?

"Yes, please and thank you," he said, not meaning it, angry he just told this dizzy bitch operator his story. He figured he would have to tell the next person as well who may or may not be another dizzy broad, but hopefully someone who could help. "How long will it take for someone to come on the line after you transfer me?" he asked with a moan.

"Well sir, there are many volunteers and it all depends on who is available. I will be placing you in a queue. Whichever volunteer becomes available next will be able to speak with you. Please hold, and good luck."

Stiv did what he was told. What else could he do?

Tranquil classical music played in the background. The soft melody soothed the unrestrained organism that he was, but nowhere near enough. He waited. Thoughts of the Nazis using classical music when herding innocent people to gas chambers before executing them went through his mind like astronomical calculations. The sheer numbers were appalling and beyond his comprehension.

In 1942 from August to October, the Nazi killing machine murdered up to 15,000 people per day. These were the deadliest, most savage months of the extermination of innocent people. Stiv thought about all those murdered souls. Their ashes and spirits floating up to the heavens in the guise of gray-black smoke. Now there was a reminder that things could be worse. So much worse. How would he react if forced to witness his wife brutalized by a group of thugs. A hideous thought and he willed it away. Stiv thought of Chopin, of Van Gogh's *Starry Night*,

Paint your palette blue and gray

The serene melody was interrupted by a croaking, guttural voice that could have been male or female. It came on the phone like an obese greasy rat jumping on a freshly set dinner table in front of a room full of guests.

"Whaddaya want?" the voice demanded in the lowest form of a Bronx accent.

Stiv quickly decided the voice belonged to a woman, what kind of female he could not imagine. Her voice was angry and evil. What did he want? Really? Seriously? The question was as stupid as Dr. Cyclops asking Stiv why he was in his office.

"Um, hello. Thanks for taking my call, I went cold turkey from Oxycodone about forty-six hours ago and I'm sick, really sick. I was taking about a hundred milligrams a day for the past fifteen years. These withdrawals are worse than I expected, like killing me, I'm so sick. Can you please help me?" Stiv sounded like a lost, hungry child.

"Help you what?" croaked the voice. "One hundred milligrams a day is weak Mickey Mouse shit. What are you, a Girl Scout?" the person shouted.

"Excuse me?" Stiv asked, stunned.

"You heard me. Now, whaddaya want?"

"Well, I was hoping we could talk about how I'm feeling and how long I'll feel this way? I'm so sad and confused. I don't want to be a junkie," Stiv moaned, really sounding hopeless.

There was a long pause from the other side of darkest callous cynicism, then, "What the fuck do I know how you're feeling, and why should I care? Do you wanna stop taking drugs?"

"Well, yes. But I thought—"

"You thought what? Thought you could call this hotline and cry like a bitch to me about going through some weak-ass withdrawals? You sound like a wimp, you know that?"

"This is the Narcotics Hotline, right?"

"Don't you even know where you called? Listen, are you a man or a pussy?"

"Well, I've got a fat cock between my legs. So I guess that makes me a man," Stiv said angrily.

"Okay, Mr. Big Cock, so if you're a man why are you calling me? Just stop taking the pills and stop feeling sorry for yourself! Man up and take the withdrawal pain, can you do that for me, sugar pants?"

"Um, well, I, I..."

"Stop stuttering at me, will you? You sound like a retard, are you a retard, a pussy, or just a stupid whining junkie? You don't need me, asshole, or anyone else. If you want to quit being a douchebag junkie, THEN STOP TAKING THE PILLS!" She shouted into her phone from her seat in the dark moldy pit Stiv imagined. "Oh, wait a second. Are you one of those spineless cunts who needs to go to rehab three, four times, get everyone feeling sorry for you, say you have a disease, get you on the road to recovery and all that patty-cake crap?"

"Aren't you supposed to help callers?" Stiv asked angerly.

"Are we having a failure to communicate here?" she yelled, sounding like Rosie O'Donnell. "Aren't I helping you, sugar britches? Mr. Big Cock, if not, then hang the fuck up!" she screamed, then waited in moonless graveyard silence.

Before Stiv could reply, the voice continued, "And just so you know, lover boy, when they busted me, I was selling and burning meth, crack, and heroin. I was homeless, living on the streets and eating out of dumpsters. CPS took my kids away when we was living in my car. We stayed in the car for over a month because I was tired of my old man pimping me out and slapping my kids around. Then the cops took my car. I didn't have shit, nothing!" she shouted. "My so-called family wouldn't help me, stopped talking to me, wouldn't do nothing! So I trusted a group of bums down by the Mission, we all need protection, right? Those bastards beat the shit outta me in an alley one night because

I wouldn't let them pull a train on me. So they dragged me to an abandoned building, tied me up and took turns fucking me on a concrete floor in a dark basement for a few days, wouldn't even share their dope. They gave me clap and one of the scumbags knocked me up at the same time. They tore me up pretty good, too. Did you ever get stitches in your asshole? Well, did you, faggot?" she screamed.

Stiv tried to comprehend what this vulgar being on the other line was saying to him. But she gave him no quarter, no time to think or respond, and continued, "I detoxed in a jail cell full of dykes who spit on me and stole my food, kicked my ass every chance they got because they said I abandoned my kids. Called me a *chomo*, which ain't true, god dammit!" She shrieked.

This caused Stiv to pull the phone from his ear a moment, but he had to go back, this lunatic needed someone to listen to her.

"I tried to fight those bitch's off me, but they were too many and the screws said I started it. So they put me in a straitjacket and solitary after I bit off a piece a one of them guards' ears. I rolled around in my own puke and piss for five days! The bastard guards wouldn't even give me a Motrin. Because of the beating I took and not eating, my baby ended up in the toilet bowl at about fifteen weeks. Just a bloody mess. A flush of the toilet as a sendoff. And you want me to feel sorry for you? What kind of weakass bitch are you?" She shouted.

Stiv was almost scared straight envisioning what this psycho woman told him. What a horrible existence. He knew about her level of humanity from working in the pawnshops, but to hear her horrific personal experiences was devastating. She was somebody's daughter, sister, mom, aunt. He really felt sorry for her and was about to speak, hearing only heavy angry breathing and possibly a sob from the other side of nowhere, but she beat him to it—again.

"Bet you live in a nice house," she said softly but the razor's edge still in her voice. "Nice wife and you become a junkie to piss it all away," she yelled. "But then again, you sound like a homo so who knows if you got a nice wife. Maybe one with a cock, huh?" she asked menacingly. "Betcha can't keep a job, can you, Mr. Big Cock? Having trouble scoring your pain meds these days? Bet you are, either way if you don't think I'm helping you then hang up and go take some drugs and die! Or don't! I don't give a bloody tampon what you do!" she thundered, rattling Stiv's iPhone speaker.

"Wow, I wasn't expecting this when I called the Narcotics Hotline," Stiv stated finally, unable to hang up due to stunned disbelief.

"What were you expecting? Mother-fucking-Teresa?" she screamed. "You wanna stop taking the drugs, then stop. Or don't. It's that simple. It's your life, your choice, not mine and not anyone else's. Only yours, buddy boy, and I think this conversation has gone on long enough. YOU'LL STOP TAKING DRUGS ONLY IF YOU WANT TO," she yelled with conviction and very possibly her only level of compassion. "Now, I have other losers to counsel and help today, so if there is nothing else, fuck you very much for calling and have a nice life, asshole," she said in what might have been her normal voice, still coarse, but not the menacing shriek.

"Wait a second," Stiv yelled into his phone. "Don't hang up yet!"

"What do you want?" the croaking voice asked, slow and guarded.

"I want to thank you for speaking with me today," Stiv said. "And I wanted to offer you a joke for your time, would you like to hear the joke? I think you'll like it," Stiv said, wanting to stab the bitch's eye out with an ice pick through the wireless phone line.

"You better not be screwing with me, faggot."

"Do you wanna hear the joke or not?" Stiv asked.

"Sure," she said, almost friendly. "Livin' in the joint an' all, might be nice to hear a joke for a change. Go ahead, and it better be worth it," she warned.

There was silence between them. Stiv could hear noises in her background, buzzers, clanking, and shouting. Then he said, "Why do they call a woman's premenstrual cycle PMS'ing?"

There was silence from the dark pit, then, "Why?"

"Because *mad cow disease* was already taken," Stiv said.

More silence. Then she began to laugh, a throaty phlegmatic cackle that continued. And with that, the witch faded to anonymity, hanging up her phone but laughing till disconnect.

Stiv sat holding his phone to his ear, wondering what the hell just happened. He was pissed so he hit the redial button and waited. Another woman answered on the other side of fuck all, her voice friendly and reassuring.

"I just talked to a person your office directed me to. I was hoping to talk to someone who could help me. Isn't this the Narcotics Hotline? What kind of animals do you have working there? Are these calls recorded? I want to report this bitch!" Stiv said to the listener.

"Sir, I am so sorry. All I do is answer the phones then put the caller on hold and in line for the next available volunteer. No one gets paid except the receptionists. The volunteers are located in different prisons around the country. You might get Alaska, New York, Hawaii, or the Midwest. We direct calls to over two thousand state and federal prisons. The convicts do counseling as part of their community service. It helps take time off their sentences, I think. Did you have an unpleasant experience?"

In his misery, Stiv had not put two and two together. The *mad cow* bitch was incarcerated. Okay then. He thought about the pleasant-voiced lady's question, about the ghoul he spoke to, or rather, got told off by. Did he have an unpleasant experience? Or was the troll on the hotline his reality, his lucidity? He suddenly had another AA moment of clarity. Through the physical and psychological pain and general flu symptoms, Stiv realized the hotline ogre did help him. Not only did she help, but she was right about everything. Stiv even understood her twisted, sinister verbal sadism. She made sense, almost the same logic as Azar the Wicked had when she refused to fill his Oxycodone prescription starting the domino effect.

Holding the phone to his ear, allowing the realizations to settle, Stiv's body shivered. The bizarre alignment of positive forces working for him, helping him were clear. This cosmic energy, the symbols and all the signs; his wife had been talking about angels and signs for years, synchronicity as well. Stiv thought of everyone involved with his life for the past few days. The whole cast of ingenious characters were in this charade together, a synchronized line of support to help Stiv kick his narcotics habit. He was sure the Sound, the dolphins, and charms of twittering hummingbirds were in on it too. Even the caw caw cawing murder of crows played a part. Of course, the players did not know they were working together, but the universe knew. Now Stiv knew too. The signs were perfectly clear. Talk about an epiphany. Stiv felt a little better, no, a lot better. He was going to be okay. Everything was going to be good, really good.

"No, I guess not," Stiv said to the pleasant voice. "I was wrong about everything. I was having a bad day and it's my fault. No one else's, I'm going to take responsibility going forward. I don't know if you can track the person I spoke with, but if you can, please tell her the pussy with the Oxycodone habit said *thank you*, and she did a great job helping me. I have a job interview tomorrow, how about that?" Stiv said to the stranger. "The woman I spoke to, I guess she's rotting in some prison cell somewhere. She said some terrible things, called me messed up names, but that's okay because she was right. I can't believe I'm saying this but another woman who was recently nasty to me may have had my best interests at heart after all. Didn't seem so at the time but I'm seeing clearly now, I can see all obstacles in my way. She might be one of the angels looking out for me. Angels have been appearing all over the place, even showing themselves, you might be one too."

"I am so happy to hear that sir. We do not get to hear positive feedback from our efforts very often. My son is struggling with Opioid addiction. He's such a good boy, I love him so much," she said, her voice breaking in pre-tears. "I'll do anything to help him. We've sent him to three different rehabilitation centers so the judge won't send him to prison. We have used all our savings, my boy does not belong in prison," the stranger said and then was silent.

Stiv sat holding the phone to his ear. What kind of celestial irony just punched him in the nose? His whole body involuntarily shivered again. Should he tell her? Explain and help her with the same universal help he received the past few days? He knew the answers as sure as he knew what love is. Stiv could help this stranger, help her understand she was wasting her time and money. Her son had to help himself; his life and future depended on it.

"Anyway, sir, I'm sorry for going on about my personal troubles. But we have no way of knowing who you spoke with. I'm glad she helped you though. Was there anything else I can do for you?" she asked, back to her pleasant voice.

"No, but thanks again, have a wonderful day," Stiv said. He was just about to hang up, then yelled, "WAIT!"

Even though he had a job interview he was excited about and a new and incisive belief that everything happens for a reason, driving back home was difficult. He could see his life in chapters, or units, and these measures of time had drugs, alcohol, and bad choices in common. Since he was a teenager, Stiv had been in some sort of trouble, always weakness based. Sobriety would not change those past tribulations, but he was going to invest all his strengths and energies not to make the same mistakes.

A new exhilarating worldview mantra flooded his mind. Like viewing a vast fertile land for the first time from the top of an impossibly treacherous mountain it took his whole life to climb. As he pulled into the parking area of the condo, he said out loud for the world to hear, "I'll drink and do drugs again someday, just not today."

He promised himself, only himself, no one else, that he would succeed. He would get completely sober. No Valium. No Nyquil. No alcohol. And no Oxycodone.

Stiv sadly knew if he professed to quit drugs and

alcohol forever his sobriety would last a matter of hours, if not minutes. Forever is a long time. He would take everything offered, take it any way he could get it—one day at a time...

Chapter 26

The Beginning of the End

5:00 P.M. Thursday, July 6th, 2017

THE SKY WAS DARKENING with sheeted black and gray thunderclouds barging in, blocking the sun and blue sky. A summer squall was threatening. The air thickened with humidity and was alive with electricity. With the blue of the sky scattering quickly, only the yellow, orange, and red end of the color scale remained, making the condos surrounding brighter, greener from the coming storm. Suddenly, violent winds whipped and blew through like huge misshapen sea monsters floating in furious upheaval. Erratic strikes of stepped-leader lightning lit up and fingered the area, striking near the condo and out over the whitecapped Sound. Cannonade-like thunder shook the area, accompanying turbulent driving rain and verifying the closeness of the storm.

Stiv loved the short-lived tempests and could watch them float across the Sound all day. A splendid beast of nature. He parked in the assigned covered parking space his wife used, indicating she was not home. The condominium was cool and empty. Exactly the way he found it the morning he found her gone.

That morning, years before, he woke in pain from the beating he took the night before, and hungover from the celebratory beers, shots, and narcotic pain medication after training. His nemesis friends fueling the fires, ordering drink after drink. His poor wife had enough of his drunken ways. She was *gone*—packed traveling like the capricious four winds and most good luck. She left a goodbye note on her easel next to her diamond eternity band she loved and never removed, until then. A violent storm raged that morning and lasted all day too, in both nature and in his bewildered heart. Her surprise departure those twelve years before sent him into a mental breakdown of sorts lasting one painful miserable drunken drugged out year.

He felt a sudden electrocuting jolt of cold death run through his body at the heart-wrenching memory. He was momentarily paralyzed with panic and fear. Was she gone again? This time for good? He dashed to her studio, pushed the door open, and saw everything was as it should be. She was still in his life, just out.

The sweet smell of oil paints, linseed, Liquin, and turpentine tickled his nose. The faint wood smell of a new palette mixed in the air, but he didn't see it. The more delicate aroma of unprimed linen canvas waited against the wall. Stiv had gotten used to the aromas over the years and enjoyed the intoxicating atmosphere of her creative haven.

His relief overwhelming, his emotions bubbled to the surface. After everything else, he could not handle her disappearance again. Her leaving him the last time and subsequent return was another story, bittersweet and perhaps beyond his ability to describe. Her studio was as neat as a working home-studio could be expected with brushes soaking in jars by the sink they installed in the room. Minty smelling Master's Artist Soap mixed in the air of aromas, a different kind of busy kitchen. She hung finished paintings on the walls like a showroom. Stiv had several favorites he hoped she never sold. Her room had a girlish artist's positive energy he loved and needed but he rarely came into her inner sanctum. More so, he was not allowed.

Rays of amber sunlight shone through the windows. On her antique mahogany easel, flaxen afternoon light showed on her most recent work. The painting was two experiences refusing rational ideas, but also expressed mutual time, love, and values of unconscious dreams and subconscious thought. The colors and imagery were electric and lovely, like honey-scented flowers. Passionate reds, burning sun orange, raindrop blues, and shaded border black radiated tonality. He recognized aspects of their life together in her brush strokes. She created mystifying beauty with controlled symbolism, her depiction of two strangely colored oceans, like in his weird dream with the pterodactyl. The abstract bodies of water were symmetrically sided with two intricate hovering hummingbirds inhabiting the work as conceptual geometric lovers. The sky's shades were varying topographical colors. The painting was undeniably alive and obviously represented their time shared, mutual love and life together.

Twoness.

The whimsical, brightly colored canvas was immediately Stiv's new favorite painting. He felt the depressing emotion rising while his heart started the Gene Krupa drum solo again. She was so talented and he was so damn lucky. He left her studio, intimidated for so many reasons, closing the door behind him. Stiv owed her everything. She loved him for so long and so sweetly even in her absence that dismal year. Yet she returned to his arms. It was scary to be so open and vulnerable, his heart and emotions unshielded. But it was also true love.

The storm had moved on continuing its disruptive yet beautiful journey. He sat on the living room couch looking out at the Sound, now dark steel blue with swells and white-caps. Birds were gliding in the high winds, he felt drug-sick but determined. In his mind's eye the memory of his thirty-second birthday popped into his head, the recollection floating through like the happiest ghost of a child.

He was living in Osaka, hopelessly in love with her while coping with contradictions. His reality was quickly becoming overwhelming. His band was getting more popular with TV appearances and their songs were increasingly played on national radio stations. He was sharing a lot of time with her when he learned she was in love with another man. Hearing this news he stopped seeing her and began self-medicate with Depas, Halcion, black-opiated hashish, and booze. He was driving down a one-way narcotic speedway in a souped-up twin-turbo factory nitrous death-mobile. A fiery collision was inevitable. They hadn't communicated in several months when she sent him thirty-two long-stemmed red roses for his thirty-second birthday. Which in turn caused a life-changing chain of events that brought him to that very couch he sat on waiting for another storm and her return home. Their love only grew and continued like a gilded path into each other's arms.

Still sitting on the couch his mind moved to another subject he felt strongly about. Stiv believed all humans possessed a singular consciousness, what the Bible and Catholicism call a *soul*.

The breath of God, body of dust

He was not sure if this was reincarnation exactly, but he believed when death occurs, we return our borrowed bodies and our consciousness enters a new host at its birth, carrying our core to the destiny set before it. No memory of past or individual experiences except in dreams and total subliminal recall. He also believed human newborns' minds hold the endless knowledge of the universe. A mother's womb, the infinity of all knowledge passed down through the ages, with unlimited capacity for all comprehension and information. Until society, cultures, traditions, folklore, languages, and social norms blocked their insights, bringing the child to a dull intellectual stop.

See Spot run, run run run

Stiv wondered what newborns saw when waving, smiling, and laughing at corners and ceilings in rooms, greeting the emptiness. He believed they see, hear, and feel what cannot be recognized by those who have reached the age of what is considered learned and trained. Their perception is lost as the high-powered fetus turns infant, to adolescent.

Chapter 27

Stiv Baker's Universe

5:31 P.M. Thursday July 6th, 2017

WHAT A DRAG AND GETTING WORSE. Stiv was dope-sick, runny nose and stomach cramping. His joints and muscles screamed, his jaw ached where he got punched. He accepted the pain and acknowledged the agony, like the old jailbird told him, making him feel exalted. Yes, he was a man of mortal flesh, but he would *not* take another Oxycodone. Not forever, but not today and probably not tomorrow. He was determined to universally maintain.

Money between friends regardless of means, or reasons, was bothering Stiv. He knew his life and marriage were going to be fine, but he harbored an anxiety about Zander's thoughtful and generous gift. Then again, the charity could have been some kind of elaborate indirect Zander diss, but Stiv didn't think so. Zander's gift came from love.

Stiv went to his desk and found his checkbook, wrote a check to Zander in the same amount he received plus $50. He put the check into an envelope, addressed and sealed it.

Dashed down to his car and sped to the post office, just making it before they closed. He bought an overnight envelope and addressed it. On a piece of post office paper he wrote,

Dear Zander, don't ever change, thank you for loving me. Stiv. PS Don't thank me or ever mention this check, those are conditions.

-Stiv

He watched the postal worker seal the overnight envelope, paid, feeling an intense individual achievement. They thanked each other. Stiv drove home feeling amazingly enlightened.

Back in the condo, the pills were shouting from their bottled confinement in the cigar box on his desk. He ignored them and kept to his plan. Sitting on the living room couch staring out at the after-storm Sound, he was trying to catalog the different pains he felt while thinking about his life and energy around him in a new light. This complex undertaking set him adrift in cosmic computations. He began to whisper apologies to everyone and everything he thought he hurt in his past. His voice ascended, the list was long and took time, but he owed gratitude and humility. First, a long meditation of unfeigned gratitude to the dope-fiend withdrawal pain and sickness he felt. Without the discomfort, how would he know? Then he thanked and apologized to his old company and the other companies that fired his junkie ass. He would not have gained this new high-stakes perspective otherwise. He sent out vocal thanks and apologies to people he knew he hurt, not people he cared about exactly, just humans who were part of his being and past.

Then, with a heavy heart, he began to thank and apologize to friends and family. As important as strangers and past acquaintances were, this level of humility was painful and made him shudder. But he made it through, including anyone he might have forgotten by name or dubious circumstance. Then he thanked and apologized to his wife, whom he loved voraciously and hurt the most. He gave everything thanks but was not done. He walked to the sliding glass door of the balcony and went out into the cool afternoon summer air smelling thick of earthy-musty wetness. The aroma was symbolic and cleansing, reminding him of the family home on the other side of the country and the summer storms that brought refreshing relief from steaming scorching dog-day afternoons. The squall had passed, the sun on the horizon winking orange, yellow, and red behind the Sound. The late afternoon sky burst alight with colors of coral, dark purple, maize, and violet-blue in a cloud formation created by artistic and talented storm gods for humanity to enjoy. Then one by one he thanked the parts of space beyond the sky he knew by name. Ones he could remember and drew strength from. The vast emptiness that held the infinite multitude like man's Boolean Pythagorean Triples, serious mathematical calculations.

Leaning against the railing, ignoring his body complaints, he looked up past the sky and thanked the troposphere, then the stratosphere, the mesosphere, and who could forget the thermosphere and exosphere? He wondered where heaven was. Then he thanked the universe and all the angels, past, present, and future. This was his new shining light, the guiding bright rays on the path of his life, the light of love and surrendering gratitude, good health, and personal sobriety. Lastly, and with substantial humility, he thanked...and then forgave... himself. This was the most difficult but most important admission. And like Scrooge said at the very end of *A Christmas Carol*, Stiv said to the Sound, and to everything and everyone, *"I don't deserve to be so happy!"*

Chapter 28

The Game of Life
6:45 P.M. July, 6th, 2017

THE SOUND of his wife's key penetrating the front door brought him out of his meditative afternoon doze. He was dreaming about nightingales singing loud with whistling and crescendos perched high in magnificent bright green trees. After his marathon of thanking and apologizing he had fallen asleep on the couch. The front door crashed opened with a bang against the wall like a SWAT team raid in progress.

"There she is!" he wanted to shout, like *Ignatius J. Reilly at the movies*, but he did not, he only watched, smiling. And there she was, in all her splendor. His beautiful wife wearing dark blue jeans, tucked-in light blue oxford button-down shirt, and white sneakers. Her long black hair was pulled back and matched the color of the thin leather belt hugging her slender hips. She was stunning. Their many years together flashed before his eyes like a beloved movie rerun. Stiv smiled to himself in the knowledge he was still intensely in love with this girl, as hopelessly in love as when they met all those years ago. He could only hope she knew his endless love and dedication to their lives together.

"I can't believe you parked in my spot, I had to carry all these groceries. Are you just going to sit there or are you going to help me? Come on!" she demanded from across the room, eyes flashing, tongue of flames.

Stiv jumped up and dashed over, helped her with the bags of groceries and a large pizza box containing their favorite pie, meat lover's special with heavy everything. Enough calories for a rotund family of five. He could not see how she'd effortlessly carried everything up herself, but she did. After they put the groceries away, they kissed and hugged. Stiv teared up with his new knowledge and surrender. He was happy with the results of the past fifty-plus hours of agony and all his new insights and enlightenment.

"Wasn't that an amazing storm, darling?" she asked excitedly, eyes ablaze. She didn't mention the parking place again. "I hope you got to see that lightning, so many stepped-leaders but mostly staccato strikes, and that thunder, like drums of the gods, it was beautiful!"

Of course she knew how much Stiv loved violent thunderstorms. Although she did not share the same passion, she did share his enthusiasm.

"I did, I was right here watching from the balcony loving it but wishing you were with me. I love watching storms with you."

"Hey, what happened to your face, your chin? It's all blackish-green and purple. You look ridiculous Stiv. Your face is all lopsided. Did you get hit last night?"

"Knocked out, actually," he said with a boyish grin. "While I was unconscious, I had that dream again."

"The Pterodactyl, the platforms, the sea?"

"Yup."

"Who hit you? I didn't see that bruise last night. I hate when someone hurts you, Stiv Baker, only I'm allowed to hurt you, your dojo people know that. I've told them a million times. I'm gonna have another talk with Sensei. That really bothers me," she said, meaning it.

"It was my fault, sweetheart. Everything is my fault. Everything."

"Yes, I know that," she said, eyeing the pizza box on the table.

"No, I mean it. Everything, sweetie. And I hope you can forgive me. I've been very selfish for a long time... and I am sorry."

She was silent, looking at him, concern shadowing her pretty face, a flash in her dark eyes. Even with his new mindset, he still felt weak physically and emotionally, but he was hoping to make love to her right then and there to reenergize himself.

"Make love to me, right here," he said finally. "Help me through this. You asked how you can help, make love to me for twenty minutes. That's how you can help."

"Stiv, I just got home, I'm tired and starving. Maybe later? That's better than no, right?"

"I want to show you something, okay?" he asked.

"Whenever you say you want to show me something you pull your pants down. I'm not interested in seeing that right now so don't bother, Stiv."

"That's not what I want to show you."

"Can you show me after dinner? I'm starving. The pizza's gonna get cold, please?" she protested.

"No, sweetheart, this can't wait. Before you ask, I'm still sick and will be for a while, but I'm definitely better than I was. I haven't taken any narcotic pain medication for almost fifty-five hours. I've come to some serious conclusions and I think I might be fine in a day or two, if not sooner."

"What happened?" she asked guardedly.

"I'll tell you everything when we're eating dinner. Now, I need five minutes of your time."

"I'm not going to bed with you," she snapped, looking luscious.

"Did I ask you to go to bed? I need to talk to you and then I want to show you something. Please, five minutes, unless you change your mind about going to bed."

"Will you please stop," she exclaimed. "You're so annoying, I'm taking the pizza to my studio. Make your own dinner."

"Okay, okay. I'm sorry, come sit on the couch, please?" Stiv pleaded.

She did, with her long legs crossed and arms tight across her chest. She wore an angry pout looking straight ahead. Stiv sat next to her, looking at her pretty profile. Then he began his long materialization of feelings built up over the years. He was beginning to feel unchained, free from the fetters of slavery to the bottle and narcotics. The freedom of sobriety was real and close; he could sense the power.

"I want you to know, I've been wrong for many years and I'm sorry, really sorry. I know I've hurt you and I can't change the past, but I can change our future for the better. I think I'm over the worst of the withdrawals, at least mentally. I've also reached a realization about my life, our lives together. No matter how long it takes, I know I'll be all right, we'll be all right. I'm sure of this."

"That's good, Stiv, I'm really happy, can we eat now?" she said, looking straight ahead.

"It's pretty rough, that's true, but I can control the discomfort. Pain can be controlled. My mind is straight. I want to thank you for coming back to me and staying through all this. And I promise here and now, I'll never take Oxycodone or any other narcotic again. That also includes drinking alcohol, I will not take another drink. And I'm going to prove it with actions and time. Now, this promise is of course contingent that we stay together, but I know we will, forever."

"Stiv, I never asked you to quit or give up anything. You know that. But I'm sure I can't stay if you don't stop being a drug addict," she said, turning to face him finally.

"Yes, I know that. And this is how I'm going to prove it. I'm quitting everything. Will you please come with me?"

"You said five minutes only. I'm starving, can't this wait until after dinner?"

"No," he said flatly.

"The food is getting cold," she complained. "I wanted to eat hot pizza. What a rip-off," she whined, using her little girl voice.

"Come on," he said, pulling her by the hand.

Stiv walked her over to his desk and grabbed his cigar box pharmacy and continued with her into the kitchen. Standing in front of the sink, he started taking bottles of pills out of the box. There was several thousand dollars in street value, money he could use, but making his point was more important. He had to prove to her and to himself that his drunken, drugged-out days were over for good. He owed this to both of them, their friends, and their families. This would be a new chapter in their lives together, a much happier one, he was sure. And once again, Beta's prophetic words echoed in his head...

Never find another like her

And yet another chapter in their mutual game of life. First, he poured out all the Valium into the sink, which made a significant pile. Then the Klonopin, Ritalin, and

303

Xanax bars. He dumped the Adderall, then the pungent marijuana buds. Stiv dumped out his Oxycodone pills, his old friends, the blue bullets. They screamed in his head, *'You traitor, pussy, bastard, son of a bitch, cocksucking loser! Just wait till you need us again! We'll pour you down a dark fucking drain, you backstabber!'*

He didn't know how many Oxycodone he had left because he could not bear to look at the screaming pills. Then the blue bullets' insults changed to cries for help, bouncing around the stainless-steel sink's interior, then down the wet dark gobble-hole drain.

When all the bottles were empty, Stiv said, "My love, would you please turn the water on?"

She did as he asked and the water made rushing noises from the faucet. Stiv looked down into the black hole end of that moment in time. His lost past-life disappeared into the void of the all-consuming watery abyss.

After the pills and grass were washed away to their uncertain destination, Stiv reached over and hit the garbage disposal switch. It roared to life with an angry determined grinding noise as the disposal's teeth did their job. Stiv considered the obnoxious grinding the first of two important metaphors, the roar equated to his years of debauchery. The grinding sound began evening out as the steel teeth masticated the contents to liquid pharmaceutical mud, washed away to the tides of time. This was the second metaphor, the one for their lives and future together, which he knew would even out too. Together they stood in front of the sink. Stiv turned the disposal off once he was certain the job was complete. He looked at his wife. She was still looking into the black hole drain of their past. Her profile causing an irresistible flame in his heart.

"I have a job interview tomorrow. I feel confident, but I

hope I'm feeling better than I am right now. I guess I can say I'm getting over the flu. That's how I feel and I'm sure that's how I look," Stiv said sycophantically.

"No, Stiv, you look so cute," his wife said earnestly as she turned to face him. "I'm so proud of you. This must have been very difficult and I know you'll be better soon. Then we can start our new life together without drugs."

―――――

At 8:30 p.m., Stiv walked down to the beach alone. The night was cool and a light rain passed earlier leaving wet foliage and concrete smells. Near the water's edge where endless ripples made gentle musical sounds on the shore, he took deep breaths of the clean briny air. Memories and emotions flooded his mind at the seawater aromas. He sat down on a massive log at the edge of the Sound. Storms floated wayward timber from as far northwest as Alaska. Some were enormous unprocessed trees, others, huge, finished logs. Gigantic and ageless tree stumps sprouting long tangled roots long since dead, landed on the shore looking like sea monsters on a lunar landscape. All the dead driftwood around him had once been living in another time and place. What he saw either escaped a log jam or a lumber barge making many parts of the Sound treacherous for boaters. The next storm or when tides changed, currents would take the delinquent floaters again drifting aimlessly like lost comets in the cosmos.

He thought about his interview the next day, glad he had the foresight to ask for the later time. Not even the cool breeze and expanse of winking stars quelled his aches and pains, his want for Opiates. But with his new revelations, he felt the discomfort was as it should be. And here he sat watching and waiting, looking at a night sky Indigenous people saw exactly as he did now, only fifty thousand years before. He heard a group of people walking up on the sidewalk. The clinking chimes of dog tags, voices, and laughter. The happy sound made him wish he could apologize to the old couple and their over-friendly duggie. He forgot them during his marathon apologies.

Tomorrow, he would put on jacket and tie, clean himself best he could, and score the job with Ocean Blues Jewelry. He really liked the company name for one thing.

He took another look at the cold summer water reflecting the stars in a dual glimmering showcase. Then he breathed in the reassuring briny aroma, looked up at the vast infinity, then said aloud, "I'm done with those damn pills no matter what."

Steven Huffam Baker made his promises to the night sky, the blinking stars and himself. He got up, turned west of the Sound where the sun sets every day, and walked forward into the future.

- END -